MY FRIEND THE DOG

At Once His Ears Went Up, Their Tulip Tips and the
Worriedly Sympathetic Glint in the Eyes Enliven-
ing His Whole Expression

[See page 54

MY FRIEND
the DOG

By
Albert Payson Terhune
Author *of* LAD

GROSSET & DUNLAP

PUBLISHERS   NEW YORK

By Arrangement with Harper & Brothers

MY FRIEND THE DOG

Copyright, 1922, 1923, 1924, 1925 and 1926, by

Albert Payson Terhune

Printed in the U. S. A.

Fourth Printing

C-E

To
My Very Dear Friend
Cynthia Dryden Kuser

In Memory of Many Happy Hours
at Faircourt and at Sunnybank

My Book is
Dedicated

CONTENTS

MY FRIEND THE DOG

I. The Gorgeous Pink Puppy

BRECK strolled toward the big puppy yard of the Kerwin Collie Kennels, his eyes on the distant masses of leaf-brown fluff sprawling asleep in the shade. His mind as well as his eyes were on these slumbering collie babies. Thus he lent no heed to Kerwin's babble as the kennel owner trudged along beside him.

"Yes, sir," Kerwin was saying, "I have just what you want. There are eight pups in the yard. All that's left unsold of two of the best litters I've had this year. You say you want the puppy as a chum for your boy. Well, these pups are fine for chums, and every one of 'em is a grand show-prospect, besides. They——"

Breck was not listening. As he watched the sleeping youngsters, one of them raised its head, the sound of voices and footsteps piercing the sleep mists, the scent of humans waking it wide.

This pup was up and alert for several seconds before its brothers and sisters so much as stirred from their noontide naps. Breck nodded approval. Here was swiftness of the senses, as well as the true watchdog instinct. He looked more keenly at the pup.

The youngster warranted a second glance; not from any outward signs of excellence, but because of its truly remarkable appearance. It was almost a third smaller than the yard's other occupants. Its deep-set eyes were a china blue—betokening merle collie blood no further back than a single generation.

Its coat was an indeterminate blend of red sable with the gray of a merle. The general effect was a dingy pink; as of a badly soiled and faded rose-colored dress. Dark splotches were strewn here and there through the pinkness—another merle heritage—and the whitish muzzle, from eye to nostril, was spattered with tiny black spots, as though it had been sprayed with ink.

Truly an amazing color scheme for a collie; and one which Breck never before had seen.

By this time all eight babies were awake and running toward the wire fence to welcome the two men. But the pink puppy was well in the lead. It moved with a cleanness and steadiness of gait, unusual in a pudgy four-monther. Still deaf to Kerwin's laudatory prattle, Breck stood looking down at the pups.

"Let me watch them a few minutes, here from the outside," he bade the breeder. "I'll go in later and examine them."

Presently the puppies ceased to note the unmoving man. Two of them went back to their doze. A third trotted to the feed dish and began to eat greedily. Two more began to play. The pink puppy ran also to the feed dish. But the much larger pup eating there growled threateningly. Undeterred, the pink puppy began to eat.

The larger pup turned and ran at it in clumsy fury. The pink puppy wheeled to meet the attack. Diving, it caught the farther of the other's pudgy forelegs and braced itself. The maneuver threw the larger baby heavily to earth. By the time it touched ground the pink puppy had it by the throat.

Loosening its playful grip as the other scrambled up, the pink puppy lunged warily from behind, wolf fashion, and caught its opponent by the base of the neck. The whole thing was done right deftly and with a keen sureness of instinct. The bigger and clumsier pup was helplessly at the mercy of its pinkish playmate.

Again, Breck nodded approval. Entering the yard, he picked up the war-like baby and ran his eye over it.

"I like this one," he said. "She has brain and pluck and instinct. She didn't start the squabble, either. But she finished it, to the queen's taste. She's true collie. How much?"

For a moment Kerwin gaped in contemptuous amaze. Then he went into action.

"You've sure got a good eye for a dog, my friend," said he. "Just at one glance you've chosen the pick of the two litters. She's the best of the lot, by far. Sired by Sunnybank Gray Dawn; no less. I refused a hundred dollars for her, last week. I was planning to keep her, for the show circuit and as a brood matron. But since you seem to have took such a fancy to her ——"

"Hold on," interposed Breck, very quietly. "Let's understand each other, please. You wouldn't dare show this mutt, anywhere; and you know it. You'd be laughed out of the ring. You wouldn't dare use her for a brood matron, either. She hasn't a single redeeming point, to a professional breeder like yourself. She is lop-eared. She has blue eyes and dew claws. She is a runt. Her color and her markings are a joke. Besides, she has an incipient rupture. She's too homely to sell as a pet and she isn't worth a nickel as a show dog or a matron. You know that, as well as I do. Those ears of hers will never come up. A blue-eyed sable can never get anywhere in the ring, and not often as a dam of registered stock. She's been a dead loss to you, and you'd have drowned her if you hadn't thought you could saw her off on some foolish novice. You never refused a hundred dollars for her or a hundred cents. I'll give you fifteen dollars, cash, for her, here and now. Yes or no?"

Kerwin's aspect of wounded dignity gave place to a sheepish grin. He realized he was talking with a man who not only spoke the cryptic language of collie initiates, but who apparently understood the breed from every angle. Yet he made one more try.

"Give me twenty," he coaxed, "and we'll call it square. Twenty, and I'll throw in a pedigree and a registration blank."

"Fifteen," calmly insisted Breck, adding: "And you know as well as I do that the American Kennel Club laws compel you to give a correct pedigree and a registration blank, free of charge, with every registered stock dog you sell. Fifteen. It is fourteen more than she is worth to you. But she is worth that to me and to my son."

"All right," sighed Kerwin, surrendering.

"Here's the cash," went on Breck. "And here's the address where her 'papers' can be sent. I'm going up into

Maine—up close to the border—for the next few months, to settle my father's estate and get his farm in shape to sell. I am taking my wife and my boy with me. It'll be wild country for the kid, away from all his friends. I want this pup as a pal for him. If she turns out the way I think she will, she'll be worth her keep, ten times over, with sheep and cattle, when I come back to my own farm, down in Passaic County. Come along, Pink!"

He picked up the puppy again, carrying her under one arm, while he led the way to the battered car in the door-yard. The pink puppy made no protest at being borne away from her kennel mates. She seemed to understand that this man knew and loved dogs, and that she would fare well with him.

Thus it was that Pink journeyed to her new owner's farm, and a week later to the Maine woods. Breck's son, Roland, was enraptured with her from the start. His father's twelve-year-old collie—two years younger than Roland himself—had died a month earlier. The old dog's passing had been a sharp sorrow to the animal-loving boy. He welcomed the puppy with open arms. To him her absurd color was a delight.

"I guess there's mighty few dogs as pretty as this one," he bragged as the three Brecks journeyed northward in the battered car, their luggage strapped gypsy-like to its sagging top. "I'll bet her mother liked her best of all the litter, because she was the nicest colored and because she——"

"I don't believe the color had much to do with the way her mother felt about her," said his father. "You see, the science sharps say that dogs don't see colors. They say dogs only see black and white. Everything looks to them as if it was a photograph or a movie. I don't know why. But that's what they claim. Still, Pink is worth more than all the rest of those pups put together, to a man who has the sense to value a collie for what's in its heart and brain and not just for a lot of silly show-points. She'll pay her way, too. See if she doesn't."

The prophecy came true in ample measure. Before Pink was six months old she had developed into a rarely keen watchdog. Also she was a natural handler of livestock and needed only the most rudimentary teachings in driving and herding. Incidentally, she and Roland were inseparable comrades.

Breck had feared the loneliness of the remote region would make the boy homesick for the New Jersey farm he had quitted and for his life-long friends. But there was no homesickness or loneliness for Roland in his new surroundings. He and Pink roamed the forests and hills together in delight, reveling in the wildness of it all. The pink puppy slept on a mat at the foot of her young master's bed.

One morning, when she was about eleven months old, Roland awoke to find himself the roommate not of one dog, but of six dogs.

Cuddled against Pink's furry side were five moist and squirmy and rat-like morsels of caninity; her first puppies, feeble little mongrels sired by a near-by trapper's rabbit-hound. To Breck they were of scant attractiveness. To Roland they were the most wonderful creatures on earth.

Breck had no intention of bringing up such a litter. Yet he dreaded to make his boy unhappy by decreeing their death.

Nature came to the rescue. One by one, within the first two days, the tiny crossbreeds began to "squeak" (in other words, to refuse food and to cry continuously) ; then, one by one, after the way of "squeakers," they died.

Pink cuddled the cold and lifeless little things to her, crooning pitifully over their bodies, licking them and trying to make them feed. Roland's grief was scarcely less than was hers. Breck solved the unhappy situation by ordering Pink out of the house with the boy, for a walk. Reluctantly she obeyed. In her absence the man buried her dead babies.

Meantime, Roland strode through the woods with his beloved collie. But to-day she did not gambol ahead and explore every hole and thicket, as usual. Instead, she crept wofully along behind him, every now and then stopping and turning back. Repeatedly Roland had to call her.

So for a mile or two. Then, halting once more, she sniffed the still air, and plunged into the dense underbrush. This time Roland did not call her back to him. She was not headed for home, but for an impenetrable tangle of rock and brier and windfall just ahead. He was glad that any forest odor could have tempted her from her grief.

Scarcely a minute later, Pink reappeared and came trotting toward the boy. From her jaws dangled a lump of straggly grayish fluff. At first glance Roland thought she had killed a rabbit and brought it to him. More than once had Pink done this. Always she had dropped the trophy in front of her young master's feet.

But she did not drop this dangle of gray fur. Indeed, she carried it as tenderly as if it were a ball of pins. Ro-

land saw the fur move convulsively. He looked closer.
The thing was not dead; nor was it a rabbit. It was
about the size of a cotton-tail, but its fur was mousier and
more dank.

Roland took the bundle from Pink's reluctant jaws.
He knew, now, what it was. Two days earlier, his friend,
the trapper, had stopped at Breck's house on his way to
town and had exhibited to the lad a big she wolf he had
just shot; as well as one of her month-old cubs he had
found and knocked in the head. The killed baby wolf
had been the image of this forlorn creature which Pink
had just brought to him.

Evidently this was an infant of the same litter, over-
looked in the tangled undergrowth by the trapper who
had slain its mother. For two days it must have hidden
thus, starving, until Pink's keen sense of smell had lo-
cated it in the thicket where it crouched.

She had not harmed the starving little thing, in bringing it to Roland. It was thin and weak, but unhurt.
Also, it snarled and snapped and growled ferociously at
the collie and at the boy.

Roland laid the wolfling on the ground again, meaning
to kill it with a stick. There was a cash bounty on all
wolves. He was minded to collect a few dollars on this
find of Pink's.

But Pink would not have it so. She had been peering
worriedly up at Roland while he held the cub. Now, as
he laid it down, she caught it gently in her mouth again,
and set off at a canter toward home. Her overpowering
new mother instinct had been too strong for the ancestral
hate of dog for wolf. She had found a new baby to re-

place her dead children, and she was carrying that baby home.

Roland did not call her back. He followed her fast footsteps. When he reached the house he found Pink had installed her nurseling in the hay-lined box that had sheltered her own pups. She did not seem, now, to miss those pups as she lay in drowsy contentment on the box floor. The little wolf, too, had lost its first snarling aversion to her. It cuddled against her furry warm underbody, nursing fast and greedily to make up for its two-day fast.

Roland was so delighted with his new pet that Breck had not the heart to obey his own first natural impulse to order it killed. Breck was a born woodsman. He knew wolf nature fairly well, and he knew a wolf has no rightful place on any man's farm. Yet, at Roland's pleading, he agreed to let the wild baby stay on for a time, and to give his son the coveted chance to try his hand at domesticating it.

Roland entered zestfully into his work of taming and training his collie's foster child. The task was by no means as difficult as he and Breck had feared. It was Pink that did the bulk of it. Had the little wolf been brought up without a dog mother, its wildness might have been far harder to cure.

But in a few days it forgot to snarl when the boy handled it. It lost its feebleness and thinness, and with them its forest ferocity. Soon it became to all intents a clumsy and non-belligerent collie pup, lapping milk from the weaning pan, suffering itself to be petted, even consenting to romp with the lad and following him clumsily about the yard.

"I've seen one or two wolf cubs that took to human training, that way," said the trapper as he watched Roland and the changeling and Pink playing gayly together. "But most of them stay mean and ornery, no matter what pains you take with 'em. Watch out for that one, too. It may think it's a dog, for a while. But some day it's dead sure to find out it's a wolf. When it does, look out!"

The warning faded from Roland's mind as time went on and as the wolf developed more and more dog traits. It was a female. The boy named her "Loup." A passing Canadian *voyageur* who stopped at Breck's for a meal told him that Loup was the French word for "wolf," and that it was pronounced like "Lou," not like "Loop."

The settling of his father's estate and the selling of the back-country farm occupied Breck much longer than he had expected. It was nearly a year from the time he came to Maine before his duties were cleared up and he was able to take his wife and son back to their native New Jersey home.

Then came the question of taking along with them the partly grown Loup. Breck was for turning her adrift in the wilderness, as Roland had grown too fond of her to endure the idea of her being shot. But the boy begged hard to be allowed to carry her back with him to the New Jersey farm. He explained that she was no longer a wolf, but a puppy, and that she had lost all her wild ways. He knew she could be taught to tend stock and to act as guard for the house and barns. He promised eagerly to be responsible for her.

Against his better judgment Breck consented at last. This boy of his was the apple of his eye. Besides, he remembered his own soul-starved childhood and his bitter sorrow when his father had killed a fox cub of his that he had taught to shake hands and to retrieve a ball.

So it was that Loup journeyed from Maine to northern New Jersey, along with Pink, in the rumble of the battered car. So it was she found a comfortable home in a region whence the last wild wolf had vanished many decades ago.

She took as naturally to her new surroundings as did her collie foster mother. She grew into a leggy and gaunt youngster, taller than Pink and heavier, pricked of ear, topaz of eye, leanly mighty of loin and shoulder. She could run tirelessly for hours, at a deceptively fast lope. Wind and rain and snow were her welcome playfellows.

When a mongrel dog flew out savagely at her, as she and Pink were jogging homeward along the highroad from a rabbit hunt, she flashed in at the charging brute with incredible swiftness and deadliness, and left him howling raucously in the roadway with a snapped ankle bone and a slashed shoulder.

But, except for this one instance of warfare in self-defense, Loup proved a splendidly tractable and gentle inmate of the Jersey farm. To the three Brecks she was eagerly obedient and demonstrative. To outsiders she maintained a cold reserve that seemed to hold no hostility.

After a single sharp lesson from Breck—when she bit the head neatly off his best Buff Orpington rooster— Loup let all livestock severely alone, except when she and Pink were herding or driving. Even then she did her herding work less vehemently than did the wise little collie herself.

Breck was forced to admit he had been mistaken and

that the gaunt young wolf promised to be an ideal farm worker. There was little to distinguish her, in manner and action, from Pink.

True, she never wagged her tail, but kept it for the most part clamped close between her legs, its furred gray tip well under her body. Also there was a furtive, almost slinking, air about her.

Her yellow round eyes held a tinge of the wild in them. Her gray coat was harsh and was faintly rank in odor. Her gait was noiseless and swift. She seemed to have the faculty of melting into the densest copses without disturbing a twig or leaf. She never barked.

To such dogs as did not molest her she maintained a grim neutrality. To those of them, like the mongrel, that attacked her, she was a murderous opponent. It was amusing to see her romp with Pink. The blue-eyed collie still held the odd wolf traits that had attracted Breck in the puppy yard. She was undersized, but she was lightning-quick and amazingly strong.

In her romps with this foster child of hers she showed a skill and a speed and an accuracy that matched Loup's own. Never did either of them lose temper with the other. Each loved the other above anything. Patiently the collie had taught Loup the rudiments of herding.

Pink herself seemed to look on her farm duties as on some hallowed trust. Neither blizzard nor sickening hot suns could slacken her vigilance in carrying out her tasks. Loup went through her own work obediently and with a certain eagerness; but not with Pink's ardent zeal.

So life went on for the two oddly differing yet oddly similar four-footed chums, during the next year. To all intents and purposes, Loup was a dog. The trapper's pessimistic warning appeared to have been absurdly baseless.

Neighbors of Breck's got over their first astonishment at having a domesticated wolf in their community. Loup became a matter of course, in the region; even a matter of some pride—to be pointed out to strangers and visitors. Even pessimistic farmers, who had threatened to appeal to the Grange to have the menace removed, were convinced of the wolf's harmlessness and of her stock-tending value.

Then, of a late twilight, Pink and Loup were sent to the hill pasture to round up and drive to the home fold a bunch of wethers that were to be taken next day to the Paterson market.

The wethers were unruly and excitable. The rounding up was not an easy task, but Pink and Loup set about it in true workmanly style. Presently they had turned back the last eccentrically galloping stray, and had bunched the sheep at the pasture gate, where Breck and Roland were waiting to follow them to the farmstead.

As Pink was steering the milling and baaing huddle through the gate, one flighty wether swung about and scampered back into the field.

"Hold them, Pink," ordered Breck, as others of the bunch showed strong signs of following the deserter's example.

Then, gesturing to the wolf and pointing to the stray, he continued:

"Loup! Fetch him!"

Before the words were fairly spoken Loup was charging after the fugitive, to head him and drive him neatly back. The wether dashed to one side, to avoid capture. The shift brought him crashing against a dead cedar stump from which projected a pointed little dead branch.

The wether hit this point of tough wood at an angle that sent the projection an inch or more through his wool and into his shoulder. It was a mere flesh wound, but it spurted diligently.

Loup caught up with the stray and headed him back toward the other sheep. The wether ran bleating and limping. Drops of blood spattered the ground behind him.

The wolf hesitated in her steady trot, wavering and coming to a stop. Her nostrils dilated. She began to tremble. Her yellow eyes took on a phosphorescent glint. A million ravenous beasts of prey, among her ancestors, were screeching their red secret to her ignorant and innocent brain.

She dropped her head and sniffed at a spatter of blood on a rock the wether had just leaped over. She licked, tentatively, at it. Then, greedily, she lapped it clean, muttering and growling under her breath.

"Loup!" called Breck, through the dusk.

The wolf heard. She shuddered all over and set off after the wether, driving him into the waiting bunch of his fellows.

On the way home she did her routine work of keeping the jostle of sheep from scattering. But always that maddening reek of blood was rioting in her brain. Always the taste of it was on her tongue. Once as the same wether bolted she drove him back.

As she sent him into the flock she licked his shoulder. She was aware of an overmastering desire to drive her curved fangs into him. But the presence of the two humans and of Pink deterred her.

That night she did not touch her high-piled supper dish.   Neither did she sleep.   Pink's sleeping-mat was on the floor beside Roland's bed.   But Loup's resting-place was the door mat on the back porch.   There, commanding a view of stable and barns and fold, she was wont to drowse with one eye open, guarding the farm and its live-stock.

To-night she lay as usual.   But she was broad awake. Once or twice a trembling went over her.   Once or twice she growled.   And ever she sniffed the air for trace of the blood smell.

At midnight, Pink jumped up, growling, from beside Roland's bed.   She sprang to the door of his room, bark-ing frantically.   The boy sprang up, too.   He could hear nothing disturbing.   Yet he obeyed her imperious scratching at the door by letting her out.   He followed. At the barred front door she recommenced her scratch-ing and barking.   Breck awoke and called downstairs to know what was wrong.

"Pink's crazy about something," called back Roland. "I'm going out with her to see what it is."

"Put the leash on her first," said Breck, getting up and preparing to follow.   "Remember the time she got ex-cited that way, last year, and we let her out and she found a skunk in the chicken yard.   Keep her leashed till you're sure it's nothing like that."

The boy slipped a leather loop over the dancing collie's head, twisting the leash's other end about his own wrist. Then he caught up a flashlight and ran out with her. She headed straight and strainingly for the fold.

And now Roland could hear a milling and stamping and a piteous bleating from behind the wattled fence which penned the wethers. At top speed he ran thither, Pink almost pulling him off his feet in her craving to get to the fold. Vaguely the lad wondered where Loup might be and why she was not on hand, as always before, to defend the sheep from any prowling enemy.

At the wattled fence he turned on his flashlight and swept its ray athwart the fold. Then the light all but dropped from his suddenly nerveless hand.

The bulk of the wethers were huddled in a far corner, jostling and baaing in mortal terror. In the trampled space between Roland and the corner lay four sheep, each in a pool of dark liquid. Crouched over one of them growled Loup. The wolf's eyes shone like yellow fire. Her jaws were dripping. She had lost all likeness to a dog.

At sight of her, Pink shook from head to foot. Then from her furry throat issued a queer sound, curiously akin to the roar of a wild beast.

Roland stood with jaw hanging and eyes abulge. Just then Breck came hurrying up. A glance told him the story. Always he had feared this very thing must happen. To his memory came the grim warning of the Maine woods trapper:

"It may think it's a dog, for a while. But some day it's dead sure to find out it's a wolf. When it does, look out!"

"Hold Pink!" he ordered. "Don't let her loose. She'd only get hurt or mix things up. Give me the flashlight."

Boldly he walked into the fold and toward the slavering wolf. As he drew near, Loup looked dazedly at him. She seemed drunk from her hideous orgy. The man called her sharply by name. Hesitant, she moved forward.

Without another word, Breck took her by the collar and led her, unresisting, from the fold and into the barn. There he locked her in a stout box stall. Then he returned to his son.

"I've lost valuable sheep," he said, harshly, "by being fool enough to let you keep that brute. Come in here and help me clean up. Wait—first go and tie Pink. Tie her in the cellar, for to-night. I don't think she'd follow Loup's example, but I don't want to take any more chances. In the morning I want you to pay your bill for this damage, as far as you can. You'll pay it by taking Loup out into the woods somewhere and putting a bullet through her. Understand? That's *your* job and it's your punishment. You said you'd be responsible for the beast."

"Yes, sir," mumbled the boy, still dizzy and incredulous.

"To-morrow morning, first thing," reiterated Breck. "I could do it myself, of course. But it's your work. It'll be a lesson that you'll maybe remember. Now put Pink up, and then help me with this mess."

Roland did little sleeping that night. He was jarred and sickened by Loup's grim reversion to the wild. Though he had none of the comradely love for her that he had for Pink, yet he was fond of her, in a way; and he had been more than a little proud of his achievement in taming and training her. And now all his work and hopes had gone for nothing—for a hundred times less than nothing.

He felt the sting and rankle of Breck's displeasure at what had happened. He felt, too, the justice of his father's command that Roland act as executioner to his disgraced pet. He did not relish the job of shooting the wolf. Yet he was sane enough to know the deed was keenly necessary. The world over, death is the only fate to be meted out to a slayer of farm livestock.

At grayest dawn he got up and dressed. Going to the closet where his father's rifle was kept, he cleaned and loaded it. Then, with steadily sinking heart, he fared forth to the barn. From the cellar where she was still imprisoned, Pink whined eagerly at sound of her young master's tread. Unheeding, the boy went on. More and more he hated the task ahead of him.

Halfway to the barn, his father caught up with him, saying, curtly:

"I'm going with you."

Roland went red. A hot retort sizzled up to his lips, and he choked it back with much difficulty. He thought he understood the reason for Breck's presence. He believed the man did not trust his son's nerve or purpose and feared that Roland might weaken in the carrying out of the job.

Sullenly, wordlessly, the two went to the stall where Loup was confined. There, handing his father the rifle, Roland unfastened the gate and stepped inside. From his pocket he drew a dog chain.

The wolf was hunched up in one corner of the stall. At sight of Roland, in the dim light, she curled back her lips and growled. For the first time since her babyhood she did not trot forth friskingly to meet him. The shell of tameness had been husked away by the night's happenings.

Breck lifted the rifle at sound of her snarl. But Roland walked unhesitatingly up to the cringingly threatening brute and snapped the chain clasp to the ring in her collar. Had he faltered, either in mind or in action, a slashed forearm or a crushed hand might well have rewarded his flinching.

His sureness and calm assumption of mastership seemed to tighten momentarily Loup's tenuous thread of connection with the days when she was his obedient follower. For at his command of "Come on!" she suffered herself to be led out into the farmyard, by the chain. Breck lowered the rifle. He saw his son was in no present danger.

Roland led the way across the fields, Loup padding at his side, Breck following with the gun. The boy was headed for a wooded hill a mile distant, a hill beyond which arose the tumble of almost trackless mountains that shut in the eastern side of the rich farmland valley.

Breck guessed at his son's motive for traveling so far afield. There was no use in letting Pink find out later what had befallen her fosterling; nor was Loup to be honored by a grave.

To the hill moved the silent little procession; then up its rocky sides to within a few rods of a spot where a ravine split the slope cleanly in two as if with a monster ax-stroke. The ravine's bottom was clogged with brier and bush, and it was nearly a hundred feet below the top. There in the depth of the cleft a dead animal could lie inoffensively until crows and weather should reduce it to a skeleton.

For the first time, Roland turned to his father. Reaching out his free hand, he took the rifle from Breck. Cocking the weapon, he bent and unsnapped the chain from Loup's collar.

The wolf had been showing more and more uneasiness as the walk progressed. Perhaps she had some intuition of what was in store. Perhaps the growing wildness of the scene stirred a responsive chord in her. At any rate, she had been hanging back on the chain, once or twice snapping viciously at it.

Now, as Roland unfastened her, she slashed at his hand, her eye-tooth grazing it deeply as he snatched it out of reach. Wheeling, she made a dash for the thicket-fringed lip of the ravine.

Roland gave her a full fifty feet of galloping start. Then he fired.

High in air leaped the wolf, with a strangled yell. Crashing to the ground, she rolled over twice, then lay sprawled and motionless. Roland set down the gun and turned away, feeling dizzy and ill. His father walked across to the fallen Loup and bent down to examine her.

"The bullet went in at her hip," he reported, "and it went clear through her. It came out at the shoulder. It was a ragged shot, but it did its work. There's no use skinning her. Her pelt is off prime, this time of year."

As he spoke Breck picked up the inert body. With a heave he flung it over the edge of the ravine. Down the steeply rocky sides it rolled and bumped, coming to rest at last among the tangle of bushes and briers at the bottom.

The man had noted the entrance and exit of the bullet, and deemed the grisly work satisfactorily done.

As a matter of fact, it was not done at all.

If Breck had had more knowledge of big-game hunting —or of human warfare—he would have known that a modern high-power bullet can sometimes drill its way entirely through a body without inflicting a mortal wound. Many a man thus wounded walks the earth to-day, sound of health.   Many a bear or wolf or deer thus hit has lived to die of age.

So it was with Loup.   The shot had bored a hole from hip to shoulder without doing more than inflict a painful but curable wound, and to shock her into brief senselessness.   Yes, it had done more.   It had snapped the last tie which bound her to civilization.   It had left her a dangerous marauder in a fat farm country.   In less than a fortnight she was on her feet again and as strong as ever she had been.

Mercifully unaware that he had been responsible for turning loose this scourge on his community, Breck congratulated himself that the wolf had been put out of the way before doing worse damage than the killing of his four wethers.   Roland tried to forget her last leap and her strangled yelp as she rolled over and over.   Pink was kept in the cellar until a heavy rainstorm had washed away the trace of the footsteps from stable to hillside.

Life went on as before at the Breck farm.   The early summer work kept father and son busy from daylight till dusk.   Pink hunted vainly and wistfully for her wolf comrade.   If she had grasped the sense of what she had seen in the fold, she had apparently forgotten it.   At the least, she did not seem any longer to associate Loup with the carnage.

Then, of a July morning, word went up and down the valley that thirty chickens had been killed and mangled, in a single night, at a poultry farm some four miles away.

All the valley believed that a killer dog was loose.   But the utter silence wherewith the slaughter had been achieved led some folk to think it was the work of fox or wild cat. For these pests kill in silence, while a chicken that is being killed by a dog can be heard for half a mile.

The next morning, a henroost, ten miles in the opposite direction, was robbed of no fewer than sixty-three chickens. Some had been eaten. Others had been destroyed in wanton mischief and were left unmarred.

The valley buzzed with fury. There could be no further doubt that this was the work of a true killer, not of some mischievous stray puppy. The distance between the two massacres went to prove that. Spring guns and poison were cunningly set. Men took turns at all-night vigils in their poultry yards.

Two nights later, a yearling Guernsey heifer was found dead in a pasture; its throat gone. Two calves in the same pasture had also been put to death. Now, few are the killer dogs which, singly, will attack a yearling. Thus report sprang up that this was no single offender, but a pack of dogs.

Six miles off, on the following night, a hill pasture was visited by the killer, and fifteen sheep remained as lifeless witnesses to the raid.

The Grange offered $200 reward for the slayer or slayers. Men let their farm work go neglected while they combed the mountains and the river gullies for the arch-enemy. They took to eying one another's harmless farm dogs askance, mutely wondering which of the canines might be the one that threw off the daytime mask of respectability by night, and ravened among the imperiled livestock of the region.

There was a week of surcease. Then came word of twelve murdered calves in a pen, nineteen miles to the west. The valley breathed a sigh of relief. The killer had wandered to other fields of destruction. But on the next morning a farmer, barely a mile south of Breck, woke to find his old sheep-dog killed. Along with him were a foldful of ten market lambs the old dog had been guarding. The whole thing had been done in utter silence.

Truly, Loup was levying heavy if belated toll on civilization. She was having a deliriously happy life of it.

No longer did Pink sleep in Roland's room at night. She was stationed on the back porch where, of old, Loup had slept. Vigilant, alertly tense, she lay there from bedtime to sunrise, except for several patrolling trips of the farm buildings, wherewith she lightened her duty of guarding.

The pinkish little blue-eyed collie seemed to understand that something was gravely amiss in the neighborhood. For of late she had an air of eternal watchfulness, by day and by night. But in the hours of darkness she was tenfold more eagerly on guard than ever before she had been.

Breck was as puzzled as was everyone else as to the source of the wholesale killings. Had he not seen the double bullet hole in Loup's motionless body he would have been certain she was the destroyer. Indeed, several of his neighbors appeared to grow increasingly doubtful as to the truth of his statement that he had shot her.

While Breck shared to a great extent his son's enthusiastic trust in Pink, yet he was not minded to risk everything on a mere collie's watchfulness. He and Roland took turns in sitting up at night, from ten o'clock till daybreak, reinforcing Pink's vigils. Three householders out of four, throughout the valley, were doing the same thing. The result was an epidemic of nervously cranky farmers and ill-done work.

On a hot night in late July, Breck sat nodding on his porch beside Pink. Dozing and waking, dozing and waking, he passed the hours of darkness. From a longer snooze than usual he started guiltily awake to find the world was no longer densely black, but dull gray, and that full daylight was scarcely an hour off.

Comfortably sure that the killer would not venture to attack, except under cover of night, he got up and stretched, preparing to go to bed. As he did so, Pink looked up from the mat where she was cuddled at his feet, and wagged her tail in greeting. The man patted her, then turned to go indoors.

On the threshold he paused. The collie's tail had ceased to wag. She was sniffing the dawn wind. Then she got to her feet and padded silently toward the fold, where again a bunch of wethers were herded for market. Thinking she was merely making one of her several nocturnal rounds, Breck went into the house. He stood there, unfastening his vest and his shirt collar. As he stooped to pull off one of his boots a tumult from outside broke on his ears. Bolting out of the house, he ran at top speed for the fold.

Silently, and with the wind in her favor, Loup had paid her first return visit to the Breck farm since the day of her expulsion. She had been belated, by reason of going first to a distant poultry farm. There she had found men on guard and the fowls safe hidden behind closed doors. Hungry and balked of her proposed prey, she made a detour on the way back to her lair—a detour which brought her to the farm she had once been wont to guard.

With inspired caution and still keeping to the right side of the wind, she made her way to the home fold and leaped its wattled fence. Clever as was Pink, the scent of the noiseless wolf did not reach her, for the wind was sharply the other way.

Then, as Loup seized the first wether, the breeze veered. At the same time another wether bleated in terror.

Pink bore down upon the fold. In happier days the scent of her foster child had been friendlily familiar to the little collie. Now there was a tinge of the hostile wilderness to it. Pink's hackles bristled as she sped onward.

She rounded the barn corner just in time to see Loup's jaws strike deep into the throat of a second wether, bearing the poor bleating creature to the ground. That was enough. Pink needed no more to show her her own duty as guardian of the fold. The fiercely fanatic loyalty of endless sheep-herding generations of collies flared hot in her soul, driving out all else.

With a yell that was strangely like a human scream Pink leaped the fold fence. Loup turned leeringly from her orgy. The collie was flashing at her, with teeth bared and blue eyes aflame. No longer were Loup and she foster daughter and mother. They were destroyer of property and avenger of property's destruction.

Loup knew it. She knew this pinkish dog was her mortal foe. There could be no quarter given or taken. For the millionth time in the history of their races, dog and wolf were clashing; in the world-old feud between these blood-cousins and sworn foes.

Rearing herself from her kill, the wolf whirled to face the madly charging collie. Then to her acute hearing came the thud of Breck's running feet. Instantly she spun about and cleared the fold fence at a flying bound. Pink was after her with a whirlwind rush. She leaped the fence, but miscalculated the distance. For an instant she swayed on the top of it, then got her hind-feet into the wattles under her and scrambled over in hot quest of the killer.

Breck rounded the barn just in time to see a grayish streak whiz across the field in the faint dawn light, the pinkish collie in mad chase. Deceptive as was the light, Breck knew at once that gray shadow. Thus had he seen Loup run, a hundred times, in search of strays. A chilly feeling crept up his spine at sight of the ghostly runner. Shaking off the tinge of awe, he gave chase.

Across the field tore Loup with that oddly mile-eating gait of the Wild. Across the field, after her, rushed Pink, straining every sinew to catch up and to wreak justice. Innumerable times had these two galloped thus after each other, in romping play. Each knew the other's speed prowess.

Loup was making straight for the nearest hill—the hill into whose ravine bottom Breck had flung her—the hill in whose deepest gorge she had her lair. Far behind, and panting with his own futile exertions, raced the man.

The wolf gained the bottom of the hill, darting upward amid a strew of irregular rocks. Close at her heels pattered the fleet little collie, soundless, terrible. Between two bowlders Loup twisted about and faced her pursuer. She could have run much farther, and might perhaps have worn out her doughty little enemy in an endurance race. But her hearing and her powers of scent told her the man was left far behind and was not likely to prove a factor in the affair. Mad resentment turned her from a fugitive to a rabid warrior. This collie had spoiled her feast in the fold and now was chasing her with deadly persever-ance. Loup was not averse to trying conclusions with the dog and to ridding herself forever of the only animal that had been able to balk her murder cravings.

So suddenly did Loup wheel about, with the bowlders shielding her shoulders and flanks, that Pink all but fell into the trap prepared for her, by blundering at full tilt against the craftily braced wolf. A ripped throat or, at the very least, a smashed foreleg must have paid for such an error.

But a collie is like no other dog. Back in his brain ever lurks the queerly wise instinct, though never the incurable savagery, of the olden wolves he sprang from.

Not by mere chance had Pink proven her instinctive prowess as a general in the puppy-play that Breck had watched on the day he bought her. Not in vain had she perfected those wolf instincts of tricky wariness and crafty battle skill, in a hundred playful romps with Loup in earlier months.

She had learned thus from the young wolf the myriad clever moves of attack and defense that are the lupine heritage.

Now, almost in midair, Pink checked her own impetuous onward rush, and changed it to a dive for the wolf's braced forelegs. Loup reared, to avoid the peril, and drove for the collie's neck nape. So had she done in scores of play fights, long ago, until Pink had learned by instinct the sidewise shift to dodge the rending jaws; and the counter-ing slash for the underbody.

Together came the two, rearing and roaring, in a whirl-wind mutual onset, at close quarters. Loup fought with all the flaming savagery and strength within her. But in the collie's clean heart blazed a red fury of vengeance against this desecrator of her sacred life trust. The hillside rocks echoed to the wild din of carnage.

Up from the plain toiled the breathless man. Breck lurched forward and came in sight of the two bowlders where Loup had made her stand. Pink had dragged her opponent out from the rocky shelter. On the patch of open ground in front of the bowlders rolled and snapped and tore two interlocked bodies.

Of a sudden, as Breck ran up, the sound and the frantic rolling ceased. For an instant the tangled bodies lay inert.

Then, slowly, very slowly, one of the two struggled from the unloving embrace and got, swaying and staggering and bleeding, to its feet. The other lay in a bloody torn huddle on the stony ground, its neck broken.

As Breck stared agape, Pink recognized him. Feebly she wagged her tail in greeting. Then she looked down on the dead wolf. Out of her china-blue eyes all the fury had ebbed. Whimpering softly, she stooped and licked the foster child she had loved.

Pink's duty was done. She had punished the raid on her master's flock. Now there was time for her to mourn the loss of her playmate.

Lifting her head, she made the hills reverberate with a wolf-like death yell; then she bent whimpering again, to lick the wounds she had inflicted.

In the midst of her pitiful task she sank helpless to the ground beside her victim. Mighty exertion and pain and loss of blood were claiming their price. Nor for another month or more was Pink fully healed of her grievous wounds.

"Come, old girl!" muttered Breck, gathering her in his arms and turning homeward. "We're going to patch you up and get you well again, if the best vets in the state can do it. You're—Lord! but you're *worth* it—you—you gorgeous pink puppy!"

II. Runaway

"AND there were bears in that dream of mine, Ronny," continued Fay. "Twenty-five bears. They were all cream-colored and they had brown eyes. They were each of them more than seven times as big as you or any other collie, Ronny."

The girl paused to let this amazing statement sink in. Coolharbor Ronald, the mighty-coated gold-and-white collie, wagged his plumed tail and looked up at her with much interest. He loved this ten-year-old little daughter of his master, and he loved her crooning voice when she talked to him as if he were another child, even though nine-tenths of her actual words meant nothing to him. He loved the way she rumpled his silken ears as she talked. Also, the constant repetition of his name flattered him.

"And, Ronny," went on Fay, "those twenty-five cream-colored bears all lived at the South Pole. I dreamed that it got so hot down there that they all chipped in and bought an aeroplane, Ronny, and they got into it and they flew

32

clear up to the North Pole, where it was ever so nice and cool, even in summer, Ronny. And they—"

The collie became aware of a malignantly mordant flea, feasting in the hollow behind his left ear. He broke in on Fay's narrative by sitting up and scratching the ear-hollow with much intensity. His wontedly clever face took on a look of idiotic vacuity as he scratched.

"*Ronny!*" rebuked Fay, indignantly. "Do you want to hear the rest of this nice dream of mine, or don't you? It isn't every day anybody has such a wonderful dream. It's worth listening to, I can tell you."

Either at her chiding tone or else because he had abated the supping flea, Ronny settled down again on the veranda floor at her feet, wagging apologetically his plume of a tail and looking in whimsical appeal at the flushed and frowning little face. Appeased, Fay took up again the flea-severed thread of her narrative:

"Well, I dreamed the bears loved it up there, in the cool and the ice and all, after it had been so hot down at their home in the South Pole. But pretty soon it began to get so cold at the North Pole that they were all shivery and chatter-teethed, Ronny. And the bears said: 'Gee, but it's cold, here! Let's get back home where we belong.' So I dreamed they all piled into the aeroplane again and they stepped on the gas. And, Ronny, what do you suppose happened? The aeroplane had frozen stiff and it wouldn't move an inch, Ronny.

"So I dreamed they all had to *walk* every step of the whole way home from the North Pole to the South Pole, Ronny. It was pretty near a billion miles. But that was the only way they could get there—by walking. By the time they reached the South Pole again their feet were terribly sore, Ronny. As sore as that new tooth of mine was, last year. Maybe sorer, Ronny."

At the repeated speaking of his name the dog's tail smote the porch floor anew, and he reached up to lick the gesticulating little brown hand. There was something so confiding and happy in the action that Fay's conscience smote her. She felt that Ronny not only understood, but believed every word of the tale. Hesitatingly, yet laughing in loud bravado, she added:

"I—I didn't really dream quite every bit of that dream, Ronny. Not just all of it. I—well, I made up a little of it, here and there."

The tail continued to slap the floor and once more the collie sought to lick the hand poised above him. Fay grew red. She avoided the caressing tongue of her canine worshiper and she said in a spurt of self-vexation:

"Now that I come to think it over, Ronny, maybe I didn't even dream any of it at all. But—but wouldn't it have been a perfectly glorious dream if I *had* happened to dream it, Ronny?"

Conscience calmed by confession, she patted remorsefully the classic head at her knee, admonishing her chum:

"You mustn't always believe everything you're told, Ronny. Learn to take a joke, sometimes."

The morning sun was striking athwart the fire-blue lake. A sluicing rain of the night before had washed the springtime world clean of a week's dust and had filled it with a hundred fresh odors. It was hard, on such a morning, to sit primly on the veranda, in one's best clothes, waiting for the car to come around and keeping Ronny from straying into the lake or over the plowed ground of the rose-garden.

Yet this was the brief task assigned to Fay Denning by her father, that day. At nine o'clock, Denning, with his wife and daughter, were to start for the hour-distant dog show at Paignton. It was an event, a tremendous event. It was the first outdoor show of the year. It was the show whereat Coolharbor Ronald was eagerly expected to win the final four points needful to the completing of his championship.

The beautiful young collie had been bathed and brushed and trimmed until his burnished gold-and-white coat stood out like the hair of a side-show Circassian beauty. For weeks he had been conditioned for the great event. His owners did not believe there was a show collie on earth that could equal in perfection this pet of theirs.

The dog-show virus is as insidious and as potent as a Borgian poison. Once let man or woman fall under its spell, and the winning of a blue ribbon seems more important than the winning of a college degree. The purple Winner Rosette is worth a fortune. The annexation of the mystic prefix, "Champion," to a loved dog's name is an honor comparable to the Presidency.

The virus had worked deep into the cosmos of Malcolm Denning and his wife since the day, six months earlier, when they had been persuaded by a friend of theirs to take their home-bred young collie, Coolharbor Ronald, to a neighborhood dog show. The collie had won a spectacular victory there and at ensuing shows; annexing with ease eleven of his fifteen championship points. To-day's show —if his winning streak should continue—would suffice to gain him his full title.

At daybreak the Dennings had been astir. Ronald had been groomed with all the meticulous care that might be lavished on a Derby favorite. Then, while Malcolm and his wife were changing into their dog-show clothes, Fay was deputed to stand guard over the collie and to see he did not stray from the veranda.

A single luxurious roll in the rain-wet grass would undo much of his painful grooming. A plunge in the lake and a homeward canter through the loam of the flower borders would necessitate an entire new toilette—the labor of at least an hour. There was not an hour to waste before departing for the show.

For a few minutes Fay found it simple enough to sit on the porch with Ronny, entertaining herself, as ever, with telling him a story. But presently the wait waxed tedious. There was a mightily potent call in the sun-blazoned outdoors. Momentarily, to the restless child, the call waxed stronger.

"Ronny," she said after a minute of silent fidgeting, "I promised I wouldn't let you get into the lake or on the wet grass or into the flower beds. But I think it would do you good to walk around the gravel paths with me. They are awfully clean and dry, Ronny. Just as clean as this poky old veranda. Daddy says a collie needs lots of exercise. Come along."

She snapped a leash to the dog's collar, lest he be beguiled from the uninspiring gravel to the damp grass. Then she descended the porch steps, Ronny gamboling delightedly around her and tugging at the unwonted leash.

Primly she strolled down the wide gravel path to the near-by summer-house and back again. Then she struck into the longer and narrower path that led to the vegetable garden behind the stables.

Past the stables she and the dog made their way, and

along the central path of the garden. Beyond were the hillside woods—full of enticing sights and sounds, but forbidden ground on this morning. With a sigh Fay turned about at the end of the garden's path and prepared to go houseward again.

Just then, out of a lettuce row whisked something brown and bounding; something with a stumpy white tail and with a fascinatingly bumpy gait as it dashed for the near-by woodland.

At sight and scent of the rabbit the collie yelped his shrill hunt cry. He leaped forward with all his sinewy strength and with the impetus of his sixty pounds of weight. Fay saw the maneuver in time to make an effort to check it. Involuntarily she tightened her grip on the leash, whose loop was around her wrist.

The dog's jump lifted her bodily from her feet and flung her forward. She came to earth prone in the green-and-scarlet center of an early strawberry bed, her pretty white organdie dress at once taking on splashes of scarlet and streaks of rich brown earth.

Checked by her fall, Ronny resorted to guile. Backing away, he slipped his neck out of the loose collar. In the same gesture he wheeled and was off like a gold-white flash, in pursuit of the vanishing rabbit.

Rubbing her chafed palms on her barked knees, Fay Denning scrambled up from her roll amid the squashy strawberries and soft dirt. Despairingly she blinked after the fast disappearing collie and at the rabbit that bumped along at full speed some hundred feet in front of him. Then she gave chase.

She was responsible for Coolharbor Ronald's safety and immaculate cleanliness. Both were in peril. All at once her sophistry . . . as to the gravel walks being as clean a place for him as the veranda whereon she had been told to remain . . . rang thin and cracked. No longer did it seem a convincing argument wherewith to face her father.

Into the woods she rushed, and through a patch of marshy ground at their border. Her quest was not long. Fifty yards within the woodland the rabbit had dived into a warren, among some stones, on the steep hillside. Around these rocks the collie was dancing, shouting wildly barked insult to his escaped prey. Ronny, too, had traversed the patch of marsh, and at a pace that had spattered his shining coat thick with black mud.

Fay called weepingly to the dog. Toiling up the slope, she plunged forward under a low-hanging bough to grasp him. Her eyes were blurred with tears. Ronny's were not. Thus it was that the collie, turning around at her call, saw what she missed seeing. He saw and, collie-like, he went into immediate action.

As she ran below the bough the top of her head brushed glancingly against something soft and yielding. It was a hornet nest as large as a derby hat—the abode of several hundred giant black hornets with white-barred tails.

Scarce had she touched the nest when Ronny flew at her. His classically chiseled skull smote her with heavy force in the meridian of her small body. The girl doubled up and rolled backward down the steep pitch of hillside far more rapidly than she had rolled into the strawberry bed.

Ronald did not so much as glance after her meteorically tumbling body. Slowly, at a deliberate walk, he began to move away in the opposite direction. He knew well what he was doing, as have other collies that have done the same thing. He knew also the price he must pay.

Out of their shaken cone-shaped nest poured the army of hornets, furious to revenge themselves on the intruder who had joggled their home.

In the second or so which had passed since Fay's head had come into contact with the nest, the child had involuntarily put several yards of hillside between herself and the hornets. Even now she was coming to a stop against a bush of mountain laurel.

The hornets saw thus only the nearer moving object— the dog that was walking so deliberately away from them. The whole buzzing white-barred troop flew at him settling down above him in a fiercely droning mass.

Now a collie's coat, in its thickest parts, is as impervious to hornet stings as is a suit of armor. But on the head and the feet and under the forelegs there is no such mattress of protection.

While the bulk of the swarm were stabbing vainly at Ronald's back and sides, a dozen or more were driving at the less-guarded parts of him. Their flame-like stings clove deep. Shutting his eyes, the dog broke into a slow canter, still moving in precisely the opposite direction from Fay, and drawing with him the whole furious hornet horde.

Thence, stumblingly, he made his way down the slope and along the water edge. In a single hurricane dash he could have distanced his torturers. But, baffled, they would have found the weeping child. Therefore, enduring the agony as best he might, he continued for nearly a furlong at the same slow canter before instinct or reason told him he had lured the hornets far enough away from her.

Then, in a spasm of relief, he plunged deep into the lake, freeing himself of his foes and gaining momentary relief from the myriad stings of fire which were swelling his head and feet out of all proportion to the rest of him. But, as collie instinct also told him, mere cold water is not a swift remedy for hornet stings. A better and a quicker cure was at hand. Swimming back, alongshore, he landed near the forest-edge strip of marsh. Into the soft cool black mud he thrust himself, shoving his swollen head in it and wallowing deep and luxuriously.

Here Fay came upon him. Herself dirty and torn and rankly disreputable, she peered tearfully down upon an object which by contrast made her look spotlessly well groomed. Coolharbor Ronald was one solid, streaky mass of black mud. Out of the mire his grotesquely swollen head and face arose like some misshapen Silurian. He was horrible to look upon.

Panic drove Fay into action. Regardless of her own appearance, she caught the dog by the collar and dragged him out into the lake. There, the chilly water up to her knees, she strove to scrub Ronald clean of some of his coating of mud. The task was not difficult, for the mire had not yet caked.

A hornet that had become enmeshed in the dog's tangle of hair came to life during the wash, sufficiently to sting her right venomously on the hand back. Ronny, too, in shifting his position as the cold water sloshed over him, staggered against her and made her lose her footing in the wet ooze.

To her feet she struggled, gasping and dripping, an unlovely and bewilderedly unhappy little Venus rising from the mud-stained deep. Pluckily she went on with the task of cleansing the dog.

At last he was superficially clean, his mighty coat sticking dankly to his suddenly attenuated body, his once snowy shirt-frill and ruff grayish with water and with the remnants of mud. His head was still swollen grotesquely. One eye was shut, with a big lump above it. His nose was bulbous; his graceful lower legs and feet were a series of bumps.

As she led the wofully disfigured brute ashore, Fay glanced at her silver wrist watch, the birthday present which was her chiefest treasure. By some miracle, it was still going. She wished it was not. For it registered ten minutes past nine.

Nine o'clock was the time scheduled for the Dennings' departure for the hour-distant Paignton show; which was to begin—so the premium list said—"promptly at ten"! Paignton was an hour away. The show was to begin in fifty minutes. The hopes of the whole family had rested on Ronny's winning his four points and thus his championship. Already his luxuriant coat was showing first signs of the summer shedding. Before the next show he would be "out of coat." An out-of-coat collie stands slim chance at any show. Six months might pass before he could hope to be "in bloom" once more. Perhaps longer.

It was she—she who loved him—who had robbed him of his championship. He had been well content to stay there on the porch with her. It was her own fault they had gone for that miserable walk. She pictured herself trying to explain to her father and mother. And she fell to wishing she were at the South Pole with the twenty-five cream-colored bears of her pseudo dream.

From her drenched pockets she drew forth the envelope she had begged her father to allow her to take charge of, that morning—the yellow envelope containing Ronald's "identification card" and collar tag for the show. They were wet and a bit pulpy.

Squaring her small shoulders, she drew a long breath. Then, snapping the leash anew on Ronald's smeared collar, she turned homeward. There was only one thing to do. Nothing was to be gained by putting off the evil day of reckoning. Open confession might prove to be as bad for the anatomy as it was good for the soul, but it must be faced. There was no least taint of cowardice in the child. Her heart was sick; but her step was steady.

The nearest way to the house, from the curved shore line whence she had emerged from the lake, was not through the woods, but by striking straight across to the road and so to the Denning driveway, a quarter-mile distant. To the road she led the drenched collie, the water still dribbling drearily from her own wrecked clothes at every step.

As she went, bits of the nightmare chase began to flit back into her memory. She recalled the route she had taken, up the hillside. She wondered at her own blind folly in following that particular course. Not three days earlier she and her father had been rambling through that very part of the woods and Malcolm Denning had pointed out to her the giant hornet nest.

The hornet nest! Then, all at once, she understood. She knew now why her chum, Ronny, had turned on her and had butted her over and sent her rolling down the steep, while he walked so slowly in the other direction. With a catch of her heaving breath, she stooped down and flung both arms around the collie's wet throat.

"Oh, Ronny!" she sobbed. "Of all the dogs that ever happened,—you're that dog! You're a—a hero, Ronny!

That's what you are. A hero. And look what I've gone and done to *you!* I've kept you from being a champion. Oh, Ronny, I'd hate to be as worthless as *I* am!"

To her remorseful senses, just then, her parents' disappointment and anger seemed infinitely less important than did the wrong she had worked on Ronald himself in cheating him out of his golden chance for a championship. From much eager listening to her father's dog talk she had become fiercely imbued with the idea that a championship was the most desirable and most difficult goal in life. And this was the shining goal from which she had deflected her adored pal, Coolharbor Ronald!

She was on the highway now, and pattering toward home. Around a bend in the road chugged a closed car— a car almost as disreputable in aspect as were Fay and the dog. The cleanest thing about its mud-dimmed exterior was the large white linen sign pasted on the windshield, a sign that read "TAXI."

It was driven by a grimy-shirted old person with a large pink face—Iry Tevvis, the local hackman. In the tonneau of the car were four wicker baskets of generous size and fanciful design.

At sight of the bedraggled girl and her lankly dripping escort, Iry stopped his machine.

"What's wrong, Miss Fay?" he asked, anxiously.

As an accompaniment to his question, a quartet of falsetto barks sounded shrilly from the four wicker baskets in the tonneau. At the sound, Ronald pricked up his ears in mild interest. Even Fay stared wonderingly. Iry explained:

"I'm taking Mrs. Biller's four Pekes over to the show. There isn't room for them in her runabout. She's gone on ahead. But whatever on earth's happened to you, missy? To the two of you, for that matter? Have you—?"

Stiffly, formally, her jaw set hard, Fay began to tell her story. Then, through no will of her own, she broke down and wailed the rest of the fearsome narrative. Iry listened, open-mouthed. Before he could comment, her conscience awoke belatedly. Just because she had ruined Ronny's career, it was no reason why the four basketed Pekes should lose their chances.

"Hurry up!" she exhorted Iry. "You're—you're fifteen minutes behindhand, now. You can't possibly get to Paignton by ten o'clock. And if you don't—"

"If I don't," finished Tevvis, with no trace of anxiety —"if I don't, I'll get there when I do get there. That's all there is to that. But I want you should stop crying. It's rotten hard luck, I know. But—"

"The show begins at ten o'clock," insisted Fay, the fate of the Pekes oppressing her more and more. " 'Promptly at ten.' It says so. And if—"

"And if it does," rumbled Iry, unconcernedly, "there'll be an earthquake and a new Congress. For there wasn't never yet a dog show that began anywhere inside of an hour of the time it was scheduled to. I've follered them for a good many years now, with my own dogs and with other folks'. And I haven't found a one of 'em that started before eleven o'clock. So—"

"But that won't do Ronny any good," lamented Fay, her personal griefs coming to the fore again, now she knew the Pekes were not to be made late on her account. "It'll take ever so long to get him clean, and it'll take weeks for those swellings of his to go down. Here I've got his ticket and everything! And he can't even go there, or to any other show till—"

"Hold on!" broke in Iry, eagerly, as her eyes filled anew. "Just don't you go a-crying again, now! There's only two things in this funny old world I can't stand to sit by and watch. And both of 'em is a scared child a-crying. Listen! You're due for a licking, anyhow, I s'pose. But the thing you seem unhappiest over is that collie missing his show. Would you as soon take your whaling this afternoon as this morning? Because if you would, hop in here with me, you and your dog."

"I—I don't understand what ——"

"You will. Here's the dope: I'm on my way to the show, aren't I? Well, you and the dog can come, too. You got his ticket and everything. If we was to drive all the way back and talk it over with your pa, we'd be late for sure. Besides, if he took one look at that dog, he'd figger there wouldn't be a ghost of a chance for him to ever look decent again. Now *I* know better. I was handling collies before your pa ever saw one. Hop in. As soon as we get to the show, I'll phone your folks. Then they won't worry what's happened to you. And if they want to come over, they can. By that time I'll have the collie a-looking like something. If ——"

A veritable squeal of delight interrupted him. Her tear-splotched face transfigured, her super-imagination fired by the prospect, Fay was swarming up into the car among the baskets, exhorting the willing Ronald to join her there.

"And I'll give you my watch," she promised, gratefully, as they got into motion. "I haven't any money with me except sixteen cents. But you can have my watch for tak-

ing us there and back. It's—it's worth ever so many
dollars. I——"

"You'll cut out that line of fool talk, missy!" ordained
Iry, roughly, "if you and me is to be feller-passengers in
this rattly old ark of mine. I'm doing this as a buddy of
yours. Not for pay. If your pa wants to slip me something, later, well—why, that's up to *him*. I'll show the
dog for you, too, if you like, in the ring. Unless maybe
you think he'll show better for you, him not knowing me."

"I'll show him!" she declared, delighted at the prospect.
"I know how. I've seen daddy do it at his other dog
shows. And I've watched him make Ronny show, for
practice, ever so many times, on the lawn at home. I know
the words that make him prick up his ears and look all
noble. *Please* let me!"

"All right!" vouchsafed Tevvis. "There's no great trick
in doing it, if a dog is a natural shower, like this one of
yours is. I saw that when I watched him in the ring at
Paterson, last fall. Besides, lots of judges kind of favors
a dog that's showed by a kid. Go to it!"

To Iry Tevvis there was nothing strikingly amiss in
the child's bedraggled costume. True, it was soaking
wet. But an hour's drive in sun and wind would dry it.
As to its several torn places and its ample brocading of
mud and strawberry juice, it was almost foppishly neat
by comparison with the clothes of his own brood of
picturesque grandchildren.

"Besides," he went on, "collies may not be judged till
late afternoon. Long before that time your pa and your
ma will be there to handle their dog—and maybe to mis-
handle you, as well," he ended in grisly wit.

The prospect of later retribution did not for an instant

mar Fay's glittering vision of the show. But she glanced
down apprehensively at Ronald as he stood in placid contentment on the floor of the car, in front of her. The rush
of sunny air from the open windows was drying his lank
coat. His fur was beginning to stand out fluffily from
chest and sides. Less and less did he look like an ema-
ciated drowned rat.

His face's contour, too, was growing to resemble that
of a collie, instead of a gargoyle. Fay was learning for
the first time the amazing speed wherewith the swelling
of an insect sting can subside from the flesh of a healthy
young dog. Already the swollen eye was open. The
myriad other lumps were losing size and aggressiveness.

Fay looked disconsolately at her own attire. Then she
leaned forward and said primly to Tevvis:

"Iry, will you please promise to keep looking straight
ahead at the road? I am going to sit down in the bottom
of the car for a little while, and hold my dress out of the
window to dry. Then if you can spare some of those pins
that are stuck in the front of your shirt, won't you please
pass them back to me? I want to do some mending."

By the time the taxi was parked in the tented inclosure
where the Paignton dog show was in progress, Coolharbor
Ronald was dry and fluffy. His paws and the white portions of his coat were still grayish, and here and there his
hair stuck together in bunches. But no longer was he
grotesque. The swellings had all but departed.

As Mrs. Biller came forward to collect her basketfuls
of Pekes, she looked in perplexed disapproval at the
daughter of her friend and neighbor, Mrs. Malcolm Denning. Her opinion of that estimable woman declined
sharply, at sight of the unkempt and altogether wretched

condition of Fay's dress and shoes and stockings. The Peke owner could not understand how any mother could let her little girl come to a public place looking like a comic-paper gutter child.

But it was no business of Mrs. Biller's. She told herself so. Later she told several other neighbors so. She gathered up her Pekes and strode away, leaving Iry to pilot Fay and Ronald past the gate and to the collie's numbered stall.

Coolharbor Ronald was anchored on his bench in the collie section—a section which some twenty-seven dogs of his breed already occupied. Owners and handlers were at work over some of them with cloth and dandy brush and talcum and other aids to beauty. Visitors were drifting along the aisles, pausing at one or another of the benches to stare at the dogs or to ask vapid questions of the nervously busy exhibitors.

Iry brought Ronald a pan of fresh drinking water. Then he departed, to telephone the garish tidings to Denning. Despite his own d'Artagnan-like assurance, assumed for the quelling of Fay's grief and worry, Iry was not wholly at ease in the prospect of explaining to Malcolm Denning that he had kidnapped the girl and the dog. Thus it was with a grin of relief that he heard at the far end of the telephone the voice of one of the Denning maids. Speaking very fast and hanging up the receiver as soon as he had delivered the message, he declaimed:

"This is Iry Tevvis. Tell your boss I've took little Fay and the collie over to the Paignton show, and they're all right and he's not to get sore. Tell him to come on over, quick, and show his dog. I'll have him in shape for the ring, before the boss gets here. G'by."

It was another five minutes before Iry returned to the bench, where Fay stood guard over the big collie. He had commandeered from other dog men a tin of water, a handful of dusty lumps of French chalk, a broken comb, and a bunch of soft rags. Fay recalled the elaborate kit of grooming appliances her father was wont to take to shows, and her confidence began to flag. But it was restored when she saw the briskly workman-like way Iry began to labor over the dog's coat.

Deftly he combed and cleaned and fluffed. Shamelessly he applied great quantities of French chalk to the spots where the grime refused to yield to gentler treatment and to the paws and the face-blaze. Under the clever grooming, Ronny began to look somewhat as he had before his disastrous walk with Fay. The swellings were disappearing fast. To increase the speed of their vanishing, Tevvis anointed the dog with witch hazel he begged from a next-bench exhibitor. A human would have carried those swellings for days. Ronald had gotten rid of them with incredible ease.

"Wasn't it perfectly gorgeous how he got himself all stung up and tortured, just to save *me?*" exclaimed Fay, stroking lovingly the shimmering coat of her chum. "Did you ever hear of a dog being so splendid? He ——"

"I did," answered Iry, without pausing from his work. "I did, once. It was a collie of my own. He did just that very thing when my own kid bumped into a hornet nest when him and her was for a stroll together. But he's dead this fifteen years. He was my pal. And he's dead. Like all dogs die, by the time they get to be a man's best chum and when he could spare fifty human folks out of his life easier than he could spare his chum dog. Just

when they've got so close to the heart of you that you feel
you can't get on without 'em, they up and die. Dogs die
too soon, anyway; and a lot of us humans don't die soon
enough. When I heard how this collie of yours done the
same stunt, this morning, I made up my mind I'd do what
I could for him here, kind of in memory of my own collie
pal."

He laid down the cloth which he had been using as a
sponge, and he went to work again with a lump of French
chalk, applying it here and there with artistic touches.

"Collie judge isn't here yet," he continued. "It's pretty
close to eleven o'clock. The judging will begin in a few
minutes. If the collie judge don't get here soon, the four
rings will all be taken by the other breeds. That'll mean
the collies can't be judged till afternoon. So your pa
will be here plenty early to fix up his dog and show him.
I'm just getting him in shape in case the ——"

Down the aisle hustled a white-coated show attendant,
droning monotonously:

"Get your collies ready. Ring Number Three. Calling
male puppy class. Numbers 225, 226, 227, 228, 229!"

Iry Tevvis stopped him as he scuttled past.

"I thought the collie judge wasn't here yet," said he.
"How does ——?"

"Just got here," replied the attendant, hustling on.
"Told the superintendent he has to catch a train for the
city at one o'clock, and he wants to do his judging job
right off."

Down the aisle he continued, calling out his sing-song
announcement. Instantly the collie section was athrob
with activity and nervous excitement. Iry glanced at the

number tag on Ronald's collar, then at the catalogue he
had annexed from a momentarily vacant camp stool.

"Number 241," he mused. "Your pa has only entered
him for the American-bred Class. That won't be called
for another ten minutes. Maybe longer. Novice Class
comes next to the Puppy class. I'll have time to finish
getting him in shape."

A vast wave of terror swept over Fay as she watched
him. It was one thing to dream valorously beforehand
of putting Ronald through his ring paces. It was quite
another to contemplate at close quarters the prospect of
responsibility for his victory or downfall. Her hands grew
very wet and her mouth waxed very dry. Then she braced
herself all over.

"Ronny," she whispered, leaning over the dog as Tevvis
fluffed out the plumed tail and breeches, "I got you into
all that nasty mess. There's nobody but me that can make
up to you for it. And I can't do it unless you help me a
lot, Ronny. You'll just have to imagine it's daddy pilot-
ing you in the ring, and act the way he taught you to."

The collie wagged his tail (much to the annoyance of
Iry, who was trying to comb it) and licked the scared
little face so close to his own. Then—it seemed only a
moment before the attendant was droning forth a new
set of numbers at the end of the aisle and Iry was lifting
the resplendent Coolharbor Ronald off his bench and handing her the leash. With numbed legs Fay made her way
toward the million-mile distant show ring, in the wake of
several other people who were leading collies thither for
the American-bred Class—a class open to all dogs except
champions.

Into the ring filed the six entrants for American-bred

honors. In the center of the roped inclosure was the low judging block, or platform. In one corner of the ring was a table bearing an open pasteboard covered judging book and a varicolored heap of ribbons. Beside the table stood a fat little man in tweeds. At the entrance to the ring another man checked off the numbers of the competing dogs.

"All in, sir," presently called this other man. The fat little judge came out of his studious apathy. Advancing from his corner, he surveyed the six collies as if he noticed their presence for the first time. Then he rasped:

"Walk your dogs, please!"

Around the ring plodded the six handlers, their dogs either pulling back on the leashes or else marching proudly alongside. Fay was familiar enough with the procedure. Presently the parade would be halted, and the judge would order one dog after another to be brought on to the block for his examination.

All this, unless some collie should be deemed unworthy of careful inspection. There had been such a collie at the Englewood show and another at Paterson. The judges then had ordered the outclassed dog taken away while the parade was still in progress.

As the procession started a second time around the ring, now, the judge stepped suddenly forward from his place near the block. Touching Fay on the shoulder, he said, none too gently:

"Take your dog out of the parade. Take him over in that corner, and keep him there."

Aghast, the child stared up at him; doubting her own ears. But with a peremptory twitch of his thumb toward

gratulation. "He done it! But then I knew he would as soon as I seen the judge send him into that corner. Ronny was so much better'n the rest of his class that he put him aside while he figgered out what dogs to give the second and third prizes to. Judges often do that. Now we'll take him back to his bench and groom him for the Winners' Class—the class for all the dogs that's won their own reg'lar classes—the class that gives the champ'nship points to the dog that wins it. Then'll come the 'specials,' after all the reg'lar classes is over you know. So it's up to us to put him at his best. Come along. Why—you look like you was asleep! Buck up! We just won the strongest class there's likely to be in this show."

It was a wrathful Malcolm Denning who hastened into the huge tent, with his indignant wife, an hour later. His first question, of a passing attendant, was whether or not the collies had yet been judged. When he was told their judging had been finished some minutes earlier, his wrath was not lessened. Stormily he made his way toward the collie section.

As he and his wife hurried along the aisle, a knot of people stopped their progress. The group was gathered around one bench in the long line. Denning peeped over the heads of those nearest him, to see the cause of so much interest. His wife, through a gap in the shoulders of those in front of her, followed the direction of his gaze. Then they both stood spellbound, goggle-eyed.

On the bench reclined their lost dog, resplendent and majestic. Close beside him in the straw sat Fay, one arm around his shaggy neck, her eyes like stars in a murky lake. In her free hand she gripped proudly a gleaming silver cup half as large as herself. Above the bench, decorated by a blue ribbon and a purple rosette and several tricolored ribbons, Iry Tevvis had scrawled on a thumb-blackened sheet of wrapping paper the legend:

CHAMPION Coolharbor Ronald; Winner and Best Collie Of Either Sex in Paignton Show.

Iry himself, glowing like a moist sunset, stood beaming on all and sundry. At sight of the Dennings he lurched forward and caught them unceremoniously by the arms, drawing them back from the crowd. There, half-trium-phantly, half-shamefacedly, he told them in dramatic fervor the tale of Fay's exploits.

Fay herself looked up from her thrilling levee to see her father beckoning to her. Instantly delirious happiness froze into terror. Yet, walking very straight, she came across to him through the clump of onlookers. Denning, without a word, piloted her to a deserted end of the tent. Then he spoke.

"Daughter," he said, in the rare judicial tone she always dreaded, "you disobeyed your mother and me this morn-ing. You abused our trust in you. You betrayed us. Have you anything to say for yourself?"

Fay fought for words. Then, in a muffled little voice, she answered right bravely: "No, sir. I haven't got any-thing at all to say for myself. I did all those things."

Denning nodded, in what might almost have seemed ap-proval, as she did not urge in her own defense the glorious fruits of her disobedience.

"That sort of thing has to be punished," went on the gravely judicial voice. "It has to be punished severely. Here is the punishment I am going to give you—a punish-ment you will remember all your life: I am going to con-demn you to spoil your prettiest dress by rolling in a strawberry bed. Next, I am going to make you stand in a cold lake and wash a muddy dog. Next, I am going to make you get a bad hornet sting on the back of your hand and be more frightened and unhappy than you've ever been. There, daughter! You've heard your sentence."

Again he paused. She was blinking at him, uncomprehendingly. He resumed:

"Of course, if you have already suffered any or all of those punishments, I am not going to be so cruel as to make you go through them again. In that case, you've paid your bill and the slate is clean; which is a good deal more than *you* are just now."

"*Daddy!*"

"I—I think I heard your mother say something, a minute ago, about buying you that pink crêpe-de-Chine dress you were so crazy about the last time we were in the city," continued Malcolm Denning, gruffly. "As a handler fee, you know, for carrying Ronny to victory today. . . . I never thought I should be so proud of anyone who is so dirty and so disobedient! Don't go getting the idea I'm pleased with you. I'm not. But—but somehow you're beginning to make up to me for the splendid little son I never had. Now stop crying and tell me about the show!"

III. The Feud

"WHAT d'ye call him?" asked Bourke.

"A collie," answered Hurd.

"H'm!" sniffed Bourke, suspecting an attempt of the better educated farmer to patronize him by use of this unknown word. "Looks more to me like a shepherd-dog."

"It's the same thing," patiently explained Hurd. "The old-timers used to call them shepherd-dogs, but the Scotch called them collies. The name has crossed over to America. I found this one down at the Rumson dog pound a couple of months ago. I went there to look for that mongrel of Kernan's. The dog had disappeared and Kernan thought it might have gotten as far as Rumson and been raked in by the pound master. His dog wasn't there. In fact, it never has shown up, anywhere, since the day it vanished. But this young collie was at the pound. He had belonged to some folks that had to leave town one jump ahead of the sheriff, and left their dog behind. The

pound master had grabbed him. I bought him for ten
dollars, and——"

"Ten dollars!" scoffed Bourke, with all a mountaineer's
contempt for such useless waste of money. "Why, man,
you could 'a' bought a trained coon dog for that! Ten
dollars for a wuthless——"

"Not so worthless, maybe," contradicted Hurd. "I've
only had him about two months, but in that time he has
learned faster than we've been able to teach him. Look!"

He nodded toward his lower pasture lot. An uneasy
heifer had been teasing a top rail of the makeshift fence
with her half-grown horns until she had pried its rusty
nails free and sent it toppling to the ground. Then she
had attacked the second rail, with equal teasing persist-
ency. As this rail tumbled she stepped through the gap,
over the remaining rail, and headed gleefully for a near-
by corn-patch. The five other head of young cattle in
the field came joyously through the gap, in her wake.

Bourke grinned. The day was sickeningly hot. The
breached fence was a full furlong distant. That meant
a fast run through the heat, for Hurd, if he would head
off the strays before they could begin to destroy the young
corn. It would be amusing to stand there on the farmhouse porch and watch Hurd race around in the sun's
glare after his absconding yearlings.

But Hurd showed no chagrin at the sight of his strays.
Without moving a step, he snapped his fingers to the
drowsing young collie at his feet. Instantly the dog was
awake and up. Pointing to the straggling cattle, Hurd
said:

"Turn 'em, Jock!"

Barking gayly, the collie dashed across the intervening

furlong of ground like a fluffy and tawny thunderbolt. He caught up with the first heifer as she set forefoot in the corn.

Deftly he halted and wheeled her back. Then, getting her under way, he made for the others. In an incredibly brief space of time he had bunched the stragglers and had them in motion. He was here and there and everywhere, barking harrowingly, nipping where gentler persuasion failed.

Reluctantly the fugitives gave up their pleasant plan for a corn feast, and began to yield to his urge toward the fence gap through which they had found liberty. One by one Jock drove them through the gap, doubling back after two bolters; nor ceasing his task until every last one of the five was safe in the pasture. Then he stood panting in the gap, wagging his tail and looking to Hurd for further orders.

Hurd whistled. The collie came bounding back to the porch.

"You can stay here in the shade," Hurd told him, speaking as to a fellow-human. "But watch 'em! *Watch* 'em!"

Turning to the interested Bourke, he added:

"He'll keep an eye on 'em, in case they try to get out again. I doubt if they'll try it more than once. Then, when it's cooler, along around sunset, I'll go down there and mend the fence. Handles cattle real pretty, don't he? Took to it from the first, like he had been doing it all his life. That's the collie of it. A lot of 'em pick up herding as easy as they pick up fleas. He's just the same with the sheep. No, Jock isn't worthless. Not by a mile. He's pretty near as useful as another hired man would be. That boy of mine thinks he's worth his weight in ——"

"Shucks!" grunted Bourke, refusing to be impressed. "I'll bet he wouldn't be wuth a dern at cooning. I'd rather have a fust-class coon dog than all the shepherds that ever shepped. Rouser is wuth fifty of him."

He lifted his lanky frame from the chair into which he had lowered it on his arrival at the Hurd farm, ten minutes earlier.

"Well," he said, stretching, "I gotta trudge. I just dropped in, like I said, to see if maybe you might 'a' caught sight of Rouser anywheres. I'm asking everyone around here. He's too good to let go without giving a good look for him. He never strayed before in all the time I've had him. I can't understand it, nohow. He ——"

A fourteen-year-old boy approached from the creek at the foot of the farm, a fish-pole over his shoulder and a string of six perch dangling from one hand. Hurd hailed him; then turning to Bourke, he explained:

"That son of mine is always traipsing around the woods, vacation-time, when his farm work's done. He'd have been more likely to see Rouser than any of us grown folks would. . . . Say, Ethan," he went on as the lad came up to the porch, "Mr. Bourke has lost that black coon-hound of his. He ——"

"Rouser?" asked the boy, in real interest. "That's funny!"

"Mebbe 'tis," rasped Bourke. "But I don't see the fun of it. That dog's wuth ——"

"No, no," protested Ethan. "I didn't mean it that way. I meant it was queer that another dog has disappeared.

That's the fourth in two months—four from just around here. And I don't ever remember hearing of any other dog being lost hereabouts till then. How long ago did you miss him?"

"Couple of days ago," answered Bourke. "I figured he had chased some fox so far he couldn't get back the same day. He did that once before, when he was a pup. But he'd never chase any fox so far that he couldn't get home again in *two* days. So this afternoon I been making inq'ries for him. You say he ain't the fust?"

"No, sir," replied Ethan, excitedly. "He's the fourth. The fourth I've heard of. The first was Kernan's little cross-breed. Dad was looking for him when he found Jock at the pound. So that was one lucky lose for us. The second was Dan Foster's beagle. That was a month ago. Then, a couple of weeks back, the Landers' old coon-dog strayed off and he hasn't ever been heard of again. And now it's Rouser. Funny, isn't it, dad? All of them were dogs that had lived at their homes for years. Not a one of them was a runaway. They couldn't all four have been stolen. Nobody would have given a nickel for Kernan's mongrel. Nobody except Kernan."

Bourke was glowering at him and slowly chewing the big mouthful of tobacco he had just bitten from his plug. The mountaineer's small eyes puckered.

"Say, bub," he growled, "unless you're making this up, there's due to be an unholy lot of trouble over it. It ain't on the free list, in this region, to go around stealing folks' dogs. I've seen knives drawed quicker over a dog-stealing than over a bound'ry dispoot. If some one's trying to be funny or to settle some grudge by stealing our dogs, he might safer have bit into a hornet's nest. Soon or late he'll get nabbed. And when he does—well, I'm only speaking for myself, mind you. But if Rouser has been stole, the cuss that did it won't be fit to put in jail if I git to him before the const'ble does. So long."

He swung his lean body down on to the gravel walk and plodded out of the dooryard. Hurd looked after him worriedly.

"Say, Ethan," he rebuked, "you hadn't ought to have put that notion in Hi Bourke's mind. He's a mossback old mountaineer. I know the breed. When he thinks some one's robbed him or done him some other harm, his first thought is that crooked old sheath knife of his, and his second thought is his bear rifle. He'll go sleuthing around now till he thinks he's found the man who stole his dog. Then there's li'ble to be work for a jury. Maybe the grand jury, at that. What makes you think Rouser was stolen?"

"I don't," returned Ethan. "I didn't say I did. I said the four dogs weren't likely to have been stolen. Two of 'em weren't worth stealing. I just said it was funny that all four of 'em should have disappeared in two months. I tell you I'm going to keep a mighty close eye on Jock and Eileen. Specially on Jock. Eileen's too old and wise to get lost anywhere."

At this second iteration of her name a diminutive and ancient red setter came slowly out from her lair in the cool earth under the porch and approached Ethan, wagging a moth-eaten tail.

The runt of an illustrious litter, she had been bought by Hurd, for a mere trifle, eleven years earlier. Under his tutelage she had developed into one of the most renowned bird dogs in the county. Ludicrously small, she made up for dearth of size by her inspired scenting powers and field skill and by dauntless courage. Now age was silvering her red muzzle and stiffening her lithe muscles. But she was still redoubtable and adventurous.

From the hour of his arrival at the farm Jock had worshiped the crotchety little old setter. And she had taken a pretty and motherly interest in him; she who was wont to snap at other dogs. They were dear chums, the old setter and the young collie. Jock was even more deeply devoted to Eileen than to his human idols, Hurd and Ethan.

Now as she appeared from her dark lair under the porch Jock advanced to meet her, tail awag. The two touched noses and trotted off together toward the creek for a swim. But, halfway thither, the collie seemed to remember his master's command to watch the cattle. He glanced sidewise down the field toward the lower pasture.

The mischief-making heifer had become emboldened by his absence, to make for the fence gap again. She was blundering through, toward the corn-field, the five other yearlings at her heels. This was no time for a swim. Barking, the collie raced after the strays.

Eileen watched him, as if wondering at his desertion. Then the heat of the day and the promise of coolness in the creek's fast waters made her trot on to her swim.

The cattle proved sulkier and more recalcitrant than before. It was several minutes before Jock was able to get them all herded into the pasture. Then, as he was departing, one of them made another break for the gap. Impatiently he headed her back. To make certain she and the rest would not try to get out again the moment his back should be turned, he cleared the rail and chased the six in a huddled bunch to the far end of the pasture.

His work done, he saw Hurd coming down from the house with a hammer and nail box. The man, at this second attempt of the cattle to escape, had decided not to wait for a cooler hour, but to mend the broken fence at once. Jock realized his own vigil was at an end and that he was free to go for his coveted swim with Eileen.

"Hold on, Jockey!" called Ethan, as the collie loped past. "I left my other pole down there. I'll go with you."

Together the boy and the dog made their way across the meadow and to the rise of tree-fringed ground which marked the nearer bank of the creek. As they went, there came to them the sound of a distant bark. Both recognized it as Eileen's. Jock bounded forward, as at a summons. To him the timbre of the bark meant more than mere excitement. Ethan whistled him back.

"Your coat's too thick to go galloping after rabbits or coons or whatever she's put up, this sizzling weather," he adjured the collie. "Take your time. Dad says Eileen's only fault is that she *will* take out after coons and rabbits and such like when he's not gunning with her. In weather like this she's too old to go racing them. Don't encourage her by chasing along after her. Come back."

Unwillingly Jock obeyed. He was keen to rush off to Eileen at top speed. A dog's bark has a dozen shades of meaning which all other dogs and many dog men can read. In that one distant bark of Eileen's the collie read much. He craved mightily to join in the adventure, whatever it might be. But Ethan's word was his law. Wherefore, fidgeting, he came to heel.

Together, at leisurely pace, the lad and the collie

reached the creek; arriving at its widest part, where was moored Ethan's boat.   There was no sign of Eileen.

Fingers to lips, Ethan whistled piercingly.   The shrill note split the hot silences of the summer afternoon.   Twice he whistled.   Then he strained his ears to catch the rustle and crack of undergrowth which should betoken the little old setter's return.   But the silence hung dead in the torrid world.

"H'm!" said Ethan, aloud.   "She must have run a big distance, not to hear that whistle of mine.   She always comes on the jump when she hears it."

He frowned, perplexed.   He knew that the stiffening legs of the aged setter could not have borne her so far in that brief time as to make his calliope-like whistle unheard.   He knew, too, that such a call ordinarily would have brought her back to him at top speed.

Again he whistled, long and shrilly.   Then he shouted. No answering bark or sound of tearing through the bushes.   He turned to Jock.   The collie seemed to have read the boy's thought before it was formed.   He was casting about, in an irregular half-circle, nostrils close to the drought-parched grass.

"Good old Jockey!" approved Ethan.   "Find her! Find Eileen.   That's right."

Like many another well-trained collie, Jock knew well the meaning of the command, "Find!"   Also he knew who was meant by "Eileen."   He was doing his best to obey.   He had been doing so before the order was given. Perhaps he, too, wondered at the setter's non-response to the call.

In another second his sniffing nostrils ceased to quest. They had found the trail they sought.

Head down, he galloped along in a straight line, alongside the creek; Ethan following at top speed. In another few rods he veered inland, quickly taking up a straight line again. Ethan understood. Eileen had detoured here to avoid a clump of brier and sumach and, having skirted it, had continued her course.

A hundred yards farther the dog swung at right angles to his former route. Here a noisy mountain brook debouched from the abruptly rising hillside and emptied into the creek. Up the hill, amid bowlders and tree trunks, sped the collie, Ethan trying in vain to keep up with him.

Well did the boy know this abrupt slope of Raccoon Mountain, the southerly limit of Hurd's farm. The brook dropped, from a spring at the very summit, in a series of rapids and tiny cataracts, spreading out into large or small pools at various narrow plateaus amid the bowlder-strewn slope.

At the first of these pools—a widish sheet of water, nowhere more than a foot deep—the collie had come to a halt. He was smelling around the rocky edges of the pool, and taking a hesitant step or two out into its stone-bottomed expanse.

Again Ethan understood. Be a dog's sense of smell never so unerring, it will not guide him through running water. There, all odor disperses. Eileen had come as far as this. Then she had run out into the pool.

Instantly Jock came back to land. He skirted the entire pool, nose to ground. But he could not pick up the scent again.

And now Ethan felt that he himself should have been as able as the dog to follow the trail. For the rocks on every side were dry and sunbaked. If a dog wades out into the water, and then comes back on such dry and grassless ground, there will be distinct wet footmarks visible for many minutes thereafter, as visible to the human eye as their scent is perceptible to a collie's nose.

But on no spot was there a single wet footprint. Eileen must have passed this way and splashed into the pool, not ten minutes earlier. Into the pool she had gone. Jock's unerring scent proved that. But she had not come out of it. There was not so much as a splash of water on the baked poolside rocks, except where Jock had tracked the moisture ashore on his own return from reconnoitering there.

The thing did not make sense.

Vexed at the mystery, Ethan took off his shoes and socks and waded out into the pool. The bottom was formed by a solid sheet of rock, slightly concave, perhaps twenty feet long by fifteen feet wide, and with its surface worn almost glass-smooth by centuries of freshets hurtling down from the mountain above.

From end to end of the pool, and across and across it, waded Ethan, the water nowhere rising above his shins. No, there was no unseen crevice down which Eileen could have slipped. Nor was there a hidden patch of quicksand that could have sucked her in. The basin of rock was unbroken.

In midpool Ethan ceased his explorations. He felt queer in the stomach. This was like the magic he had read of in story-books. Eileen had run up the hillside till she came to this pool. She had run out into the pool. There she had disappeared, though not even a lively cat could have drowned therein. The water was crystal clear against the bottom of pale-gray rock. Ethan could see every inch of the shallow basin. There was nothing in it; not so much as a minnow.

Then his sense of awe departed and he grinned sheepishly at his own absurd fear. Why, the thing was simple enough!

At the pool's lower end the water filtered down in a thin cataract to the brook below. At its upper end it was fed by the brook from above. At this end the water brawled down a steep slant, perhaps three feet wide, for a distance of some thirty yards, over bowlders and gravel, to the lip of the next pool overhead.

Naturally, since Eileen had not come out of the pool at any of its sides, she had swarmed up that slant in the brawling bed of the brook, pursuing whatever thing had chanced to be her prey.

Left to herself, she would have chosen the easier going, on the bank of the stream. But the creature she was chasing had apparently stuck to the brook bed—perhaps with an instinct of obliterating its own scent—and Eileen had not dared risk the loss of time involved in detouring by the longer and easier route.

The pool above was smaller, but much deeper, and with serried juts of rock sticking out far below its surface. Ethan knew the place well. He had bathed there, sometimes, when August heat had made even the cold creek waters too warm for comfortable swimming. There, too, he had barked his legs against the sharp shelves of rock and shale which jutted out at several places along the lower portions of the five-foot depths.

Still grinning at his momentary feeling of superstitious dread, he climbed the slope, close alongside the brook, till he came to this second pool. Jock ran beside him, still fruitlessly sniffing.

The pool lay black and peaceful, save where the falling waters from the steep slant above churned it to bubbles and froth.

No sign here of the missing Eileen. Summoning Jock, the boy made him circle the pool and then the brookside above it. Try as he would, the collie could pick up no scent.

Then, without warning, Jock shuddered violently all over, as if smitten with a convulsion. Sitting down, he lifted his classic muzzle to the sky, shattering the still afternoon air with a succession of eerie wolf howls so ear-splitting and unearthly as to make the astounded Ethan shout angrily to him to be still.

The boy felt his own scalp crinkle at the horrible sound. Trying to shake off the unbidden terror of it, he said:

"Well, Eileen will hear that, anyhow, if she's in the same county with you. It'll bring her kiting back to us, if anything will. But what in blue blazes ails you, Jockey? Have you gone crazy?"

The collie, still shivering convulsively, crouched with head adroop and tail between his legs, his eyes half shut. From his furry throat came sounds strangely like human sobs. To the startled boy this manifestation was more creepy than had been the deafening outburst. Ethan glanced nervously about him.

Aroused by the racket, a huge and elderly raccoon had thrust forth his comedy mask of a face from a cleft in the tumble of rocks above the pool. Now, at sight of the boy and the dog, he drew coyly back into his stony lair, like some ludicrous jack-in-the-box.

Ethan was not interested in the raccoon. Had the season been autumn or winter, he would have impressed Jock into service, then and there, as a coon-dog, and would have tried to hustle the stones far enough aside to dislodge the beast. For raccoon pelts, in prime, were worth from $8 to $8.50 apiece, from any near-by dealer.

But at this stiflingly hot season raccoon fur was far off prime. The raccoons themselves were hog fat and of poor flavor for food. There was nothing to be gained in digging out this obese creature. So Ethan left it to its interrupted nap and shouted again for Eileen.

There was a quaver in his voice as he yelled the missing setter's name. He was beginning to be genuinely troubled as to her fate, the more so because of Jock's amazing behavior. The boy knew enough of collies not to discount the almost psychic phases that sometimes possess them. He did not like those eldritch death howls, nor the subsequent shuddering and sobbing.

To quell his own disturbed fear, he called sharply to Jock and pursued his climb. Eileen had come part of the way along the wet course of the brook. It might be worth while to follow the brook upward and find at what point she had emerged from it. Damp footprints on the dry rocks would surely apprise him of the exact spot where she had emerged. After that it would be simple for Jock to track her.

The collie needed a second sharp summons from his young master before consenting to follow. Then he crept along listlessly, ever looking back and refusing to take any interest whatever in the hunt.

At last, after a hot and breath-taking climb, Ethan reached the summit and the bubbling big spring which was the mountain brook's source. Nowhere had he seen trace of Eileen. He looked around. Jock was no longer at his heels. The collie had turned and started downhill.

Ethan called him peremptorily. With much reluctance, the collie trotted uphill toward him. For another half-hour the boy searched the mountain, Jock following sullenly, at his repeated orders, but taking no part in the hunt, nor so much as sniffing. Ever he kept turning back toward the second pool.

It was sunset when Ethan and the dog reached home. There the boy called once more to Eileen, half-hoping to see the silver-muzzled little red body come wriggling out from under the porch to greet him.

"Listen, Jock," he said to the collie, as they tramped up the walk, "she isn't here. She isn't ever coming back. She's gone. Just as those four other dogs went. You knew that, before I did. It don't make sense, but it's true. She disappeared somewhere on the side of the mountain. There's Something up yonder that isn't good for dogs. You've been trying to get back there every time I looked the other way. You're not going back there. Understand? I'm going to put you in the old calf paddock for the night. It's wired, and you can't get out of it. To-morrow I'm going to keep an eye on you till my chores are done. Then we're going back there together. With the rifle, maybe. There's no bears or panthers or even wild cats around here. So there's nothing that could have killed those dogs or hidden them too close for them to get loose and come home. Just the same, they didn't come home. Yes, we'll take the rifle."

As ever, he talked to the wise young dog as he would

have talked to a human. Jock as a rule was highly flattered at such conversation. To-night he gave it no heed. Nor would he eat his supper. Twice, before he was shut into the disused calf paddock for the night, Ethan found him trying to creep away in the direction of Raccoon Mountain. The gay collie had undergone a grim change that the boy could not understand.

Hurd and the rest of the family sought at first to make light of Ethan's fantastic theories as to the vanishing of Eileen. But when day dawned and the setter had not returned, Hurd himself took the morning off, to look for her.

Old as she was, Hurd felt she could not have been done away with by any wild animal. In the first place, there was no wild thing within miles that was as large as she or that could have conquered her in a stand-up fight. And even had she been set upon and overcome by a bear, the sound of battle must surely have reached Ethan, at the creek, and he and Jock must have seen unmistakable signs of such conflict when they followed her trail. No, she had disappeared in a way wholly beyond her woodsman master's experience or conjecture.

On his way back from the fruitless search, Hurd chanced to meet Bourke, who also had been wandering the hills and farms for sign of his beloved coon-hound, Rouser.

Hurd told him of his own loss. The mountaineer's thick brows folded down over his small eyes.

"That boy of your'n has got sense," he declared. "It ain't in reason that five dogs would all stray off from the homes where they'd always lived, and fergit to come back. There's been foul play, I'm telling you. Eth was right. Somebody's a-tryin' to be funny or else to pay off some grudge. Nobody that wanted to steal a dog for profit would 'a' stole Kernan's mutt; nor yet that no-count beagle of Dan Forster's. That dog was a plumb fool. Nope. A smart Alec or else some grudge-toter is doin' this. Likewise I aim to find out who he is. When I do, I'm—well, I'm a-hopin' there'll be enough dog-owners on my jury to let me off easy."

"More feuds have started, in these mountains, over dogs than over everything else put together," said Hurd. "Think careful, a couple of times, before you start another, Hi. Don't go off half cocked. Like as not, you and my boy are both clean wrong in your notions. Keep your head."

"Keep my head!" mocked Bourke. "Easy enough for you to say that. Eileen was past her day. You told me you wa'n't going to hunt her ag'in. But how about Rouser? That coon-dog was in his prime. He was the best in the county, bar none. Why, he was ready money to me! I don't git robbed of spot cash without gitting arter the skunk that robbed me."

Hurd could realize what the loss of Rouser must mean to the impoverished mountaineer. Bourke was a renowned coon-hunter. He paid his taxes and paid for such repairs as his farm was lucky enough to get and for many a square meal, out of the raccoons and red foxes he was able to shoot or to trap in winter-time.

From at least one firm of furriers in the ten-mile-distant city of Rumson there was ready market and fair price for all the raccoon and fox pelts Bourke could get hold of. By a trick well known to the trade, but known neither to Bourke nor to the public, a strange and profitable amalgamation was made of these two dissimilar types of fur.

Cleverly were the red fox pelts dyed a lustrous black, except for the white tail-tips and an occasional single white hind-foot. Then the long silvery "guard hairs" of the raccoon were inserted deftly, here and there, into the dyed pelt, with an electric needle. The result was a pelt so closely akin to that of the rare "silver fox" that none but an expert could tell the two apart, and then only by sense of touch.

Undeterred by his father's failure, Ethan prepared to set off on his own account, as soon as his farm work was done, that afternoon. All morning he had kept Jock close to him. Sulky, half rebellious, Jock had accompanied the boy here and there. Always his wrathful eyes kept turning toward Raccoon Mountain. More than once he growled under his breath.

Jock had worshiped the little old setter that had mothered him so prettily. Her disappearance had changed him to a sullenly wrathful brute whose only desire was to get back to the scene of her vanishing. Not even Hi Bourke was so ridden by the sense of feud and revenge as was this sunny-tempered collie.

Moreover, Jock's nostrils had told him more than could be gleaned by the mere woodcraft of any human. It had not given him a positive clue to his setter chum's fate, but it had given him something to connect it with. Nor was this in any way akin to the odd canine sixth sense which suddenly had apprised him that the loved setter was dead.

All afternoon, boy and dog ranged the mountain, following the pools and the brook that linked them. The dog had been frantically eager to get to the mountain. Yet when he reached the second pool he merely sniffed its banks, snarling the while, under his breath; and was persuaded to continue the search from there only by Ethan's imperative command.

Tired and discouraged, Ethan brought Jock home at nightfall. They had drawn blank.

Weary as he was, Ethan slept badly. The night was stickily warm and breathless. He awoke at first gray tinge of dawn. Not for another hour was he due to get up. Yet he was restless and hot and unhappy. It occurred to him that a swim before breakfast would brace him for the day's work.

Silently he put on trousers and shirt. Then he crept downstairs and out into the dew-soaked dooryard. On the porch stood the squirrel rifle, where he had left it when he came home. Perhaps there might be a gray squirrel or so, at this early hour, in the creekside trees. The boy picked up the rifle, loaded it, and slipped a few spare cartridges into his pocket. Then, letting Jock out of the paddock, he started for the creek.

The collie did not bound forth at him, as usual, in eager greeting, but trotted out, head down, paying no heed to Ethan, and heading at once toward the base of Raccoon Mountain.

Ethan caught him by the scruff of the neck and scolded him into walking alongside, instead of deserting him for a silly return to the pool. Together they made their way down the meadow and to the rise of ground which marked the edge of the creek.

Ethan stuck an exploratory bare toe into the water. The hot days and nights had made the wontedly chill creek warm to the touch. The boy recalled the icily limpid second pool where sometimes he bathed. The added coolness would be worth the climb. He set forth to the spot where the brook ran into the creek, and thence he began to follow it up the hill.

At the second step of his ascent something fat and grayish and shapeless scuttled out of sight, up a turn of the brook bed, a few rods in front of him. The listless Jock at once gave furious chase. Ethan's lips parted to call him back. Then he decided to let the dog go ahead.

His own fleeting glimpse of the gray creature had been enough to tell him it was a large raccoon that had been hunting for crayfish and minnows in the shallows of the brook. Probably it was the same raccoon whose comic face had peered out from the rock cleft above the second pool, two days earlier. The collie might tree him or might more likely lose him among the scores of rock-holes along the way. In either event the excitement of the chase might lift Jock from the glum misery that had been his since the loss of Eileen.

So he allowed the dog to continue the race, quickening his own steps up the rough incline, and letting the rifle hang idle in his hand. There was no sense in shooting the coon. Far better let him alone till the beast's fur should be prime and his flesh more palatable.

The noisy scramble of the dog's feet amid the loose stones came clearly to the climbing boy. Then all at once the scrambling sounds ceased. There was an angry growl, followed by a gurgling noise, then a splash, and dead silence. Ethan broke into a run.

Up the brook bed had fled the raccoon. Close behind had dashed the collie. The raccoon, like its big cousin, the bear, is an unwieldy-looking creature. But at a pinch it is capable of brief spurts of really creditable speed. The nature of the ground aided this fugitive's slithering gallop, while it impeded the rush of the dog.

No raccoon can maintain a lead over a collie for any distance. This the pursued coon, with the wisdom of the wild, must have known. For raccoons have brains—queer, wily, half-human brains—when they care to use them. Clown-like in aspect and in superficial mental processes, yet they are capable of uncanny processes of mind and of action.

The coon did not take advantage of any of the several rock-crannies or overhanging trees to escape from his foe. He stuck to the brook bed; flowing, rather than running, up its stony center. The collie plashed after him, gaining at every leap.

Thus they came to the first pool and tore through its shallows. Up the brook toward the second and far deeper pool raced the coon, the dog's snapping jaws now at his ringed fat tail.

At the edge of the second pool the raccoon whizzed about, shifting sidewise to avoid the snap of Jock's teeth at his back.

As the collie lunged forward in his averted assault, the raccoon slipped, eel-like, under the charging bulk. Both his arms went about the collie's furry throat, in a constrictor grip, the agile black hands meeting. The razor teeth dug deep into Jock's neck. The braced hind-legs heaved.

It was all done in the fraction of a second. The unbelievably tight grasp of the arms cut off Jock's breath. One fierce snarl alone escaped him—even as a single bark of angry surprise had come from Eileen's squeezed throat, two days earlier. Then he was wrestling and thrashing about on the pool's slippery brink, striving in vain to close his jaws on his elusive enemy.

The raccoon would have made a fortune, as a human, on the wrestling mat. Every secret of leverage and of balance was known to his crafty brain. Now, with hind-legs iron-braced, he seized the opportunity to enforce Jock's first forward pitch by throwing all his own twenty-six-pound weight and supple strength in the same direction. Under the double urge, the collie staggered across the slimy verge and into the pool.

With a mighty splash he fell in, the raccoon with him. As he went, one curved eyetooth succeeded in slashing deep into the coon's back. But the tush-point penetrated little beyond the tremendous rolls of fat which upholstered the other's body.

The raccoon was similarly impeded. When he had gotten his strangle hold on the four other dogs, it had been no great feat for him to nuzzle his sharp nose through the fur and to send his teeth to the jugular. But a collie's throat is armored with a mattress of well-nigh impenetrable hair—outer and undercoat combined. The jugular is not easy to pierce. The murderous rodent teeth toiled busily. But they made scant progress.

Moreover, this collie was far larger and stronger and faster and more aggressively vigorous than had been any of the coon's four other victims—even the redoubtable little Rouser. More by luck than by maneuvering he had gotten Jock into the water. The throat-cutting promised to be impossible.

Yet this did not greatly disturb the murderer. By instinct and by experience he knew he could stay alive under water much longer than could any dog. Wherefore he devoted his weight and strength and skill to preventing Jock from rising to the surface.

The collie fought like mad, for a moment or so. Then he realized that the water was strangling him far more quickly and effectively than were the coon's tense arms. He battled wildly to rise to the surface. But the coon had gripped the lowest of the several outjuts of under-water rock with his prehensile hind-feet and was clinging to them viciously. In vain did the collie fight to tear free. The hind-feet held the rock ledge. The arms encircled the dog's neck. The teeth held their chewed mouthful of throat-fur and skin.

Jock gave over his struggles to escape. Turning on the coon, the strangling collie fought insanely to rend him.

It was this scene which met Ethan Hurd's staring eyes as he came swarming up the brook bed in the gray dawn. The pool was lashed to foam and whirlpool. But as it was bottomed and lined with dirtless rock, no roiling of the waters hid from the boy's unbelieving sight the warfare a foot or so beneath the surface. Into his memory flashed long-forgotten and disbelieved tales of trappers concerning raccoons which lure pursuing hounds into the water and drown them.

Dropping his rifle, he flung himself on his face at the pool-side. Down he thrust his right arm and clutched the half-drowned collie by the nape of the neck. With one mighty heave he pulled upward the battling Jock and the raccoon. The latter, looking up through the water, saw the boy. At once he loosed his strangle hold and teeth grip and sank to the bottom of the pool.

Ethan dragged Jock out of the water and on to the

rocky bank. There the dog sprawled, sneezing and gulping, the water pouring from mouth and nose.

Ethan got to his feet, picking up the spattered rifle and standing at ease, looking down into the depths. On the boy's face were grimness and quiet determination. He could see the coon, five feet below him, its black hands holding fast to an irregularity of rock, to keep from rising to the top.

"Take your time," Ethan addressed the upstaring creature. "You've drowned better animals than you are, in that pool. Let's see how long you can stand it down there. If—"

His words broke off in a choke. The fight of the dog and the coon had turned the placid basin into a furious whirlpool, whose clawing fingers had whipped every side of the basin to foam. These eddies had done more. They had swept the two or three wide under-water ledges as compellingly as a groping arm.

Now, from under the broadest ledge, forced outward by the centrifugal eddies, slid into view a half-shapeless little mass of reddish fur. Behind this came floating out what was left of a long-dead beagle.

"You—you devil!" panted Ethan. "You drowned 'em, and then you shoved 'em under those ledges, so they couldn't ever come to the top! It's Eileen! And it's—"

More ghastly canine remains were slipping into view, under the urge of the whirlpool. But Ethan did not stop to note them. For, slowly, unwillingly, the raccoon was coming to the surface. His supply of breath at last was giving out. Sooner than drown, he was coming up, to take his chances with the human and with the collie.

With deadly calm Ethan cocked and raised the rifle.

The raccoon stuck the black tip of his nose a half inch above the water and took a long breath. Then with bewildering speed he swarmed up over the lip of the pool and sped for the rock-cleft from which Ethan had seen his face emerge two days before.

The boy did not hurry. He was not minded to risk a snap shot even at that range. Indeed, the raccoon's nose was in the cleft before Ethan pulled the trigger.

At the report the coon's body doubled and jumped high in air. Then it slumped lifeless at the entrance to the cleft.

"Your feud is off before it's on, Hi," explained Hurd, an hour later, lifting the dead raccoon by the tail for the benefit of his before-breakfast guest. "Take a good look at this critter. The second biggest I ever saw. Forty-two and a half inches from tip to tip. Twenty-six pounds, three ounces. And the brains of an Apache Injun."

"Huh!" growled Bourke. "My Rouser would 'a' made one mouthful of him! He—" He broke off with a grunt, as of physical pain, as he remembered the story Ethan had just told him. "Mebbe I'll git me a collie next time," he ruminated, sadly. "They seem to be luckier. What price do you put on that big collie of your'n?"

"Eight million dollars and nine cents!" spoke up Ethan, before his father could answer. "And, now this coon's death has cured him of grieving so for Eileen, he's dirt cheap at that. Hey, Jock?"

IV. The Destroyer From Nowhere

HIS sire was Champion Greyfield Giant. His dam was Imported Lassie of Lothian. His brothers and sisters were destined to make collie history at a hundred bench shows. He himself was worthless.

He was worthless because he had no chance of fulfilling the purpose for which he and his immediate ancestors had been born. He was a 100-per-cent liability in a kennel which was run for assets only and in which sentiment had no place.

His nose was snubby, his eyes were round and pale topaz in color and large, his golden coat was kinky, his tail was short and bushy like a wolf's. His head was domed like Daniel Webster's. Moreover, he was the smallest of the litter—a litter whose other members gave promise of classically chiseled wedge-shaped heads and slanting small dark eyes and long tails and wavily harsh outer coats.

There are such "throw-backs" in many a high-born litter. They are useless to professional breeders. Sometimes they are sold for pets. Sometimes, when they are atrociously bad-looking from a technical viewpoint, they are destroyed, lest their presence on earth give a bad name to the registered kennel which bred them.

Such a pup was this. One circumstance, and one alone, kept him from immersion in a water pail before his eyes were open. His mother and another famous female collie had puppies within a day of each other. The second mother's babies were but three in number. They died before they were twenty-four hours old—on the mystic plan which makes a collie the easiest or the hardest dog on earth to raise.

The worthless pup of the other litter was put into the brood nest of the bereft mother, to console her for the loss of her own young. Thus, up to six weeks, he was allowed to live. Thus, up to six weeks, he got all the nourishment that ordinarily would have been divided among several puppies. He waxed strong and large and fat under these extra rations.

But at six weeks he was homelier and more faulty of physique than at birth. Wherefore the kennel-owner bade one of his men to take the miserable specimen to the river, tie a stone around his neck, and toss him in.

The kennel man obeyed. He was in a hurry to get home at the end of his day's work. A delivery car had called at the kennels with supplies and was just starting for the village, two miles away, where the man lived. By availing himself of a proffered ride he could save a hot two-mile trudge at the end of a hard day. He was not minded to lose the chance just because he had a useless puppy to drown.

Snatching up a stone and a cord in one hand and the unsuspecting puppy in the other, he clambered aboard the delivery car. A mile away, the road crossed the bridge that spanned the river. By the time the fast-driven car had come to this bridge the kennel man had one end of the cord tied around the puppy's furry throat and the other end around the stone.

As the car sped swiftly over the bridge he threw the puppy and the stone and the cord far out over the coping and into the water. Then, his work done, he settled back to full enjoyment of the homeward ride.

Brant Millar had had a hard day, too. He had been haying, under a grilling sun, in his south pasture, which sloped down to the river edge. He was tired and he was soaked with sweat. His thin clothes stuck to him. He felt as if he was smeared with mucilage.

It is a pretty picture—to ride past in a covered car or to sit on a shaded porch and watch a sunlit field where haying is in progress. But the pleasure is all in the watching. There is scant bliss in tossing hay into a wagon, hour after hour, when the thermometer is in the nineties, and then to stand in a suffocating loft, catching and distributing the forkfuls that are flung up from the wagon. Heat and hayseed and heavy labor, and dust in the throat and nostrils: these are some of the less poetic and more real experiences of haymaking.

These were the things in which Brant Millar had been wallowing since as soon after sunrise as the hay was dry enough to pitch.

At six o'clock the last load was in the barn. Brant sent home his hired man. Then, while the horses were cooling down enough to be fed and watered for the night, Millar headed for the south meadow again and across it to the cool river at its foot.   In one hand he carried a torn towel, in the other a pair of shabby swimming trunks.

It was good, past words, to strip off his stickily damp clothes and to dive into the cold water.   It was good to stretch out on his back and float drowsily downstream with the current, looking upward at the flaring blue sky and the setting copper sun from between half-shut eyes as the water gurgled and rippled in cool caress around him.

Under the bridge he let his tired body float.   For a moment the glare of light was cut off by the dim gray under vault of the stone span.   Then he floated out into the sunset light again.

As he did so he fancied that two large fish broke water, one on either side of him, with an egregious splash that deluged his face.   At the same time something thin pressed sharply across his upturned throat, cutting almost through the tanned flesh.

Instantly, and with a snort of amaze, Brant Millar ceased to float languidly downstream.   His feet groped for the rocky bottom of the river and found it.   He stood up, shoulder deep in the fast-flowing water.

From one of his broad shoulders hung a stone.   From the other wriggled a wet and indignant baby collie.   Binding the two was the stout cord which had pressed against his throat.

The kennel man might have made that same cast fifty times without lassoing the unseen swimmer below the bridge.   The car had chugged on and had rounded the turn beyond the bridge.   The kennel man had not bothered to look back.   He had seen the puppy and the

stone go hurtling over the coping into the stream.   That
was enough for him.   He had obeyed orders.

Had he looked, as the car rounded the turn, he would
have seen a dumfounded young farmer standing shoulder
deep in the drought-shallowed river, and festooned grotesquely with that same stone and puppy.

Brant Millar's momentary astonishment faded.   He
understood what had happened.   He had heard the rumble of a car above the bridge while he was floating under
it.   The puppy and the stone, tied together, told their
own story.

Millar looked down at the helplessly but gallantly
struggling pup hanging across his arm on the end of the
deep-cutting cord.   The little fellow did not whimper.
Baby as he was, he made no outcry at the pain and shock
of it all.   He fought mutely, with all his pudgy baby force,
to get free from the strangling cord.

"Plucky little cuss!" approved Brant, half aloud.
"Must be good blood back of him somewhere.   Most pups
would be squalling bloody murder."

While he talked he tucked the stone under his arm, easing its pull from around the collie's neck.   Then, deftly,
he untied the cord's clumsy knot from the fluffy throat.
The stone glugged noisily down into the river, the cord
hanging to it, but no tortured little dog was dragged down
by the soggy weight.

Holding the puppy against his chest and out of reach
of the hungrily lapping water, Brant waded upstream
with him to where he had left his clothes.   There he de-
posited the collie on the bank and began to dress.

"I don't rightly know what I'm going to do with you,
youngster," he addressed the pup.   "I've gotten on

pretty well without a dog since old Bruno died. When he went, the wife and I both said we'd never be able to find another like him, so we'd go without. But I can't leave you here for some weasel or fox or mink to get. That'd be worse than leaving you to drown. Nor I can't give you away, I suppose. If you had been worth having, your folks wouldn't have chucked you into the creek. Well—come on home, anyhow, for to-night. I'll give you some bread and milk and you can sleep in the shed. Maybe the wife can figure out what to do about you, after then."

He finished his rudimentary dressing and picked up the puppy once more. Then he started across the meadow for his house, a half-mile distant. The pup did not resent being caught up and carried. He was still at the age when all the world is a friendly and delightful place, populated by friendly and delightful folk who are wonderful playmates.

His brief experience with the river had not shaken this faith. Wherefore he licked Brant's lean face ecstatically, and sought to chew his fingers and otherwise to lure the man into a romp. Millar petted him, absent-mindedly, and continued his homeward way.

On the narrow front porch of the farmhouse sat a sweet-faced girl, a basket of mending in her lap. This was the young wife whom Brant had married two years earlier.

Her day's work was done. Supper was on the table, a green mosquito net guarding it from the flies. She had come out here, in the sunset, to watch for her husband's return from his swim.

Rising to meet him as he plodded up the path, she

noticed for the first time the queer little burden he carried. Brant halted and set the puppy on the ground. The pup took one interested glance at everything around him. Then his topaz eyes fell on Helen Millar, coming down the steps.

Pricking up his lopped ears, he cantered eagerly toward her with the gait of a fat rocking horse.

"Oh, Brant!" Helen was expostulating. "We decided we would never have another dog, after Bruno! Why did you bring home this crazy-looking—"

She got no further. The puppy's clumsy run had brought him to her. His fat fore-paws on her apron, he was peering up into her face with adoring friendliness. For some strange reason, the confidingly loving look and action of the absurd youngster made the woman's throat contract.

On impulse, she stooped and gathered him into her arms. There the pup cuddled, crooning and clucking in great contentment, softly licking the hand that held him.

"I'll try to find some sucker who'll be fool enough to take him off our hands, to-morrow," promised Brant, sheepishly. "If I can't, I'll put him out of the way as painlessly as I can. I—"

"You won't do anything of the sort!" she declared, with fleet shift of mind. "This is *my* dog. He's elected me as his owner. We're going to keep him. Where did he come from, anyhow? He's all soaking wet."

Brant blinked at her, wondering at her abrupt change of feeling toward the newcomer. Then he said:

"The little cuss came out of the sky. Anyhow, when I was floating on my back, over yonder in the creek, he dropped down on me like a ton of brick. That's true, Honest, it is."

He did not think it was necessary to add the details of the cord and stone and the hurrying delivery car. He saw the puppy had caught his wife's fancy, even as he had caught Brant's own. He thought that a spice of mystery might add to the woman's new interest in the collie and make her the more willing to keep him.

"What in the world are you talking about?" demanded Helen. " 'Came out of the sky'? What—"

"Well," compromised Millar. "Maybe he didn't come from quite so far up as that. It isn't the kind of weather, anyhow, when it rains cats and dogs. I wish it was, now that the hay is in. But he dropped down on me, just as I told you, while I was floating there. I didn't see anyone on the bank. There wasn't any airship overhead— At least, come to think of it, I never even looked up to see if there was. Maybe he tumbled out of an airship. Anyhow, he landed, plop! right onto me. So I brought him home."

"Out of the sky!" mused Helen, her imagination struck by the oddity of the idea. "Probably he was being carried somewhere in an airship and fell out. How lucky you were there! The poor baby might have been drowned! What kind of dog do you suppose he is?"

"Well," ruminated Brant, "considering the direction he came from, I'd say he's most likely a sky terrier. What'll we call him?"

"Let's feed him first," suggested Helen. "He'd rather be fed than named. I'm sure he would. Wouldn't you, baby? Come along in here."

She set him down and led the way into the kitchen. The

puppy followed at a wavering canter, trying at every step to seize the hem of her alluringly elusive skirt.

Helen poured out a saucer of fresh milk and crumbled into it a handful of stale bread. The puppy fell upon this feast ravenously. At the kennels one of the men had taught him to lap milk, off and on, during the past fort-night—not as an accomplishment, but to wean him the earlier, so that he might the sooner be drowned.

"I've got it!" cried Helen, as she and Brant stood watching amusedly the greedy feasting of their new pet. "I mean I've got the name for him. I've been trying to remember it ever since you told me about his dropping down out of the air."

"Fire away!" exhorted Millar, as she hesitated with puckered brows.

"It—it was in a poem we had to learn in high school," she said, slowly. "A line of it was—was—was— There! I can't remember the poem, after all. But now I remember the man's name—the man who was tossed down from the skies in mythology times. His name was Vulcan. That was it. Vulcan. And that's what I'm going to call our puppy here. Isn't it a pretty name? And queer, too."

"It's queer, all right, all right," admitted Brant. "But if you're looking for a pretty name, what's the matter with Ponto or Rover or Shep or Tige or—"

"His name," said Helen, sweetly, but with calm finality, "is *Vulcan.*"

The puppy had finished his supper. Feeling that he could eat much more, he turned suddenly from his empty dish and ran over to Helen, who had given him the bread and milk. By sheer coincidence he chanced to gallop across to her just as she had uttered the word "Vulcan."

"Oh, Brant!" exclaimed the woman, in delighted astonishment. "He answers to his name the very first time he hears it. I never saw anything so clever in my life. That settles it. Vulcan he is. That's his name."

Thus it was that the worthless cull of a royal collie litter became the pet and chum of two people who understood dog nature well enough to bring out the best in him. Thus did his training and life work begin.

A clever collie pup—well and wisely and kindly raised by people who can give much time to his education—is capable of unbelievable mental development. Vulcan's brain expanded well-nigh as fast as his well-fed and well-exercised body.

At six months he could handle sheep and cattle like a veteran. At a year he was a giant in body and in strength and was the loved and honored housemate of his owners. Brant used to brag that the collie could do the work of a hired man with sheep and cows, and that he was a better guard for the house than a company of militiamen.

An artist, stopping at the farm for a drink of milk, first told them Vulcan's breed. Hitherto they had been in doubt as to whether he were shepherd-dog or retriever or mongrel.

"He's a collie," said the artist. "I've bred them all my life. He's a collie. Pure bred, at that."

Noting Helen's pride in her canine chum, the artist forebore to add the information that Vulcan was the worst specimen of collie, from a bench-show point of view, that he had had the bad luck to behold. Gravely he listened to Helen's narrative of the dog's dropping from the heavens upon her swimming husband's shoulder.

"If they raise good collies Up There," he said to himself, "I don't blame them for throwing this one out."

It was at the end of Vulcan's third year that the Valley was scourged from end to end by a pest which threatened to offset the prosperity of a bumper crop by demolishing the livestock of the entire community.

Nobody knew what the creature might be that was causing all this devastation. A thrill of superstition possessed the Valley at mention of it. None had seen it. None had been able to find track of it.

Clem Robard, a sheepman who lived two miles up the Valley from Brant's homestead, went into his upper sheep pasture one morning to find thirty of his yearling ewes and wethers lying dead, their throats torn out. Three more were missing. The remainder were huddled in fence corners, quivering with mortal terror. In midfield lay Clem's aged sheep-dog, his neck broken as if by giant pincers.

Up and down the Valley sped the black tidings that a killer dog was loose upon the world. The farmers hastened to view the carnage. They trooped into Robard's upper pasture in scores, scanning the dry hardpan of earth for tracks, examining the torn sheep, making Sherlock Holmes investigations—and learning nothing.

News of an epidemic of some mortal disease carries no more terror with it in a crowded city than does the report among grazers that a killer dog is at large. The term "killer" does not apply merely to some mischievous cur that chances to chase and kill a sheep or two.

It is the phrase used to describe such rare dogs as chance to go insane on the subject of slaughter. Once in a while a trained sheep-dog will do so. Incredible cunning goes with this form of canine mania. A killer will wreak awesome havoc in a field, for the pure love of murder, and will vanish, leaving no clue to his identity. The next night he will harry a flock or a herd twenty miles away. Sometimes he returns to his own home; living there, unsuspected, in intervals between depredations.

There could be no doubt that Clem Robard's sheep had fallen victim to such a killer. Three of his victims he had lugged away—nobody could find where. But the remaining thirty he had killed from pure lust of slaughter and had left them where they lay.

All summer, in the hitherto immune Valley, the flocks and herds had wandered at will, through pastures and woodlands. Chickens had roosted at large or in unguarded hen-coops. House dogs had been deemed sufficient protection to barn and fold and hen-roost.

Now, in a breath, all this changed. From morning till late dusk that day farmers and their men tightened and strengthened inclosures into which their livestock were to be driven at night. Volunteers made ready to patrol the Valley all night and every night. Innocent dogs were eyed askance.

Brant Millar alone made no such panic preparations for the safety of his flock. Beyond driving the sheep into the home pasture for the night, he did nothing to insure them against the killer.

"Vulcan sleeps on the porch, these summer nights," he told his nearest neighbor, Harvey Blane, who remonstrated with him against such carelessness. "And he sleeps with both ears and one eye open. Why, a lamb can't bleat or a hen can't flutter off a roost in the night or a horse can't cast himself in his stall or a heifer can't get to stamping, but what Vulcan's on his feet in a second and off to see what's wrong. He patrols the whole home tract a couple of times or more every night, too. He's a born watchdog. My critters are as safe, with him on guard, as if they were in one of those steel vaults they've put in over at the Paignton bank."

"H'm!" grunted Blane, who had come across from his adjoining farm to borrow nails for the extra palings he was putting on one of his paddocks. "H'm! Maybe so. Maybe not. Every fellow blows about his own cur. I'm not taking chances. I got my forty head of registered-stock Guernsey calves to look out for. I'm not trusting to any dog to keep them from the killer, either. Know my calf paddock? Well, into that they go to-night, the whole forty of them. What's more, I'm running an extra line of planks around it, on top of the reg'lar fence. I'm putting a line of barbed wire on top of that. I aim to have a stockade seven foot high and topped with barbed wire, all around my calf paddock, by nightfall. If any dog—killer or no—can shin up that seven-foot wall and over the wire—well, he'll do more'n any dog I ever seen or heard of."

Brant watched his neighbor depart on his stockade-building expedition. Then he noted that Vulcan was standing close beside him. Millar stooped and patted the dog's broad head.

"The killer that tackles you, old boy," said he, affectionately, "will think he's bit into a couple of hornets' nests and a rattlesnake. I'll take my chance on your guarding anything Helen and I have got. Anything from Baby to my best bunch of Merino lambs."

He passed his hand appraisingly along the collie's head

to the mighty-muscled shoulders and the deep chest and slender loins. Vulcan was built with the powerful grace of a timber wolf. In more than one fight with marauding curs he had shown himself as terrible at warfare as he was gentle to the defenseless animals he guarded.

Out from the house toddled a little gold-and-white bunch of fluff which, as it came into the sunlight, resolved itself into a three-year-old baby girl—the Millar's only child and Vulcan's worshiped deity. Stanch as was the collie's love for Brant and Helen, he idolized Baby May above all the world.

Now, at sight of May, he trotted forward in wriggling joy to greet her. The baby squealed with pleasure at seeing her dear playmate. She seized him by both sensitive ears and hugged his shaggy head to her tiny chest. The dog suffered the rough handling with utter delight, and pressed close to her side as she moved forward.

But as May reached the edge of the porch, on her outward progress, Vulcan slipped quickly and unobtrusively between her and the two-foot abyss toward which she was toddling. Very gently he pushed her away from the edge and toward the more negotiable flight of shallow steps.

Brant nodded approvingly.

"As good as a machine-gun company, for guarding," he said to himself, "and ten times better'n a hired nurse girl for keeping baby out of danger, and better'n any one hired man at handling stock. Gee! That was one lucky swim I took, three years back!"

Yet next morning, at sunrise, Millar made the rounds of his farm with greater care than usual and with some slight anxiety. Despite his assurance of security, in his talk with Harvey Blane, the thought of the killer had made his night's sleep fitful.

He might well have spared the worry. His livestock was intact. No harm had come to them in the sinister hours between dusk and dawn. Again Millar's hand rested approvingly on the wide head of the dog which paced majestically at his side during his rounds of inspection.

As Brant and Vulcan were returning to the house for breakfast, some one came running in from the roadway and up the path toward them. At sight of the furiously running man Vulcan growled. He stepped menacingly forward, as if to protect his master from possible harm. Then he dropped back to Millar's side again. For he had recognized the excited intruder as Harvey Blane.

Blane's face was purple. His eyes were goggling and bloodshot. He was all but blubbering. Millar stared in amusement at his wontedly calm neighbor.

"What in blue blazes—?" began Brant.

"Twenty-two of them!" blithered Harvey, deliriously. "Twenty-two! And not a one of them worth a cent under—"

"Twenty-two *what?*" demanded Brant, perplexed at the outburst. "What are you talking about?"

"Twenty-two of my registered-stock Guernsey calves!" roared Blane. "They—"

"I thought you were going to put them all in a seven-foot stockade, with barbed wire on it," said Millar. "You don't mean to say the killer—?"

"I mean to say the killer climbed the stockade or else he flew down into it!" stormed Blane. "Wire and all, he got in, and he killed twenty-two of my calves. Killed them without their making enough noise to wake me or any of us. Then he got out again, the way he came. Got away *clean!* Never left a trace. Dropped down from the sky, looks like, and then flew back again. No critter without wings c'd jump a seven-foot fence with barbed wire on top of it. Come along with me, Brant. I haven't touched a one of them. I left them as they was when I found them, ten minutes ago. I came over here to fetch you, as a 'disint'rested witness' that the law calls for, so as you can testify for me when I ask the county for dam'ges."

Brant fell into step with his neighbor, without a word, and started with him toward the near-by Blane farm. Well did Millar know the state law regarding the slaying of livestock by an unknown animal. If such killing can be established, the county must pay the owner a fair value on the slain animal or animals. A disinterested witness's testimony is required, to avert fraud.

Vulcan bounded along in front of the two until they reached the gate. Collie-like, he welcomed this chance to go for a walk with his master. But the opening of a door behind them made the dog glance back. Baby May had toddled out on to the porch. As usual, she was making straight for its edge. With a rush the collie regained the porch and was interposing his shaggy body between the child and a fall.

As Helen did not come out to relieve him of his nurse-maid responsibilities, Vulcan stayed where he was, instead of following Millar.

Brant found trouble in keeping pace with his hurrying and sputtering neighbor. Panting, they reached Blane's home and went past the house and barns and back to the reinforced calf paddock. At the open door of the inclos-

ure was standing a little group of horrified people—
Blane's wife and his two sons and his hired man—all gaz-
ing into the yard.

Brant noted the awkward but highly efficient way in
which the four-foot paddock fence had been transformed
into a seven-foot stockade. As he approached he studied
the wooden wall carefully. It offered no slope or foothold
whereby a dog could take a preliminary run and then
scramble up the sides of it. Here was a perpendicular
wall, seven feet in height, and with a strand of barbed
wire running some six inches above it.

"The door was shut and locked when I got here this
morning," Blane was assuring him. "I can take oath to
that. So can my man. He was with me. I had the key
to the padlock in my pants. Nobody nor nothing could
have got in. You c'n see that yourself, Brant."

They came to the doorway. The group divided and
Millar entered the paddock. The place was a shambles.

Some eighteen beautiful red-and-white Guernsey calves
were milling and lowing in a tight-packed jam in its far
corner, leaving the rest of the inclosure bare. This open
space was heaped with the carcasses of twenty-two dead
calves. One and all, their throats had been torn out and
mangled. No attempt had been made to devour any of
them.

Millar examined carefully the hideous damage done to
his neighbor's livestock and fortune. He scanned the
hoof-scored ground for print of a padded paw. But the
myriad pattering and stamping feet of the frenzied calves
had obliterated any trace of alien presence.

Next, Brant walked about the stockade from the outside, seeking claw-marks on the boards or bloodstains on the line of barbed wire. He found nothing.

"Dropped down from the sky, he did, I tell you!" raged Blane. "He couldn't have got in any other way. *Say!*" he broke off, abruptly, wheeling on Brant. "What was that rigmarole your wife told mine, a couple or three years back, about your collie dog 'dropping down from the sky'? How about it? If he could drop down from the sky once, why couldn't he—-?"

"Oh, that was just a joke!" said Millar, astonished at the frantic man's credulity. "I explained it all to her afterward. Vulcan was thrown off the bridge with a stone tied to his neck. Some one tried to drown him. I was swimming underneath and he fell on me. That was all there was to it."

"H'm!" grunted Blane, scowling at the dead calves. "Maybe so. Maybe not. Anyhow, you'll testify to what you've seen here?"

"I sure will," promised Millar. "No 'fraud' about this thing. I'll swear to that. . . . And no explanation about it, either, worse luck!"

Again up and down the Valley surged the hideous tidings. Again farmers made stout their fences and cleaned their guns and appointed guards. The county Grange offered a reward of $300 for the killer.

Yet that night—within a hundred feet of a patrolling guard—the henhouse of Abner Cobban was entered and sixty of his best fowls were killed. They were killed without a sound of the wholesale slaying reaching the patrolling man outside. Five of them were eaten. Many strewn feathers and a few chewed bones attested to that. The other fifty-five had been killed in wanton murder lust.

The heads of most of them had been bitten off. The killer had burst the flimsy lock of the henhouse, presumably by the simple expedient of pressing his heavy body against it. The rotting wood around the lock had given away with too slight a sound to be heard by the guard.

For the next three nights nothing happened anywhere along the Valley. But the tense waiting began to get on the men's nerves more acutely than had the actual killings.

On the fourth morning Baby May elected to go for a walk. Her mother saw her trudge sturdily across the dooryard toward the meadow. Helen was about to call her back, when she saw Vulcan get up from his mat on the porch and trot after the child, ranging alongside her and accommodating his pace to hers. With one chubby hand clenched deep in the fur of the collie's ruff, to steady her, May struck out at a better gait.

Helen did not interfere. She knew the baby would be safer with the great dog than with any human, and that when Vulcan should decide May had gone far enough he would herd her gently back. He had done so a score of times.

The morning was cool and bracing. A ramble across the meadow and to the shade of the woods beyond would be pleasant exercise for the little girl.

Helen herself had been planning to go to the wood edge for ferns for the rock garden she was making. Putting on her sunbonnet now, and taking her trowel and a basket, she prepared to set out after the baby and the dog. A telephone call detained her. When at last she started, May and her escort were at the end of the meadow and almost in the shade of the woodland.

Brant looked up from a log he was chopping in the dooryard as his wife passed by him.

"I'm going after those ferns I told you about," she said. "Baby and Vulcan have gone on ahead."

It was a few seconds later that Brant looked up again. This time his ears had caught the clump of several pairs of approaching feet. Around the corner of the house came Harvey Blane and his two sons. The faces of all three were grim. Blane carried a shotgun in the crook of his left arm. Without a word of greeting the trio advanced on Millar.

Harvey held out his right hand. Brant, wondering, held out his own. Then he saw Blane did not intend to shake hands. In his flattened palm he exhibited a tuft of tawny hair.

"Well?" queried Millar, puzzled. "What's the idea?"

"The idee," answered Blane, speaking slowly, "is that my boys and me were taking down that length of barbed wire, just now, from the stockade, to put up an extra line of stakes. On one of the barbs, over behind the corner stake, we found this."

He nodded at the hair tuft in his palm.

"Well?" queried Brant, still mystified.

"This here is a bunch of hair," expounded Blane. "Hair off'n the critter that jumped my stockade and killed my calves. Nothing else could have put it up there, seven foot above ground. The killer hopped the fence. As he was going over the wire, a jag of it tore off this bunch of his hair."

Brant whistled.

"I see!" he said. "Behind one of the corner stakes, hey?

That's why we didn't notice it when we looked, I suppose. But—"

"There's just one critter here or hereabouts," went on Harvey, "that has longish and yellowish hair, that color. That critter is a dog. That critter," his voice slower and deeper—"that critter is your collie dog!"

"Nonsense!" scoffed Brant, contemptuously. "Why, Vulcan is—!"

"Vulcan is the killer," finished Blane. "Likewise, we're here to kill him, or to force you to kill him, like the law says."

"The law says nothing of the kind!" blazed Millar. "And if it did, you'd have to kill me before you got through to my dog! It's the craziest foolishness I ever heard. Because you find a tuft of brownish yellow hair on your fence and because my dog happens to be brownish yellow—"

"That's the idee," said Blane, curtly. "Where's your dog?"

"It's none of your business where he is!" shouted Brant, in sudden rage. "If you lift that gun against him, you'll find yourself on your back with a broken gun barrel hammering your skull. You and your two hulking sons as well. That dog of mine would no sooner kill—"

The wrathful words died in his throat. All four men whirled about. From the direction of the woods echoed a distant sound of strife—wild, confused, hideously discordant.

Followed a woman's scream of mortal horror.

Without a word the men broke into a run, Brant still unconsciously gripping his ax and Blane swinging his forgotten gun.

Across the meadow they ran at top speed, toward the fringe of woodland. But Brant Millar was far in the van. He raced along like a madman, his eyes glassy, his brain sick with dread, for he had recognized Helen's voice in that terrified shriek.

May and Vulcan had made their leisurely way across the meadow, the child clinging to the collie's coat and using him as a support for her none-too-certain feet. Presently they reached the woods and passed into the cathedral-like shade of the lofty pines. There, just ahead, the child caught sight of a glowing patch of cardinal flowers clustering about a tiny spring at the base of a high mass of rocks.

She ran forward to play with the glowing flowers. Vulcan did not join her at once. He had come to a sudden halt. Stockstill he stood, his sensitive nostrils sniffing the still woodland air with growing aversion. The stiff hairs between his shoulder blades began to bristle. A white tusk showed from under an up-curling lip. His near-sighted topaz eyes glanced in every direction to locate the odor which had assailed him.

Far too faint to have been registered by human nose nerves, yet this scent was strong and increasingly distinct to the dog. Far back in the atavistic recesses of his subconscious brain it awoke a strange hostility. At last his suspiciously wandering gaze focused among the higher reaches of the rocks, above and directly in front of him.

There, as by a giant sword, the rock had been cleft and cleft again into fissures and crannies and caverns. It was on one of these caverns that Vulcan's eyes riveted themselves. But only for the briefest instant.

Then with a wild-beast roar he hurled himself forward at Baby May.

The child was knee deep in the patch of cardinal flowers, pulling them up by the handful and chuckling happily to herself. Vulcan rushed at her and seized her by the shoulder of her gingham dress.

His mighty jaws did not so much as bruise her flesh as he spun her about and thrust her far behind him. She lost her footing and rolled over and over among the crushed red flowers.

It was this insane attack upon the child Vulcan loved that Helen Millar first saw as she entered the woodland. She stood thunderstruck at the incredible sight.

But as May fell, a yellow-tawny thunderbolt launched itself from the rocks above. With a thud it landed on the spot where the baby had been standing when the collie tossed her out of the way of the impending leap. Helen stared, aghast.

Scarcely had the creature landed among the flowers when Vulcan was upon it. Before the momentum of the futile bound gave the intruder a chance to recover balance the dog was at its throat.

There was a multiple roaring and screeching as the two tawny bodies crashed to earth together, struggling murderously. Helen screamed in fear as she recognized the brute that had tried to pounce upon her baby.

Never outside of a circus tent had she seen such an animal. But at a glance, now, she knew it for a panther.

(Ten miles away, at Paignton, the owner of an itinerant one-ring circus had sworn in loud fury at the careless attendant who, a week earlier, had left the Rocky Mountain puma's cage door insecurely latched after the evening

performance. The exhibit was neither rare nor expensive.
Yet its loss meant much to so poor a menagerie.)

As though Helen's scream frightened it, the puma
broke loose from the battling collie and sprang back to
the base of the rocks. Bleeding, torn, bruised, the dog
gathered himself together for a fresh assault.

Never before had Vulcan seen a puma. Yet his wolf
ancestors, for thousands of years, had been the foes to this
and all other members of the cat tribe. Into Vulcan's
wise collie brain, now, seeped a glint of hereditary knowledge as to those ancestors' tactics in fighting the mountain
lion.

Instead of rushing blindly into battle as before, he
sprang at the snarling puma, which bounded forward to
demolish him. But midway in his charge the collie veered
sharply to the left with the speed of light. The puma's
crushingly raking claws missed him in their double stroke,
one of them whizzing within a hair's-breadth of his head.

Then, in what seemed to Helen to be the same motion,
the dog spun in, to the right, just behind the smiting paws,
and drove his terrible teeth into the base of the puma's
neck. Here and here alone could he or any other dog hope
to compete on anything like equal terms with a mountain
lion.

By that skull-base grip had countless wolves averted
death from themselves, from the rending claws of such
great cats; and sometimes they had been able to grind
their own tusk-like eyeteeth into the spinal cord of their
enemy.

This, now, Vulcan was essaying to do. But the puma
was one swirl of dynamic fury. Around and around it
spun, in mad effort to break the grip and to rake the dog

with its saber claws. Twice the claws found a glancing mark on Vulcan's shaggy sides, tearing through to the rib bones. But the collie's jaws had gained their one possible hold, a hold that the furious cat could not yet dislodge.

Then into the woods stormed the four panting men. Up went Harvey Blane's gun, after its owner had given one unbelieving look at the battle in front of him. But he hesitated. To shoot one of the gyrating combatants, without risk of killing the other, was impossible.

Brant Millar did not hesitate. In he ran, ax aloft. As he ran he smote. With all the force and skill of a veteran woodsman he struck.

The panther's skull was split to the brain. One last convulsive heave that hurled Vulcan against the rocks in a breath-taking impact and the giant cat lay kicking and trembling.

Slowly the wounded dog relinquished his grip. Slowly he got to his feet, lurching over to where Baby May sat weeping unheeded. Gently Vulcan licked the wet little face and whimpered in loving reassurance. Then with a long sigh he lay down and closed his friendly eyes.

Nor, until a veterinary had toiled over him for nearly two weeks, was the collie able to stand up again and to resume the burden of life.

"The—the creature dropped down from that cave up there, in one leap!" exclaimed Helen, shuddering.

"H'm!" mused Harvey Blane. "And he must have got up there, first off, in one leap, too. No other way for him to do it. That cave's a good eighteen inches higher'n my stockade. Neighbor Millar, I figger I've played the fool. If I'd shot that dog of yours, and then found out,

I'd have used the second barrel on myself. The killer is
kilt. And—the man who ever speaks bad of Vulcan
where I am—well, there's still two ca'tridges left in this
gun! . . . Lemme help you carry him home. He c'n have
my best spare-room bed to lay on, if he's a mind to."

V. A Couple of Miracles

AS PEAKE strolled past the armory, on his way to the station, a block distant, he paused to look up in mild interest at the sign that flared in red letters on white oilcloth across the arch above the door.

Peake had several spare minutes wherein to catch his train back to Hecker, whence a half-mile walk would carry him to his farm. But always he liked to get to the station well ahead of time, on these few business trips of his to the overgrown young city that was the county seat.

He hated the smell of smoke and dirt. He hated the gritty feel of pavements under his stiff town-going boots. He hated the clamor and the crowds and the hustle. These things jarred his country-bred nerves and vaguely frightened him. They were a distress to him.

All his life Abner Peake had lived on the farm that had been his father's and his grandfather's before him—all his life except for his three busy exile years at the agricultural college. Peake was one of those not-rare men whose love for the soil and for their own land and for the successful tilling of that land was as deep as their love for their home folk.

Thus it was that Abner to-day had hurried through with his routine business at the commission house and at the bank and at the county agent's office, and then had turned his face toward the station, better content to sit in the stuffy waiting room there than to risk losing his home-bound train by staring in shop windows and being jostled by the crowds.

The sign over the armory made him stop for a minute in curiosity. The red-lettered legend announced that the first annual dog show of the local kennel association was in progress. Faintly heard, from within the building, emerged the echoes of multiple barks and yelps, attesting to the presence of some three hundred thoroughbred dogs on the benches and in the rings.

"Poor brutes!" muttered Peake, whimsically, to himself, as he moved on toward the station. "Maybe it's all right for a dog that's been penned up in a professional's kennel all his life and don't know anything better. But it must be rotten for country-bred dogs to be cooped up in there all day long, with that racket and the crowds. They must hate it 'most as bad as I hate coming to town. They—"

He paused. Between the armory and a business building was an alleyway. At the back the alley broadened out into a rubbish-filled vacant lot. Abner glanced idly down the strip of paved walk, in the direction of this unlovely open space.

As he looked a large and heavy man was leading a dog out through a back doorway of the shallow armory and down the few steps that led to the lot. At least the man stamped down the steps, and then turned to face the dog he had led out. The dog, a shimmeringly gold-and-white young collie, stood at the top of the steps, his dainty white forepaws braced, a look of worried unhappiness in his deep-set dark eyes.

The next event proved his look of worry was well justified. The man did not wait for his hesitant dog to descend the steps. Instead, with a savage yank at the chain he pulled the collie through the air, down to him. The dog landed in a heap on the stone flagging, but scrambled up at once and drew back apprehensively to the full length of his chain. Then Abner saw for the first time that the luckless collie was muzzled.

By the time the dog had gotten up the man was drawing from a coat pocket a curled rawhide whip. With calm deadliness he brought this down swishingly across the collie's back. The dog shivered with pain, but did not make a sound. The muzzle prevented him from retaliating in any way to the cowardly brutality. At the chain's length he stood his ground, without whimpering or cringing. Steadfastly he looked up into the fat face of his torturer as the stingingly cruel whip made a second hissing descent through the air and smote him athwart the loins.

Then Abner Peake did something that was wholly outside his customary stolid good-nature. He could not explain it to himself, even as he thought it over coolly afterward. At sight of the torture and of the victim's gallant endurance of it he went into unpremeditated action.

As the whip swung aloft for the third time, a compactly powerful bulk interposed between the punisher and the punished. The man stared in amaze. Abner was bending above the dog. A second later Peake was standing aside, the muzzle dangling from one of his hands.

"There!" he said, drawlingly, to the astounded man with the whip. "I've unmuzzled him. That'll make it a trifle fairer. Likewise I've unsnapped his chain. I've heard of men who were skunks enough to tie up a dog and muzzle him before they dared to lick him. But I never saw one of them before. Now if you've got to go on lamming him, he'll have a chance to duck or to fight back. My old dog that died last week never had to be whipped but once. That was when he was young. I did the whipping. It was a light whipping at that. But he didn't act the way your dog does, so I figger you haven't had him long. He—"

Abner Peake got no further. The fat man broke in on his drawled words with a sizzling torrent of blasphemy. Purple with fury, he punctuated his profanity by brandishing the whip threateningly at the unruffled farmer. The dog stood still, head on one side, tulip ears cocked, his keenly interested eyes fixed on the face of the man who had set him free.

"Clear out of here!" bellowed the fat man when he could shift from swearing to distinct speech. "I've a good mind to beat you up, for butting in on me like this, you—"

"I guess maybe I wouldn't, if I was you," was Abner's placid response as he gave back not an inch before the inflamed face and the whistling rawhide. "You see, I'm not muzzled, nor yet chained. It wouldn't be such a safe outdoor sport as lashing this poor dog. . . . Well, it isn't for me to stand between any man and his fun. If you think you've got to lick the dog, I've fixed it so he'll have more chance. By the way, what were you licking him for?

Not that it's any of my business—as you were going to
say."

The fat man gurgled for a moment. Then the memory
of his grievance outweighed his immediate urge to thrash
the impudent stranger.

"I paid one hundred dollars for this cur!" he stormed.
"Bought him, last week, from a dealer who told me the
mutt couldn't help but win everything in the collie classes
at this show to-day. If he did that, I figgered I could sell
him, before I left the building, for one hundred and fifty
dollars. Maybe more. Well, he didn't win anything but
a couple of measly second prizes, the swine! So, of course,
I never got an offer for him. I was stung good and
plenty. And some one is due to pay for stinging me.
He—"

"Oh," observed Peake, "I see! The dog couldn't win
over dogs that maybe had better show points than he had.
So you aim to lick him? You're pretty near as fine a
sportsman as the cuss who sold him to you. I've always
said the rottenest skunk unhung is the man that takes out
his own dirty temper by hammering some innocent animal. Not wishing to hurt your feelings any. But—"

He stepped out of reach nimbly, but barely soon enough
to elude a slash from the whip. Instantly Peake's drawling good-humor departed. With a speed of action
remarkable in so easy-going a man he made a snatch at
the end of the whip just as it reached the farthest extent
of its stroke. The suddenness and strength of his clutch
tore the rawhide out of the fat man's unprepared grasp.
Abner flung it far out into the lot, then faced its recent
wielder.

"You paid one hundred dollars for the dog," he said,

as he advanced. "Good! I'll fight you for him. If you win, you keep the dog and I'll give you my check for one hundred dollars. It's a good check. If you lose, I take the dog. Put up your hands. It isn't on the free list to hit at me with a whip."

The fat man was only too willing to assent to the plan— or at least so far as the fighting went. His fury swept away the last remnant of his self-control as Peake deprived him of the whip. With a yell he sprang to meet the smaller and lighter farmer, slugging ferociously for Abner's face with his ham-like right fist as he rushed him.

Peake did not block the blow. He had no need to. There was ample scope for ducking and countering. His foe was as slow as he was formidable. Subconscious memory of his own boxing prowess at the agricultural college gym lurked in the back of the farmer's brain and guided his swiftly efficient body. Moving his head barely enough to let the elephantine blow whiz harmlessly past him, he struck.

Peake's left fist did not travel twelve inches in that jerky uppercut into which he put all his strength and weight. But he smote his adversary flush on the point of the jaw. The fat man, charging at him, added to the blow's force by his own heavy momentum.

There was a jarring impact that numbed Abner's left arm to the elbow and well-nigh unbalanced him. Then the fat man was wallowing in the mud of the alley, his red face blank and foolish, his thick limbs twitching. It had been a clean knockout.

Peake glanced about, attracted by a confused noise of feet and voices. In from the street several men were running, drawn by sight of the brief conflict. At their head

was a policeman who had chanced to witness the assault
as he was walking past.

The collie had vanished. He had been there as his
owner attacked Peake with the whip, and he had snarled
in angry protest, making as though to spring forward to
Abner's aid. But as the blow had missed and as the fat
man had been disarmed, the collie had halted in his punitive advance. Apparently he saw that his new friend
could take ample care of himself without canine aid.
But now, before this onrush of new arrivals, he had disappeared, in that baffling way a collie has of obliterating
himself silently and suddenly from a scene in which he
does not want to take part.

Abner Peake had no time to consider the dog's vanishing. He was in imminent danger of arrest for street fighting. A comparative stranger in the city, he had knocked
down a presumably respectable resident of the place, and
a policeman had witnessed the assault. With all a born
outdoor man's horror of jail, Abner turned and fled.

He hurdled the spread-eagled body of his late foe as
the fat man grunted and strove to sit up. The policeman,
following close after, also tried to save distance by hur-
dling the fallen body. He leaped just as the fallen man
heaved himself to a sitting posture. Over this huge obstacle stumbled the policeman, coming to earth with a breath-
expelling crash.

Peake darted across the rubbish-strewn yard, vaulted
the four-foot wooden fence, dashed through the adjoining
yard and out into the street through another alleyway.
He was running with no aim in view except to avert arrest
and a night in a cell. His was purely the instinct of the
fugitive.

But as he swung out into the street he saw his home-bound train drawing into the station, a block below. Head down, he sprinted for the tracks. The train's stop would not be a long one, he knew. If he could get aboard, before the hue and cry should pick up his trail, he might yet escape arrest. At full speed he ran.

The train started. As its last car drew past the end of the station Abner Peake swung himself aboard the rear platform, glancing back to see if his line of flight had been observed and followed.

He was well-nigh pushed off balance as he turned. For something else, running at top speed, had leaped on to the rear platform's steps and jostled roughly against the swaying farmer.

It was the collie he had saved from the fat man's beating.

The dog had slipped behind a pile of broken boxes in the armory's back yard as the policeman and the others ran into the alleyway. When Peake sped past him in the dash to escape, the dog had followed eagerly in the wake of the stranger who had rescued him from his owner's merciless beating.

Now, reaching the top step of the platform, he wagged his tail and his whole body in vehement greeting to his new friend. Abner stared dully at him for an instant. Then, in dire need to get out of sight before the pursuit should emerge into view from the back yards and alleys, he hurried into the last car. The collie slipped in with him and stood beside him at the rear of the swaying train, his furry coat pressed confidingly against Abner's knee.

"You'll have to take your dog into the baggage car," announced the conductor, bearing down on Peake. "No animals allowed in the day coaches. You ought to have gotten a dog check for him, at the station. The baggage-man can give you one. Two cars ahead. Ticket?"

Seated on a trunk in the dim baggage car, with the collie cuddled comfortably at his feet, Abner found chance, for the first time, to consider his own situation. By rare luck he had gotten clean away from trouble. But what was to be done about the dog? He had not the remotest idea of his opponent's name or where the man lived. He had no wish to incur jail or fine, or both, by returning by the next train to the armory to make inquiries. What was to be done?

Then his forehead lost its worry crease and he smiled in whimsical relief at the collie.

"It's all right," he whispered down at the friendlily upraised face. "I just happened to think. Remember I told him I'd fight him for you? Remember that, doggie? I said I'd keep you if I won, and that I'd give him your price if *he* won. Remember? He agreed to that, too. At least he sailed into me with that double-size fist of his, the second after I said it. Well, I won. And even then, I didn't take you. You've brought yourself along. But I'm not going to take you back to be beaten to death by him. I won you fair. I made the offer. He took me up. I won. And here we are."

The dog's plumed tail was smiting the dusty floor of the baggage car with happily resounding thumps as Abner talked to him. The man's voice and intonation were such as an animal likes. The collie licked the calloused hand that stroked his silken head. Mutely, a bond of chumship was established between the dog-lonely man and the ill-treated dog.

"No way of guessing at your name, I suppose," went on Abner, still talking as if to a human. "So I'll have to give you a new one. If you're anything like most collies, you'll learn it in less than no time. Let's see, now. What'll it be?"

Eyes half shut, he considered briefly, the dog watching him in affectionate interest, as though wanting to hear once more the pleasant voice he was growing to like so much. As Peake remained silent, the collie sat up and gravely laid one snowy forepaw on the farmer's knee. Abner glanced down at the shapely white paw. Then he grinned.

"If that's a hint," he told the dog, "I'll take it. Your name's going to be Whitefoot. I had a Guernsey heifer with that name, once, and she won me a passel of ribbons at the Paterson Fair. She was a beauty, too; but she wasn't any prettier'n you are. Your name's Whitefoot. Understand, son? *Whitefoot!* And if you've got the sense and the disposition that your eyes say you've got, you've had your last whipping. We're due to be chums, you and I."

Thus it was that the lonely young farmer and the lonely young dog began their acquaintanceship. Like most show-type collies, Whitefoot knew nothing of farms or of farm work. But, like most show-type collies, sanely taught, he learned his daily duties with almost bewildering speed.

Within a month he was driving the cows to and from pasture and was rounding up and guiding the farm's bunch of sixty sheep. True, he still worked with a certain raggedness and over-vehemence, as do nearly all new-taught young collies. . . . But daily he was steadying down into a valuable herder and house-dog. Daily, too, he grew more happily devoted to the man he had chosen as his master.

There was much for Whitefoot to learn, apart from his workaday duties. He had been born and brought up in a professional's breeding kennels. There, apart from his short daily exercise gallop, he had been confined in a wire runway, his meals doled out to him by kennel men who scarce bothered to chirp to him or pet him. His gayly vibrant collie brain had never been developed. He had not been able to attach himself whole-souledly to any human master, which is a collie's birthright.

Sold to the fat man who had bought him as a speculation, he had had a week of torment and abuse. Then had come his dramatic release—a release due to the pleasant-voiced farmer whom now he accepted as his god. All his present life was as new to him as it was delightful. With pathetic eagerness he sought to adapt himself to it. But it had dozens of puzzling details. For instance:

At one time he was welcome to walk into the house and across its clean floors. At another, simply because it was raining and he had been trotting across muddy ground, he was forbidden to come in. Instead, he must lie on the chilly kitchen porch until instinct told him to lick clean his white paws of the clogging black mud that smeared them.

Again, he was permitted, even encouraged, to bark harrowingly at tramp or peddler who slouched into the dooryard, and to stand as a growling barrier between such visitor and the house. Yet, if a neighboring farmer chanced to drop in for a chat with Peake, the dog was scolded for standing fiercely between such a guest and the hospitable doorway.

When Peake's sheep broke fold, Whitefoot was patted and praised for rounding them up and driving them back and standing guard at the fold gap, until his master could arrive to mend the breach. Yet, when a flock of strange sheep was passing along the main road, on its way to market, Whitefoot was rebuked sharply for dashing out of the yard, thrashing the dog that guided them, ignoring the yells of their shepherd, and forcibly herding the entire flock into the Peake fold.

Yes, there was much to learn. Yet rapidly the young dog was learning it. Also, he was devising queer innovations and improvements on the things Abner taught him. This, too, is the way of the best type of collie.

On a morning in early January a motoring photographer, out to get snow scenes, passed the farm just as Whitefoot was guiding a bunch of sheep out of the barn fold and driving them to where Abner had smashed the ice off the deep watering trough. The photographer took a picture or two of the pretty sight, including a "close-up" (to the collie's infinite disgust and Abner's concealed pride) of Whitefoot standing in front of the sheep.

Two weeks later this artistic picture appeared in the rotogravure sections of no fewer than five Sunday papers. It was the sort of snapshot that rotogravure editors revel in. Beneath was Abner Peake's name—once more causing him vast pride—and the name of the township wherein lay his farm.

Among the thousands of newspaper readers, that Sunday, who focused a more or less idle gaze on the pretty bit of art work was one Caleb Falk—an obese and red-visaged man who held a small political office in the county seat's courthouse. Falk's tiny eyes contracted as they studied the clearly etched face of Whitefoot. Instinctively he lifted a ham-like hand's thick fingers to the point of his jaw. Long since, that jaw had ceased to be swollen and agonizingly painful. But never had the memory of Abner Peake's knockout blow ceased to awaken in Falk a fury of vengeful yearnings.

Peake had gotten clean away after thrashing him. Nor had a search of the city's various resorts and hotels succeeded in locating him. Hitherto, Falk had supposed the dog had run away independently. Indeed, he had advertised for the straying collie.

But now, vividly recognizable, the dog was depicted as standing in front of a huddle of sheep. At his side, grinning into the camera, was the man against whom Caleb Falk had sworn revenge. So, not content with thrashing Falk, the scoundrel had stolen Falk's hundred-dollar collie! And the fool had even given the photographer his name and address, to render the tracking more certain.

Falk sat brooding in grim enjoyment for a few minutes. Then his plan was made. The countryman could be punished now, not only for assault, but for grand larceny as well. As for the dog—Caleb smiled happily as he picked up a rawhide from the table and ran its cruel length caressingly through his fingers. It was not a pretty smile.

There was a new excitement, nowadays, not only at Peake's farm, but throughout all his rural neighborhood. Whitefoot became more and more aware of this, as a highstrung dog always does when something out of the ordinary comes into his life. He did not know what it was, but his master and occasional visitors had begun talking eagerly about something that seemed to thrill them. At the store, too, when Whitefoot trotted down there at Abner's heels, on Peake's trips for provisions or tobacco or for a chat, there was that same air of growing interest and of concentration of thought upon one theme.

Whitefoot felt the electric current of this neighborhood thrill, without in the least guessing at its cause, but with a collie's pleasurable little throb of excitement in the excitement of others.

Then on a vividly clear morning the dog awoke as usual at grayest dawn, and fared forth with Abner on the morning chores. Peake was up an hour earlier than usual, and he was hurrying through his work. The dog noted this with puzzled interest. But almost at once he forgot to notice it. He became more concerned in something else—something he could not define. Some queer thing was impending. Whitefoot had no idea what it could be. But even as he (like many another animal) could foresee a thunderstorm or a cyclone, hours before its arrival, so now he became aware of something abnormal in the air.

It troubled and excited him. He sniffed the icy morning wind in vain for a clue to it. Overhead, the new-risen sun was shining brilliantly on a world of dazzling snow. There was no portent of coming disaster, as when the breathlessness of the air and its electrical twinges foretold to him a thunderstorm twenty-five miles away. Yet there was *something*. Every animal on the farm seemed vaguely to feel it.

The morning barn-work done, Peake went back indoors, Whitefoot with him, and sat down to breakfast. The farmer ate hastily, now and then glancing at the mantel clock. In half his usual time he had finished. With another glance at the clock he went out-of-doors again, making for the windmill that stood on the summit of a knoll some two hundred yards beyond and above the house.

This windmill was erected on the stilt-supported storage tank which provided the farm with water. On top of the tank was a flat surface, perhaps ten feet square, from which arose the metal frame of the windmill tower. A ladder led to it from the ground.

To this tank platform Abner Peake made his way. In his hand he was carrying carefully something dark and irregular of outline. As ever, Whitefoot followed him. When Abner mounted the steep ladder the collie looked disappointedly up after him. Then, with true philosophy, he lay down to await Peake's return. He knew Abner must descend the same way he had gone up. As the ladder was too steep for the dog to climb, he needs must await his master's descent.

Always Whitefoot was Abner's adoring shadow, wherever the farmer might chance to go. But this morning there was more than mere affection in his desire to keep as close as possible to Peake.

Even during the short time he and Abner had been indoors at breakfast, the oddly unexplainable *something* had increased tenfold in intensity. Now it had begun to undermine the collie's high-strung nerves. He was fidgety, uneasy, vaguely troubled. He wanted to be as near as possible to the man who was his god—to the human who was all-wise and all-powerful and who could protect him if need be.

But Abner was paying no heed to him. To the watching collie the farmer appeared to be doing nothing except stand there and, occasionally, to look up at the sky. Every minute, that mysteriously uneasy feeling fastened itself tighter and tighter about Whitefoot's heart-strings. Something was happening; he did not know what. It troubled him increasingly. He got to his feet and whined softly, far down in his furry throat.

The sun was not shining now in glaring intensity, as a few minutes earlier. And through the healthful chill of the January morning seeped a draughty series of wind gusts that seemed to come from no special direction.

The garish light waned and the air took on the livid tinge that comes before a thunderstorm. Again Whitefoot whimpered softly. Again he glanced appealingly up to where his master stood. But Peake gave him no heed. The man was standing facing the sun, shading his eyes from it with a big fragment of smoked windowpane.

An almost soundless rustle, as of great muted pinions, swept over the world. With it came another swirling little gust of ice-wind from nowhere. The sunshine was dwindling to sinister early twilight. Blue shadows streaked the snow. The day was dying—the day that had scarce begun.

And now Whitefoot realized that he was no longer alone in his knowledge and dread of the hideous change that was engulfing his wholesome workaday world.

In the farmyard below he could see the busily scratching chickens give over their work of food-hustling and troop dazedly toward their roosts. Being semi-idiotic creatures, the fowls saw in the waxing darkness nothing but the approach of their sleeping-time.

A junco came fluttering past with nervous haste and plunged into the recesses of a juniper bush which was his nightly roosting-place. Six crows, winging eastward across the sky, broke into frantic cawings and flew in every direction, settling gradually toward earth.

From the stables came the scared lowing of cows, punctuated by the bellow of Abner's mighty Guernsey bull. The sheep were milling in their fold, bleating piteously.

With a crash a wide-antlered deer broke cover from the near-by woods, and came zigzagging across the open, galloping aimlessly, head tossed back, tail clamped down. He passed, unheeding, within ten feet of the dog, and scurried off across the hilly ground, snorting and bleating.

And now the sun was dead. Around its black body shimmered a ghastly pearl-white hoop of light. From the dark zenith stars winked into view, as though shamed at being caught out at such an hour. Whitefoot, shaking all over as with a chill, stood looking appealingly up at his master as if beseeching the unheeding man for a word of cheer. An owl hooted raucous welcome to the premature night.

Out from one edge of the black disk flared a diamond-bright pin head of light. The eclipse was passing—the forecasted miracle which had roused Abner and his neighbors to such excited comment and conjecture during the past few days.

Whitefoot could not know it was passing. On him the awe and terror were still crushingly heavy.

Then all at once he caught a series of sounds that brought back to mind in an instant his newly taught education as a farm dog. There was a splintering of far-off timbers, followed by a thunder of galloping hoofs. Around the side of the barn appeared a truculent shape.

In the vague light loomed Jupiter, the farm's prize

Guernsey bull, smashed slivers of his stall door still hanging to his auburn shoulders. Jupiter was a bull of great value and of murderous temper, as unsafe a brute as any stable could harbor. His stall was stoutly reinforced, to prevent escape. Yet to-day his horror-rage at the eclipse had given him strength to batter a way out.

Now, no cattle belonged in the dooryard. That was one of the earliest things Peake had taught his collie. More than once a cow had gotten out of stall or barnyard and strayed thither. Abner had praised the dog for his deft speed in turning and housing the stray.

So, in the midst of his own fear, Whitefoot saw duty forcing itself on him. Hating to depart from the protection of Abner's presence, he spun around and cantered down toward the bull, to drive him back where he belonged.

At the same minute two men turned in from the road and walked toward the front door of the house.

Saturday was the one time in the work week when Caleb Falk could leave his courthouse job at the county seat long enough to accomplish such a mission as was now his. True, Saturday, January 24, 1925, chanced to be the day of the eclipse. But eclipses meant little to Falk in comparison with revenge and a hundred-dollar dog. The only morning train from the city was due at Hecker a few minutes before nine. Accordingly, Falk had come out by that train, bringing along a county detective who was a chum of his. At the station they had had no difficulty in getting directions to Peake's farm.

Undeterred by the ever-darkening sun, and indeed scarce troubling to glance up at the miracle of it, Caleb

had hurried along the icy byroad, exhorting the less purposeful detective to greater speed.

Into the dooryard the two turned; just as Whitefoot,
nearly a furlong off, began his canter toward the escaped
Jupiter.

The bull, raw-nerved and bellowing, stood, in the
ghostly light, pawing the snow and glaring about for
some living thing on which to vent his nerve-scourged
fury. On the instant he spied the two men advancing
toward him. Here was glut for his murder-rage!

With lowered head, the mad bull charged.

At the same time Whitefoot's canter merged into a
whirlwind rush as he saw the men and the danger that
threatened them.

Caleb Falk came to a bemused halt when he beheld the
red-and-white bovine avalanche launch itself at him. He
was a city-bred man and unused to rural surprises such as
this. His friend, the detective, did not halt. He had
begun life as a farm lad. Moreover, he was spare and
agile.

In a mighty upward bound the detective caught a low-
hanging bough of an oak that grew in the dooryard.
Though the slender branch cracked and bent under his
weight, he drew himself up on it and clung there, thin
arms and legs gripping the limb. He was safe. He had
scope, thus, to look down and learn what fate had befallen
his fatter and less resourceful friend.

Falk's moveless instant of amaze had passed. One does
not need much lore of the farmland to know a charging
bull is not a safe playfellow to await supinely. With a
screech, Caleb wheeled about and ran for the road.

By the merest luck, he swerved sharply to one side as

his ungainly body got into motion. This saved his life. A bull, as a rule, charges in short rushes and with tight-shut eyes. Jupiter thundered over the spot where Falk had stood, missing the running man by a matter of inches.

Then the bull turned, opening his eyes; and again with lowered head he hurled himself at his victim.

Falk, in screaming flight, stepped on a bit of ice. Heels over head he fell, directly in the bull's path. Jupiter plunged to the slaughter. As he did so he was aware of something that flashed between him and his prey. An agonizing pain shot through his sensitive nostrils. A whalebone weight of something like sixty pounds tugged the tortured nostrils sharply to one side. The bull swerved in his rush, even as Caleb Falk had swerved when first he essayed to flee. His flying hoofs grazed the fallen and shrieking man as the giant body lurched over him.

Then, snorting and bellowing, the bull wheeled again to attack. But again Whitefoot was between him and his victim. The collie was everywhere and nowhere; nipping, barking, slashing the tender nostrils of the bull, easily evading his horn lunges. It was a pretty sight and it was an exhibition of perfect collie science.

Again and again, Jupiter lunged and sought to launch himself into a charge. Ever the harrowing dog was in front of him to deflect the rush.

Falk scrambled to his feet, still squealing like a stuck pig. He saw the front door, behind which lay the protection of the house. He made for it at a shambling run, stumbling up the two steps of the low porch.

Jupiter, seeing him on the eve of escape, bored past the detaining collie and charged after his fleeing prey. Falk grabbed the door-knob and twisted it. The door remained shut. Having read of the danger of sneak thieves during the time when householders might be watching the eclipse, Abner Peake had locked both front and back doors before going to the windmill observatory.

Caleb dropped the resisting door-knob as if it had been red hot. He turned, yelling, to seek other escape. The bull was all but upon him. As the man sought to run around the porch he slipped again, this time on the icy boards; and he fell prone, rolling down the steps.

For the second time in less than a single minute Whitefoot proceeded to save the life of his olden tormentor. Overtaking Jupiter, he seized the ragged and bloody nostrils afresh, swinging the lowered head far enough to one side to miss the rolling and shrieking Falk.

The young dog's blood was up. The bull had broken away from him once. Jupiter was not going to get a chance to do it again. Like a furry tornado he was at the brute. Biting, rushing, eluding, even leaping over the lowered horns and landing on the tumultuous back and nipping a heaving thigh before jumping down again to earth to confront the bull, he goaded his opponent to mania.

Hitherto Jupiter had regarded the dog merely as an obstacle to his killing of the man. Now it seemed the dog must be gotten rid of before the man could be gored. Jupiter charged thunderously at the collie. Whitefoot fled, keeping just in front of the pursuing bull, and egging him on by insulting barks. Stupidly, the bull gave chase, Whitefoot easily keeping out of his way and drawing him farther and farther from the house and toward the barn.

From the tail of his eye, Whitefoot could see Abner

Peake running down the knoll toward the scene of conflict. The dog acted accordingly. Straight for the barnyard he loped; Jupiter following with murderous vehemence. Into the barnyard scuttled the dog, the bull close at his heels. Then, as the oncoming Peake snatched up the bars and began to put them into their sockets, filling the gap through which dog and bull had entered the barnyard, Whitefoot slipped between two rails of the high fence and rejoined his master.

The collie was in glorious spirits. He had done well in this jolly game of hide-and-seek with death. He wanted his master's praise and friendly petting. He had deserved it. Moreover, the sinister shadows were passing. The sun was beginning to flood the world again. All danger was gone.

But Abner did not stop to pet him. As Peake had run past the house he had recognized the shoutingly hysterical fat man at the edge of the steps. Now, with shoulders squared, he went to meet him.

He found Caleb Falk sitting in a huddled and shuddering heap on the steps. The county detective had dropped lightly from the oak branch and was moving toward him, pale and tense.

At scent of his former owner, Whitefoot stopped dead short, his hackles beginning to bristle and his white eye-teeth glinting from beneath his upcurled lip. A collie dog does not forget. Hitherto the dog had been too busy and too excited to recognize Falk. Now he had leisure.

"Well?" defiantly asked Peake, walking up to the shuddering Caleb.

As he spoke he laid a detaining hand on Whitefoot's bristling ruff. The fat man did not answer. He sat trembling, and trying to get hold of his shattered self-control. The county detective broke the brief silence.

"Falk," said he, "is that the dog we came out here to get?"

Speechlessly Caleb nodded, his jaw slack, his eyes wandering glassily.

"Then listen to me," ordered the detective, "and listen good and hard. That collie saved you, just now, from being pounded and gored to Hamburg steak. *Twice* he saved you, that way, and he risked a goring to do it. See how he's snarling at you? And see how loving he cuddles up against this feller who won him from you?"

Falk made no answer.

"On the way out here," resumed the detective, "you spent most of your time telling me how you was going to whale the flesh off'n this dog's bones when you got him home. Well—you aren't going to get him home. Understand? I saw what I saw, just now. And it's a story I'm going to tell to everyone who'll listen to me. Inside a week there won't be a politician, from the Big Boss down to Humpy Pieters, who won't know it. It'll be in the papers, too. I'll see to that. Get me?"

Falk tried to speak. Only a gurgling babble issued from the fat and wabbling lips.

"Now, then," finished the detective, "you and I are going to streak it for the station in time to hop the ten-o'clock express back to town. Likewise, we're going without this dog. Likewise, we're going without serving the warrant on this man. I've saw a fight this morning that has done things to me, inside-like, and I've just told you what we're going to do about it. Likewise, if you ever make another try to get this dog or to arrest the cuss who taught him how to handle cattle like that—well, you can figger out the line of treatment you're due to get from a he-man like the Big Boss, and how all the papers will roast the fat off'n you. I guess you don't need to have a diagram drawed of it. Come on home."

Abner Peake stood watching the two visitors as they disappeared down the icy road. Then he turned slowly to Whitefoot.

"I—I guess the eclipse isn't the only miracle that's happened to-day, old friend," he mumbled, dazedly, as he caught the collie's classic head between his rough palms. "No, nor, as far as *I'm* concerned, the eclipse isn't even the *BIGGEST* miracle that's happened to-day. Gee, but you're one grand dog, Whitefoot!"

VI. Parsifal, Unlimited

"I'M—I'm kind of giving up my job with you, Mr. Bates," announced Maskell, a tinge of awe in his drawling voice. "As soon as you can break somebody in to do my work, I'll—I'll be glad if—if you can break somebody in to do my work. Because I'm giving up my job with you."

He stopped there. Pretty much everything seemed to have been said and even resaid. The declaration of independence was uttered.

Now that the words were out, Horatio—otherwise Rashe—Maskell was disappointed. He had not meant to couch his resignation in such lame terms. Fifty times—like every wage-earner on earth—he had visualized such a scene as this. He had rehearsed, from a score of angles, what he would say if ever the golden hour should come when no longer he needed the uncongenial job which fed him.

At such times as Bates had scathed him for laziness or for incompetence, it had been balm to Rashe's smashed

self-esteem to conjure up a vision of himself swaggering
into his employer's office and declaiming fiercely:

"You've bullied me for the last time, you big stiff.
I'm THROUGH!"

Then to his stricken overlord he would announce the
inheriting of a million dollars or the proffer of a dazzling
job or his appointment as postmaster of Paignton—something, anything, that should lift him forever above the
purely hypothetical slave whip of Thaddeus C. Bates,
(Hay, Feed & Lumber, Light Trucking, etc.). Yet,
now that the moment had come, he found himself as sub-
servient to his paunchy boss as though he were asking for
another afternoon off.

"Yes," repeated Maskell, fretted by the brief silence
wherewith Bates greeted his announcement—a silence
Rashe sought hopefully to construe into thunderstruck
horror at his prospective loss—"yes, I'm—well, I'm
leaving."

"So you said," answered Bates, any tinge of horror
successfully wiped from his comfortably thick voice; "so
you said. Well, good luck to you, Rashe. Don't bother
about sticking around till some one else is broken in.
This is the light season. Dugan can carry your job and
his own. Go as soon as you like. I suppose you want a
reference from me to your new boss?" he finished, with a
shade of uneasiness.

"I'm not going to any new boss," replied Maskell,
proudly. "I'm done with work. I'm going to take life
easy after this."

"H'm!" mused Bates, wholly unimpressed. "You've
picked out a bad time of year to start in on it, haven't

you? The snow is all gone and the grass hasn't started. What'll you find to eat?"

"I'll have you know, Mr. Bates, that I don't need to eat either snow nor yet grass!" flared Rashe with a rare spurt of annoyance. "The fact is I've come into a legacy."

"Good for you!" approved Bates, looking at Rashe almost as at a fellow-mortal. "Who's it from? How much is it?"

"It's from Aaron Coyle," said Maskell, "and it's nine hundred dollars a year. That's seventy-five dollars a month. It's an annuity. I get paid it by the month. Saul Boden's got to pay it to me. Mr. Coyle's nephew. He's the executor of the will and the administrator of the estate and all that. Yes, he's got to pay me seventy-five dollars a month. I'm figuring he enjoys doing it pretty near as much as if it was those sparse teeth of his."

Rashe smiled peacefully at the thought.

"Along with my little house dad left me," he pursued, "that ought to keep me pretty snug. And I can raise garden truck if I'm a mind to. Then—"

Bate's breathless amaze found belated vent in words. He broke in:

"Hold on! Sit down, Rashe. Have a smoke? Now, then, what's the main idea? Spill it. Take one of these cigars without the red bands on. They're the best. Got a match? Now, then, spill it."

Rashe launched upon his tale. As the recital began somewhere in the middle of its own action and worked alternately to one end and then to another, with endless repetitions of the less vital details, it was pesteringly long in the telling.   Stripped of the bare facts, the gist was as follows:

Aaron Coyle had been reputed the richest and stingiest man in the six-thousand-population townlet of Paignton. His sole weakness was for an obese and doubtful-ancestried and straw-colored collie dog which in a flight of imagery he had misnamed Parsifal.   This cur he had accepted, along with other and more practical chattels, in part payment for an uncollectable debt.   Coyle had planned to sell the dog for two or three dollars, if possible. In the meantime he had harbored it.   In less than a week the collie had wriggled a tortuous path into the very core of the lonely old man's heart.   He was the one mushy spot in Aaron's granite.

But Parsifal tended to sag, in his own rôle as party to the second part in this mutual-adoration league.   He was addicted to straying from home and neglecting to return until found and haled back.   He was one of those miserable rarities—a born runaway collie, with no homing instinct.   It was Parsifal's one besetting sin.   In any joyously striking dog-like characteristics he seemed wholly lacking.   He was a bleakly colorless specimen of the most colorful breed on earth.   The oftener he ran away, the deeper grew Coyle's grieving affection.   The old man was miserable during his chummiless chum's frequent absences, and he scoured the region anguishedly for him.

At last he hit on the plan of keeping Parsifal tied up when he himself must be away from home.   On the first afternoon of this new régime Aaron came back to a desolate dwelling, to find the collie had gnawed his long clothesline tether in two and had decamped, with something like twelve feet of line still dangling from his collar.

For three entire days there was no sign of the absentee. Coyle gave up every waking minute to the search. On the fourth morning Rashe Maskell was passing through a strip of bramble-choked woodland, on the way to a Sunday's fishing in the river, when he stumbled and fell heavily over some invisible obstruction beneath an upheaval of briers.

Parsifal, in clumsy pursuit of rabbits, had entangled the flapping end of his length of clothes-line around a cedar stump in the center of the brier patch. His mad efforts to get free had wound him tight to the stump and had cast over him a superficial pall of uprooted brambles. There, for three days, the hapless dog had lain, helpless to move or even to howl, by reason of two loops of the line which had passed respectively over his back and around his jaws. The suffering brute was well-nigh dead from thirst and famine and fright.

Rashe Maskell knew little about dogs, and cared less. But he was a kindly chap. He recognized Parsifal, having seen him parading the streets of Paignton at Aaron's heels. He realized the dog was at the last gasp. Wherefore, abandoning his fishing plans, he picked up the fat sufferer and carried him to his own inherited shack at the edge of town. There he heated milk for Parsifal to drink and fed him in small and slow portions the chuck steak which was to have formed his own Sunday dinner. After which he left the replete and still feeble collie to sleep off his fatigue, and went to tell Aaron Coyle of his find.

Coyle was enraptured. He hurried to the shack with Rashe. There he beheld his lost treasure slumbering sweetly on a blanket, flanked by the empty milk pail and the steak dish. So overjoyed and grateful was Aaron that he all but gave Rashe a dollar, by way of reward. Overwhelming the embarrassed rescuer with thanks, Coyle departed, taking his recovered pet with him.

"That'll have been pretty near a year back," continued Rashe, nearing the end of his recital to Bates. "I didn't ever think anything more about it. Then Mr. Coyle up and dies. And what do you suppose one of the codicils of his will says? Says there never was anybody but me who showed kindness to his dear dog, Parsifal, and that there isn't anybody but me that he'd be willing to trust him to, in case Mr. Coyle should die first. So he's fixed it that I'm to have Parsifal and that I'm to have seventy-five dollars a month for taking the best of care of him, so long as he lives. That's right, boss. If you don't believe me you can ask Saul Boden. I've been to Lawyer Ebbet, too. Him and my dad were chums. He says it's all legal."

"The old cut-up!" chuckled Bates. "I mean Aaron Coyle. He must have split his sides a-laughing, when he made that codicil. He had to leave his cash to somebody, and he always hated charities. So he left it to Saul Boden, as his next of kin. He knew Boden would hang onto it as tight as Aaron himself ever did. It wouldn't be squandered. But he fixed it so as Saul will have to sweat seventy-five dollars a month of it. Saul loves to pay out money pretty near as much as Coyle loved to. He's still got the first dollar he ever earned, and pretty near all the dollars his clients ever earned, too. It'll be a goshawful torture to Saul to keep on paying you that money all the time, maybe for years and years. Yep, Aaron played one grand joke on him, and he arranged an easy life for his dog, too. He knew you'd cosset that cur along, like he was diamonds, so as to keep earning your seventy-five dollars. He knew Saul Boden would ride herd on you, too, to see the dog was alive and well treated. Aaron played it both ways. By the way, suppose the dog up and dies on you? What then?"

A shadow marred the vacuously happy smile on Rashe's mouth.

"Why—why, the will says the annuity stops when the dog dies," he confessed, adding hopefully: "But dogs live to a terrible old age, sometimes. Ma's uncle had a coon-dog, down near Paterson, that lived to be—"

"Well, take it from me that no dog ever had time to pile up all the fat that's on Aaron Coyle's yellow collie, in less than ten or eleven years. Maybe you've thrown over your job a wee peckle too quick."

"I guess I'll take the chance, Mr. Bates."

"By the way," continued Bates, "just keep one eye on Saul Boden. I've known Saul since a couple of years before he was born. I know all about him, and I don't know much of it that's good. There's this you can tie to, though: As far as the letter of the law goes, he's honest. He won't kill the dog and he won't steal him. He's too near square for that. But he'll do anything legal or half-way legal to keep you from going on drawing that monthly cash. Watch out for him."

Parsifal, the corpulent, was duly installed in his new abode—a converted packing box, clean and large and well bedded, in the center of a high chicken-wire inclosure some twelve feet square. A sprawly oak tree, just outside the yard's edge, supplied adequate if fitful shade from the sun's hottest rays.

The more Rashe studied the dog the deeper into his memory and nervous system sank Bates's warning that Parsifal was well stricken in years and that he might at any time deprive Maskell of a career of untoiling luxury by dying from some senile malady. At last, driven to desperation by the fear, Rashe spent two dollars on a visit from the local veterinary, begging him examine the dog, with a view to finding out his approximate age and general prospects of health. The vet made the examination with a thoroughness which nearly reconciled Rashe to the loss of his two dollars. Then he gave verdict.

"I thought this was an old dog when I saw him around the streets with Coyle," he said. "But he isn't old. A dog is only as old as his teeth. His teeth aren't even beginning to yellow or to wear down. The gums haven't started to spread. I can't say for sure, but I don't believe he's a day over three."

"Then he's only a young dog yet!" exclaimed Rashe, in joy, "and he's liable to live ten or twelve years more. Maybe longer. Ma had an uncle, down near Paterson, who had a coon-dog that lived to be—"

"Well, this dog isn't going to live another ten years," interrupted the vet. "No, nor another two years; not unless you stop stuffing him with all kinds of food and keeping him penned up like that all the time. He's due for heart trouble or asthma or any of a dozen diseases, as soon as his youth stops counteracting his fat. Why, even now he's beginning to wheeze! If you want him to go on living, you've got to switch the way you're treating him and the way Aaron Coyle treated him. How often does he get fed?"

"Four times a day."

"No grown dog needs more than one meal a day," declared the vet. "Give him one good big meal, along about sundown, and nothing else to eat. Do that when he gets in shape again. Till you've trained him down, just give him a couple of dry dog biscuits every evening. Nothing else—except all the drinking water he wants. After the way he's been pampered, most likely he won't touch the biscuits just at first. But when he gets good and hungry he'll eat them fast enough. Till then he can live on his fat. Keep that diet up till I tell you to switch to a regular meal of table scraps, without potato in them, once a day. And give him five miles a day of steady road work. Do it in the cool of the day, of course, not in the hot sunshine. That's all. It'll cure him."

With dire visions of a vanishing legacy to spur him on, Rashe threw himself into the new course of training. He, who hated violent physical exercise, tramped at top speed daily for five miles, convoying an equally uncomfortable Parsifal on a forward-yanked leash. He, who hated to see anyone or anything go hungry, had to look on while Parsifal sniffed disdainfully at his two non-luscious dog biscuits at eventide, and then while the empty-stomached collie stared up in pathetic appeal for more edible food. But the wise training course began to take effect.

Once, as Rashe and Parsifal were returning homeward through Paignton's Main Street from a breath-takingly fast hike, they met Saul Boden. The lawyer had been waiting for them. At a peremptory move of his skinny hand, Maskell and the dog came to a panting halt.

For a moment the lawyer did not speak. In morbid appraisal, he was eying Parsifal. Now, stooping, he passed a speculative hand over the uninterested dog.

"By the terms of my uncle's will," he said, oracularly, "you are to provide his dog with a good home and kind treatment. Two months ago he was a plump and healthy-looking dog, much as he had been in my late uncle's time. To-day I see a half-starved skeleton, with every rib sticking out like a barrel hoop. The poor brute is being starved to death! You have deliberately broken your share of the—"

"I have not!" shouted Rashe, with the courage of a cornered guinea-pig. "I'm saving his life. That's what I'm doing. Go back into your office and phone Doc Finper! He'll tell you. You try to cut off my annuity and I'll have Doc get up in court and swear I'm following his orders, to make the dog live years longer than ever he could have kept on living if I'd kept on stuffing him with all that food and letting him lay around and sleep all day. You ask Doc Finper. I guess there isn't a vet in the state that's any higher thought of than Doc is. You go ask him."

Saul Boden did not "go ask him." He had no need to. A dog man himself, he had rejoiced in the unwieldy fat which had encompassed Parsifal and in the waddling gait and the incipient wheeze. With genuine alarm, of late, he had noted the striking change for the better in the dog's aspect. And now he had failed to bluff Rashe Maskell into letting the collie lapse back to fat and to a prospect of ultra-brief life.

Saul began taking daily walks on his own account. Every day he strolled past the Maskell shack, checking his pace to a crawl as he scanned the kennel yard and its occupant. Watching from window or from porch, Rashe grew vaguely and increasingly uneasy. He found himself harking back to the warning of Thaddeus C. Bates:

"Keep one eye on Saul Boden. . . . He won't kill the dog and he won't steal him. . . . But he'll do anything legal or halfway legal, to keep you from going on drawing that monthly cash."

One morning Bates was startled to see his employee emeritus come determinedly into the office of that local king of the Hay, Feed & Lumber, Light Trucking industry. By the leash Maskell led Parsifal. Facing the magnate, he said:

"I hear you fired the man who took my old job. Get anybody in his place, yet?"

"Nope. Why? Want the job?"

Bates laughed at his own exquisite wit. But Maskell did not laugh.

"Yes," he said, defiantly, "I do. I want it bad. I won't tell you why. You'd only laugh at me some more, or maybe think I was crazy. It's enough for you to know I'm not broke. I still get my seventy-five dollars a month and I'm due to keep right on getting it. But—well, I want my job back. Do I get it? Hold on a second, before you answer. You've got that fenced yard out yonder. You aren't using it for anything. If you take me back you've got to let me put a little dogcoop out there and keep Parsifal in it all day while I'm working here. I'll take him home with me, nights, of course. How about it?"

"Well," said Bates, meditatively, "I might give you another try at it, Rashe. But I want to speak plain to you first, so you can't say later that I fired you unfair. You did a heap of loafing and mooning when you were here before. I put up with it because I figured you needed the work pretty bad. But you don't need it bad now. So if you come back here you've got to keep up on your toes, right from the sound of the gong. It's got to be a case of hustle every minute and every second. You gotta work; not moon. Understand that?"

"Yes sir," said Rashe, in real gratitude.

Not for double his promised wage would Maskell have confessed to Bates that he sought the job as a one certain way of avoiding Saul Boden's daily snooping inspection, and to fool the lawyer into a worry as acute as his own.

With himself busy at the office and with Parsifal safely ensconced in the high-boarded fence at its rear, where Maskell could cast a watchful eye on him every minute if need be, there was nothing to fear, during work hours, from Boden's espionage. The lawyer could work Parsifal no harm when the dog and the dog's master were guarded thus. To Rashe the plan seemed sublime in its security.

In other years his duties under Bates's rule had been abhorrent. Now, to his astonishment, they waxed almost pleasant. He began to take a real interest in his work. Rashe, after months of crass idleness, found himself taking the same sportsmanly interest in the upbuilding of his job as might some leisure-weary athlete in the improvement of his golf stroke; or a mental idler in wrestling with a knotty cross-word puzzle.

Parsifal lay moodily in the office back yard, all day and every day. After work hours or early in the morning Rashe still gave him daily five miles of fast walking— sharp exercise which cleared the man's own brain and sharpened his appetite and set his blood atingle with energy.

Six times within six months Saul Boden found flimsy excuse to stray into Bates's office, and to gaze through the window at Parsifal.

On one of these office visitations Saul turned from the window and crossed to Rashe's desk.

"Parsifal looks kind of peakéd and poorly, to me," said he. "He doesn't look very well or very happy. Do you call that back-yard coop a 'happy home,' Maskell? Do you think it's treating him kindly to—"

"Yep," snapped Maskell, "I do. He's comf'table there. He gets a good square meal a day, now; not just the two biscuits. He's in dandy shape. He gets his five-mile tramp every day or every night, too. I can prove that by Doc Finper. I go past Doc's house every time Parsifal and I walk. I had him look the dog over again, the other day. He says he's in one hundred per cent condition."

"Looks poorly to me," insisted Boden. "Looks as if his digestion was bad. Ever try sprinkling a little powdered glass in his meat? Or giving him a good meal of chicken bones? They say that is good for—"

"For poisoning a dog?" finished Rashe, ablaze with indignation. "It is. Powdered glass is sure death. It's an awful death, too. I know, because Doc Finper told me, last week about a dog he was sent to see—a dog that some blackguard had given powdered glass to. He says chicken bones are pretty dangerous for a dog to eat, too. Mr. Bates, you heard that, didn't you? You heard Mr. Boden advise me to give Parsifal powdered glass? You can testify to it, if the dog is ever poisoned."

Boden walked loftily from the office.

"Look out for him," counseled Bates. "He didn't happen to get you on that. But he'll floor you on something else. I know him."

Rashe did not answer. Hardly did he hear, and not at all did he heed, his employer's croakings. He had held his own against the man who so long had been making him shake in his shoes. He had seen through the great Saul Boden, and answered him back fearlessly; had routed him. Maskell could scarcely understand this new self of his.

And, as ever, pride went before a smashing fall. That night was swirlingly rainy. He went to bed early, planning to take Parsifal for his daily five-mile walk at daybreak.

The dawn wind dispelled the clouds and the day broke in fire-and-crimson. Out of bed jumped Rashe eager for the five-mile top-speed hike which, with his new zest in work, was building up his ramshackle mind and body. He sloshed two pails of cold water over himself, rubbed down with a rough towel, and then got into his clothes. After which he sallied forth, leash in hand, to Parsifal's kennel yard.

Yard and kennel were empty. Parsifal was gone.

Beneath a side of the loose-stretched wire gaped a shallow hole in the soft wet earth. Parsifal's paws had been busy for a whole midnight hour in hollowing out that simple means of escape from the yard, which was even more monotonous than the back yard behind the Bates office. Beyond lay the whole rain-washed world—a world of fascinating smells and clues and adventures and unsupervised exercise.

A half-year and more of wise training had brought back Parsifal's sense of adventure as well as his shape and his interest in life. The olden runaway spirit had flared up. Yes, Parsifal was gone.

Rashe spent two hours in searching the neighborhood and the surrounding country. He dared not ask questions. Some one might blab to Saul Boden that the dog's owner had been looking for him.

When Thaddeus Bates reached the office that morning, Rashe hailed him loudly.

"I've been fixing up a—a—now, a kind of coop, down cellar," said he. "Fixing it up for Parsifal. After what Lawyer Boden said about powdered glass and chicken bones, I'm scared he'll sling something over the fence to make poor Parsy sick. So I've fixed up that old corner coal bin for him to rest in while I'm at work. That bin is empty these days, you know."

"All right," agreed Bates. "Only it's so dark in that corner he can't see anything."

"No," agreed Rashe, voicelessly, "and nobody can see him, either, nor know for sure whether he's there."

To Maskell's newly awakened powers of thought and action, this ruse had presented itself as the one possible way to keep secret the knowledge of Parsifal's flight.

In early afternoon Boden drifted in. He looked into the yard, as usual, then turned to Rashe.

"Left Parsifal at home to-day?" he asked, blandly.

"Look here, Lawyer Boden!" blazed Maskell. "I've put up with a whole lot from you. You been snooping past my house every day, and you've been coming in here just when I'm busiest. You're pestering me all the time about Parsifal. Now you got to quit it! See? You got to quit it! There's nothing in Mr. Coyle's will that lets you plague me like this. You've seen for yourself that Parsy is alive and you've seen he's treated good. That's all the law calls for. Now suppose you leave me be for a while!"

"The purp is down cellar, just now," chimed in Bates, as the lawyer strode past him toward the street. "Run on down and have a nice look at him, if you like. I pretty near bust my own head on the beams and I barked both shins on the boxes, in the dark, down there to-day. Maybe you'd like to—?"

But Boden was gone.

For three hours, that night, Rashe maintained a useless groping search of woodland and of streets. He did no sleeping. At dawn he was astir once more. Again he drew blank. An hour before he was due at the office he paid another perfunctory visit to the Paignton dog pound.

On his yesterday's visit that unlovely symbol of canine tragedy had been empty of prisoners. To-day there was one lone dog in the inclosure—a stray the dog-catcher had come upon at dusk, nosing the lids off a line of alley garbage cans. With high-beating heart Maskell ran to the pen and peered over its high top.

Then he settled back on his heels; and his shoulders slumped, along with his hope-stiffened spine.

The lone and morbid occupant of the pound was a nondescript black brute that bore not one trace of resemblance to the lost Parsifal. Rather did he seem a throw-back in shape to some mongrel greyhound ancestor, and in color to a blend of Newfoundland and Manchester terrier.

Except for a few ragged patches of tan on his cheeks and upper forelegs, and grimily whitish chest and feet, he was a lusterless coal black. His hair was as short as a pointer's. His arched underbody and rat tail gave credence to the greyhound ancestry. He was an unbeautiful and miserable brute, as he stood with head and tail adroop in the dirty pen whence he was scheduled to pass so soon to the dog-hereafter.

"Poor cuss!" philosophized the pound-keeper, a lanky person who beguiled his many hours of leisure by reading a pile of second-hand educational books he had bought at an auction; and who as a result had begun to think .44-caliber thoughts with a .22-caliber brain. "I kind of hate this job of killing dogs. There'd be no need for pounds if folks would only stop preaching eugenics for humans, where it can't ever be enforced; and preach it for dogs, where it could be enforced real easy."

Rashe did not hear. He was in the grip of an inspiration so audacious, so breath-taking, that the Rashe Maskell of six months ago would have shrunk screeching from it. Slowly he exhumed from his trousers a ten-dollar bill and handed it to the pound-keeper.

"I'll buy that cur, and I'll take him along with me," said he, Napoleonically. "One dollar of this ten is his purchase price, by the laws of Paignton township and borough. The—the other nine dollars is yours, friend, on condition you keep your mouth shut about my buying him. I don't aim to get laughed at for spending money on a mutt; nor yet to be called an easy mark. But he looks—he looks so kind of desolate in there. Besides, he'll be comp'ny for my Parsifal. If anybody asks you, remember you haven't ever seen the cur. Nope, I don't aim to be laughed at."

Down the main street of Paignton, he led by a rope the

apathetic and cowed nondescript. To the office he hastened. As usual, he was the first to arrive. Furtively he
hunted for Bates's shears. With these he proceeded to
clip, raggedly and with purposeful awkwardness, several
swathes of the dog's already too-short hair. The marks
of this shearing showed the dirty skin under the dirty
black coat.

Next, faring to the cellar, Maskell gathered generous
handfuls of soft-coal dust and rubbed them vehemently
into the whitish portions of the animal's coat. His work
done, he turned the dog into the back yard and washed
his own filthily grimed hands.

Bates came in a few minutes later.

"Say, boss!" rasped Maskell, waving an indignant hand
toward the yard. "Look what a day in your corner coal
bin did to poor Parsy! Just look, will you? He must
have spent the whole day rolling in what dust was left in
the bottom of the bin. I couldn't get it out by washing.
It seemed to itch him so and tease him so bad, that I took
pity on him this morning, and I sheared him. But the
coal must have sifted clean through into the skin. He's
pretty near as black as he was before he was sheared.
Gee! but it's awful!"

Bates crossed to the window. Rashe breathed deep.
He had made his fast-rehearsed speech without forgetting
a word or a tone. The battle was on. Bates looked long.
Then he laughed longer.

"Wait till Saul Boden sees him!" he guffawed.

"Well?" shrilly challenged Rashe, his back to every wall
on earth. "Well, what then? What kick has Lawyer
Boden got coming to him? I haven't broke the terms of
the annuity, have I? You can testify I brought him to

the office every day, because I figgered he'd be safer than
he'd be at home and have more comp'ny here. You've
seen for yourself how well I've treated him while he was
here. You heard what Lawyer Boden said about powdered glass and chicken bones. You can testify I put
Parsifal down cellar because I was afraid he'd maybe get
poisoned. You can testify I've done every single one of
those things for his own good and his own happiness and
health. I cut off his hair because the coal in it hurt him
so and made him scratch and fidget himself. It isn't my
fault he looks like he does. He's still alive, isn't he? And
he's in good health, even if he does look like a scarecrow.
There wasn't anything in the will about not letting him
lie in the coal or about making him keep on looking
pretty. What kick has Lawyer Boden got? He can't
do a thing, and you know he can't."

Bates nodded and went back to his desk, still chuckling.

But Rashe was increasingly worried. Boden knew
much about dogs. If he should chance to know that a
close-shaven collie did not have a figure anything like
the dog in the office yard, then trouble must follow, with
much speed and in large quantities.

Rashe thought, and thought fast.   Then he went out
into the odds-and-ends shed. Ten minutes later Bates
saw him binding about the gloomy dog a makeshift blanket, formed of a cast-off burlap bag and several lengths
of twine. When this was girt in place, only the head
and neck and tail and legs of its wearer remained in
view. The rest of him might have been the size of a
prize hog or of a fence rail, for all the blanket's voluminous
folds revealed.

"He seemed kind of chilly," explained the red and

breathlessly triumphant Rashe as he came back to his
desk. "That burlap will keep him from catching cold.
So Lawyer Boden can't accuse me of neglecting him, can
he?"

Of old, Bates would have rebuked his employee roundly
for wasting so much office time on a mere dog. But now
he said nothing. He could not afford to scold or harass
Maskell, lest the man quit; and Bates could not spare him.
Rashe was becoming more and more useful every week.
In little more than a half-year he had, inadvertently, made
himself almost indispensable around the office and storeroom. He had blossomed into such a worker as employers
dream of and wake to miss. Bates had told his wife, in
bewilderment, of the change. She had answered:

"There's nothing queer about it. Hulda was a lazy
pest, when she worked regularly for us. Now, when she
comes to town for a day and drops in to see the children,
she fairly works her arms off, tidying up the house and
cooking surprise dinners for us. Lots of other house-
keepers can tell you the same thing about their maids.
Rashe Maskell hated to work, because he had to work
or go hungry. He'd never learned the fun of it. When
he didn't have to work any more, he learned that there's
heaps more fun in the right kind of a day's hustling than
there is in moping around the house. He's got the habit.
He couldn't stop now if he wanted to. I'd give him a
raise, if I was you, Thad. If you don't he's liable to
try his hand at working for someone else. Plenty would
hire him. Or he may start a feed business of his own."

Just before noon a vexingly familiar step sounded in
the little hallway that led from the street to the office.
Rashe had been waiting for it. Unostentatiously he got

up from his desk and went into the storeroom, leaving the door ajar. From that hiding-place he heard Bates's amused greeting as Saul Boden sauntered in. He heard Boden go over to the window. Then he heard the exclamation of stark amaze he had been waiting for; followed by Bates's laugh, punctuated expounding of the situation. Boden strolled away—again without a word.

Rashe nodded contentedly. The story, as told by Bates, was likely to carry more conviction than if he himself should tell it to Boden. For Bates related it with a full belief in its truth. To the best of the hay-and-feed man's knowledge, Parsifal had spent the preceding day in the cellar. To the best of his knowledge, Rashe actually had clipped him. There was confident belief in every word of the tale he was telling.

Maskell knew that even Bates's good-natured and heaven-sent credulity must crumple under the strain of believing that a permanently black and short-haired dog was the straw-colored and long-coated Parsifal. In time the worst coal dust departs from a coat. Something must be done. That was certain. Equally certain was it that there was nothing to do. Maskell's brain began once more to race.

During the afternoon Rashe made excuse to go over to the corner drug store, there to make purchases which called for all his new assurance. He recalled a process described to him by his long-dead sister to account for a sudden change in the color of her hair.

Maskell took the unresisting dog home that night, on the end of a rope. He led him indoors and moored him to the kitchen table. Then, filling the tub with warm water, he dowsed him into it. The dog kicked and struggled mightily, after the manner of most dogs thus immersed. But Rashe struggled with greater strength and infinitely more science. The scrubbing was achieved, with vigor.

The water at last gloomed black as ink. From the tub was lifted a dog whose white portions shone lustrously in the faint candle light, but whose black regions were if anything rustier and uglier than before. While the victim was still wet, Rashe fell to work on him with a stiff brush which he dipped every moment or two in a shallow bowl filled with two parts of peroxide of hydrogen to one part of ammonia.

At last the task was finished. Maskell had been working by the dim light of one candle, set at some distance from the tub, lest a splash of water put it out. He had not wished his labors seen from the road, so he had avoided needless illumination. Now he lighted the kitchen lamp and set it on the table, alongside the tub. As he did so he noted that the dog's front teeth were busily scissoring the thin cord by which Maskell had moored him to the table leg. Rashe scarce heeded this move. His eyes were fixed in stark astonishment on the dog himself.

Then, with a jerk, the frayed cord was parted. In a single shambling rush the dog had gained the unlatched kitchen door and had hurled himself forth into the night. With a bellow of incredulous horror, Rashe Maskell snatched up his flashlight and tore after the fugitive. Ahead of him seemed to stretch an eternity of nightmare dog-chasing.

Saul Boden entered his law office, above the Imperial

Motion Picture Theater, at nine o'clock next morning, to find Rashe Maskell awaiting him.

"Next time you nobble a dog, Lawyer," began Rashe, his eyeteeth showing under an uptwisted lip, "there's a couple of things you want to remember. First, get a dye that won't come off when hot water and ammonia is rubbed hard into it. Second, don't get a blabber to do the job for you while you hold the dog."

"Are you drunk," blustered Boden, "or only just crazier than usual?"

"Maybe both," answered Rashe. "Maybe neither. It's none of your business which I am. For the sake of argument, suppose we say I'm just a boob who had the wit—or the fool luck, or both—to put two and seventeen together and get the answer. Now you'll cut out all that noble indignation and you'll listen to me. If you don't, I'll go back to Lawyer Ebbet and let him go ahead with what he said he'd do if you wasn't reasonable. I called at his house late last night, and he gave me the advice I'm going to take. He says it isn't just legal, so he couldn't do it professionally. But he says he thinks you'll stand for it; and if you don't we can always go to court with it. Going to listen?"

With elaborate scorn, Boden nodded derisive assent. Rashe continued:

"Ever since you began having to pay me that seventy-five dollars a month, you've been honing for Parsifal to die or get lost or be bad treated or anything so's you could keep the cash. Well, he didn't die nor get bad treated, but he did get lost. You found him hunting for garbage on the street behind your office here. You grabbed him. You didn't have the nerve to kill him, or maybe you weren't crooked enough. But you figgered out a way to get him lost for good and all.

"You phoned to Doc Finper's roustabout—the cock-eyed chap that takes care of Doc's stable and his boarding kennels—the one you paid fifteen dollars to, last year, to dye the white gobs on your two Boston terriers' faces, so's they could get prizes at the Paterson show; and to fake the bridle of the rest of their coats. Doc heard about that terrier stunt, and he said he'd fire the roustabout if he ever did anything like it again. Remember? But you took chances on being able to bribe him to help you out once more. Likewise he did; he being a weak-kneed cuss at best. He came over here and he worked on poor Parsy for a couple of hours, shearing him and rubbing that terrier dye into him. You gave him thirty-five dollars for the job.

"Then you turned Parsy loose. You figgered his own mother wouldn't ever recognize him, looking like that, and that *I* sure wouldn't. Nobody would. You figgered rightly that he wouldn't have sense enough to go home; and even if he did, I wouldn't know it was him. You figured he'd get run over or get killed in the pound or go some place else, or even if he stayed alive, hereabouts, that nobody'd recognize him. I'd think he was a goner. You'd call on me to produce him. I wouldn't be able to. You'd stop paying me my annuity. Oh, it was all thought out grand! Only it didn't work.

"Then you saw that black dog in Bates's yard yesterday. That must have hit you hard—knowing I'd found him. You couldn't prove he wasn't Parsy.

"I took the dog home last night, and I gave him a good wash. Well, that wash turned him pretty near back to

his own color.   Then he makes a break to run away.   I
followed him.   He ran straight into his kennel yard and
inside his coop, and he turned to the right side of the coop,
where I always put his food dish so's the pigeons can't eat
what's in it.   Now no dog in the world but Parsy could
have known where that dish is always kept in the coop.
He went to it, straight.   He didn't stop to sniff around for
food.   He knew where I always put it.   I knew then it
couldn't be any dog but Parsy, no matter how he looked.
He was half starved.   I tied him up, there, with a chain.
Then I looked at the brush I had scrubbed him with.
It was all black with a smelly stain that wasn't coal dust.

"I hopped over to Doc Finper's with that brush, and I
told him all about it, and I asked him was it possible for
a collie to look like a skeleton greyhound if all the hair
was clipped off him.   And Doc said that's how a new
clipped collie 'most always looks.   So that settled that.
Doc smelt the stuff on the brush.   Then he sends for his
roustabout.   It seems it isn't a very common kind of dye,
and Doc knew the roustabout had had bottles of it in his
room in the barn.   Well, Doc sure sweated that feller
for a goal.   By the time Doc had got him like a wet rag,
him and I takes the roustabout over to Lawyer Ebbet's
house.   They drawed up a statement, and he signs it.
Then we hunted up old Sim Zabriskie.   The roustabout
says Sim was passing your door here when you and him
was turning Parsy out into the street, after nobbling him.
Sim remembered it.   That's another witness, Lawyer.
Now shall we talk terms?"

"Are you trying to blackmail me?" thundered Boden,
in his best police-court voice.

"I sure am," beamingly assented Rashe.   "Here's the

main idea: Doc Finper says a dog as strong and healthy as Parsy ought to have nine or ten more years of life in him, if he's well took care of—which same he will be. Now I'm sick of having you on my heels all the time and trying to pry Parsy loose from me and pry me loose from my annuity. It—it kind of pesters me. Here's what I'm asking you please to do—I'm asking you to sign some such a paper as this one that Lawyer Ebbet just gave me. It says that you'll compromise on that annuity business, if I'm willing to. Likewise, I am. It says we'll both sign a writing that you're to pay me my seventy-five dollars a month for six years longer, whether Parsy lives or not. At the end of six years, if Parsy is still alive, I'm to go on taking good care of him for the rest of his life, for no cash at all. Hey! don't go tearing that paper up, Lawyer! I'd have to go all the way back to Lawyer Ebbet and tell him to start my suit against you for whatever kind of fraud and malfeasance he told me it was; and I'll have to let him write that letter to the Bar Association about you that he said he wouldn't write unless you refused my terms. How about it?"

A full hour later, Rashe Maskell strolled into his employer's office. His face was one huge peaceful grin, punctuated by a long and garish cigar.

"He was fine about it," Maskell reported to the eagerly questioning Bates. "Didn't swear hardly at all. Not more'n twenty minutes or so, at most. Then, when he'd got all those bad words and hard names out of his heart, him and I went around to Lawyer Ebbet, and the paper was drawed up in due and ancient form, and we both signed it. I'm to get my cash every month for six years, whether Parsy gets over that cold from running outdoors after his hot bath or whether he don't. I'm—"

"Say, Rashe," cooed Bates, vaguely worried by the new air of independence his underling was exhaling along with his cigar smoke, "I been thinking it over, this morning. How about a third interest in this dandy little business of mine? Pay in your seventy-five dollars a month as you get it, and draw your salary till it's all in—plus a third-interest-percentage on the profits, of course—and," as Rashe hesitated, wordless, "and a raise of thirty-five dollars a month on your present pay? Think it over. Think it over mighty careful before you refuse."

Rashe thought it over, for the best part of a second, before closing with the offer. The delay was caused by his need to adjust the proposition to one he had been planning to make, along similar lines. But Maskell had dreamed daringly of asking for a fifteen-dollar-a-month raise and 20 per cent of the profits.

"Of course you can keep Parsifal in the back yard here, as usual," added Bates, by way of allurement.

"What'd I want of a measly dog here?" scoffed Rashe. "Let him stay home, where he belongs. It'd only waste our help's time, staring out of the window at him and petting him, and the like. I don't want any loafing around here. Let's understand that from the start, Thad."

VII. Ginger

DOWN the Closser hill bumped and squeaked Abel Shunk's rattletrap pound wagon. On the front seat of the sinister vehicle slouched Abel Shunk himself, the Hoytsburg pound master.

The antique wagon was closed solid with ripped but reinforced tarpaulin everywhere except at the back. There the tarpaulin was pierced by a little wire-covered door, skewered shut just now by an iron pin through its staple.

Abel Shunk would have polled just one vote in a contest for most popular man in Hoytsburg. That vote would have been his own. Not only was he a peculiarly dislikable man, but he plied a peculiarly dislikable trade, and he plied it in a peculiarly dislikable manner.

Every community must have its dog pound. That seems to be a needful misfortune. But Shunk took a delight in his dogcatching job; and he made it mightily remunerative.

He received from the village one dollar each for all dogs he caught. He received one dollar more for every

160

dog he put to death. In order to glean all possible dollars, he scoured the township in his ancient wagon, for stray dogs. He did more. He kept a sharp lookout for any dogs that chanced to wander unnoticed to the edge of their owners' premises. These he grabbed and clapped into the wagon, hurrying on, lest the kidnapping be detected. Many a dog reached the pound that did not belong there.

Then, complying with the law, Shunk sent out post-card notices to such people as were known to have dogs impounded, warning them that their pets must die unless the license fee and the pound fee were paid in forty-eight hours. But he had a way of neglecting to mail these cards early enough to allow of the redeeming of the dogs. He received no share of the license money or of the pound fee, and he craved the dollar for putting the captives to death. Altogether, he was making a good thing of his job.

To-day while Shunk rattled down the Closser hill on the beginning of his rounds, Ray Closser came out of the woods just as the cart jogged past. Ray halted, scowling instinctively at the driver. Shunk was not loved by the boys of Hoytsburg. More than one of their chum dogs had been seized by him and hurried to too-quick execution.

Shunk ignored Ray's glare and drove on. He was used to glares. Then, fifty yards farther down the hill, he yanked his bony horse to a sliding halt. Trotting up the road toward him was a collie pup.

The collie was perhaps eight months old. He was red-gold and white, and had sorrowful dark eyes and a whimsical expression. From the smear of mud on his left side and shoulder, it was not hard to deduce that he had fallen out of some speeding motor car which had rounded the sharp bend at the hill-foot with more speed than was safe for the equilibrium of a puppy standing up on the rear seat.

Unhurt and having recovered his breath after the fall, the collie was trotting up the hill in pursuit of the vanished car—whose driver had not thought to look around and assure himself his dog was still safe on the back seat.

It was the sight of this handsome young collie that had brought Shunk to a stop. Here was a potential two dollars. Out of the wagon climbed Shunk, grasping his big net. Cautiously and with honeyed words he sidled toward the puppy.

Now, in all his eight months of life the collie had known nothing from mankind except friendliness. True, this shambling and sidling and chirping human did not impress him at all favorably. Yet the man was a representative of the race which had always been the puppy's friend.

Therefore, waving his plumed tail, he advanced politely to meet Shunk. In another instant, he was struggling in the meshes of the net. A half minute later Shunk had dumped him, head over heels, into the darkly smelly recesses of the wagon, and was clambering on to his seat and gathering up the patched reins.

Seeking the only bit of light in that black and musty cavern, the astounded puppy ran to the back of the cart and peered out at the sunlit world through the wire door. His sorrowful dark eyes fell on Ray Closser, who was standing in the middle of the road behind him, mouth open and face working with helpless indignation. There was no other dog in the wagon. Thus the collie had full view through the wires.

Ray's irate gaze met the level glance of the pup. Ray had just finished his second reading of Dumas' *Three Musketeers*. Something in the grieved young collie's expression reminded him of the sorely beset Athos' brief look of appeal to d'Artagnan in the fight with Richelieu's guards —the look of one in dire need of aid but too proud to whine for it.

That was enough for Ray Closser. Scarce knowing that he had put his lawless impulse into action, he dashed after the slow and noisily lumbering wagon. The racket of wheels and creaky boards drowned his lightly running tread. Up on the rear step of the vehicle he leaped.

With one hand he drew out the fastening pin from the door's primitive iron latch. With the other he swung wide the door. Then he jumped back to the ground, snapping his fingers at the collie.

Instantly the puppy accepted the invitation. With one bound he had escaped from his jolting prison. But it is not easy to judge distance in jumping backward out of a moving vehicle. Ray was still clawing for balance in the soft dirt after his own descent from the step when a mass of dynamic red-gold fur landed from the open doorway square in the middle of his chest.

Ray sat down hard and suddenly in the dust, the dog atop him. The cart rumbled noisily on, its driver so busy scanning the highway and the fields ahead of him that he failed to note the loss of his two-dollar captive. A wagon whose bolts and woodwork and junctures are loose makes far too much noise in going down a bumpy hill to permit its driver to hear so silent a rescue as Ray Closser had effected.

Boy and dog rolled over in the dust for an instant. Then Ray sat up. So did the puppy. The latter seemed to regard the adventure as a most delightful romp. He offered Ray his two white little paws, one after the other, in fast succession, licking the boy's dusty face the while and wagging the plumed tail in high amusement.

Then Roy was up and had gathered the squirming puppy under one arm and was bolting into the roadside woods whence so recently he had emerged. There was danger lest Abel Shunk happen to look back, and Ray was resolved the pound keeper should not regain his lost prize.

True, an athletic fifteen-year boy can outrun the average middle-aged man, but he cannot outrun the law; and Shunk was certain to set the law on the track of his captive's rescuer if he should catch sight of the two there in the road. No need to try vainly to catch them by running. The law would do his running for him. It was best to avert trouble by getting out of the way while Shunk was still peacefully ignorant of the escape.

Keeping a screen of woodland between the dog and the departing cart, Ray set forth homeward. Here a new ordeal promised to await him; and he braced himself for it. His father had the name of being a hard man and, above all, a man who was fanatically upright in his dealings.

Ray would rather have taken a chance of Shunk's arresting him for theft than to face his father with the story he must tell if he wanted to keep the pup. Almost he regretted the impulse that had made him release the doomed little collie. Then he stiffened his shoulders and marched on, his lips very tight, his clenched hands very wet.

The puppy was swift to notice this subtle change in his new friend. Collie-like, he had the queer gift of reading even the best-suppressed human emotions, when he cared to. Now he whimpered far down in his furry throat as he trotted close to the boy's side, and he thrust his cool muzzle against the clenched hand nearest him. The contact gave Ray fresh resolution. Drawing a deep breath, he turned in at the lane that led to the rambling Closser homestead, atop Closser hill.

His father had just come in from overseeing some work in one of the lowest of his fields. Hot and a little tired, he was sitting down on the porch for five minutes' rest before going indoors. Here Ray came upon him.

Mr. Closser's eyes focused in surprise on the dog that was trotting along beside his son. In his youth he had bred collies for his own diversion. In this puppy he saw the best points of a high-quality show specimen, as well as the true "look of eagles" that marks the finest type of collie.

Before he could speak, Ray went straight up to him and began breathlessly to tell what had happened. His father heard him in silence, his eyes still on the young collie. The boy glossed over nothing he had done, but told the bald truth in as few words as possible.

"I was thinking," he finished, "that maybe you'd let me pay Shunk the two dollars out of my wood-chopping money, and—and keep the dog. He's awful good comp'ny. Not Shunk. The puppy is. I—"

"Shunk was going down the hill yonder?" put in Mr.

Closser. "You're sure that's where he picked up the dog? Think!"

"Yes, sir. Not more'n a furlong below here. Just alongside the wood-bunch down yonder. Do I have to—?"

"Shunk is pound master of the incorporated village of Hoytsburg," said Mr. Closser. "Of Hoytsburg and of nowhere else. The village boundary line is two hundred yards below the foot of the hill. If Shunk caught this dog halfway down the hill he was outside his own jurisdiction. He had no right to the dog."

"Dad!" exclaimed Ray, in unbelieving rapture. "Then I c'n keep—"

"And you have no right to him, either," went on the judicial tones. "From this mud on his shoulder, and the fact that the only mud puddle left within a mile of here is at the bottom of the hill, he fell out of some car that went around that turn down there too fast. It isn't the first time a dog has been spilled out there. Two of them were pretty badly hurt, last year, you'll remember. This dog belongs to the people who had him in their car, not to you."

The delight faded from Ray's face. Then he said, resignedly:

"Well, it's better'n if I had let Abel Shunk keep him and kill him. The people wouldn't ever have found him then. And for the matter of that, how are they going to find him now? That car may come from a hundred miles away. It may belong in New York or in Tuxedo or in—"

"Wherever the car belongs, its collie doesn't belong to you."

"But if the folks don't come back to look for him—if

maybe they don't think he's worth coming back to look for," hazarded the boy, "then could I please keep him, sir? He's such a grand little chap, and I—"

"How much do you suppose he is worth?" asked Mr. Closser.

"Him? Oh, quite a lot. He's a beauty. Most likely he'd be worth ten dollars. Maybe even fifteen. But if you'd let me take my wood-chopping money to pay them for him if they come for him and if they'll sell him to me—"

"You'll chop a good many cords of wood at the sum I pay you before you'll chop enough to pay for him. As high-class a collie as this one would be dirt cheap at two hundred dollars. I've seen worse pups sell for much more than that."

Ray's jaw dropped. His eyes bulged. Eagerly he scanned his father's face to see if Mr. Closser was joking. Then the boy stammered, incredulously:

"Why, dad, that's more'n a pretty good horse would bring, these days! A dog—"

"A typical registered stock collie costs a great deal more than 'a pretty good horse,'" his father explained, amused at the lad's crestfallen look. "For instance, if this pup keeps on as he has begun, and doesn't 'go coarse' or get snippy or thick or get a second coat that isn't as good as his first—in another six months he may be worth as much as five hundred dollars. Perhaps as much as a thousand dollars. He is a perfect show collie. Now do you think his owners aren't likely to make inquiries for him?"

The boy sighed and turned disconsolately away. The dog had sat down beside him and had laid a friendly forepaw on Mr. Closser's knee. Now he jumped up to follow his new master.

"Where are you going?" asked Mr. Closser.

"Down to the post office," answered the boy, glumly. "I'll put a notice there, about him. Folks always stop at a post office, when anything's been lost."

His father nodded approval.

"Leave the puppy here while you're gone," said he. "While Shunk has no sort of right to him, he may claim him if he sees him down there. Put up the notice. Describe him as a 'sable-and-white collie about eight or nine months old; blaze on foreface; full collar.' You can keep him till he is claimed, if you like. But don't get too fond of him. A dog like that isn't going begging, long. And we'll watch the 'Lost and Found' ads, too. That's all we can do about it."

For once Mr. Closser was mistaken. Weeks passed, and the puppy continued to "go begging." Despite Ray's neatly written signs on the bulletin boards of three near-by post offices, nobody arrived to claim the high-bred young collie.

Those weeks were a pure joy to Ray. For the first time in his fifteen years he was entering into the rightful heritage of every boy—the ownership of a dog. Since the death of the elderly mongrel which had guarded the Closser house for twelve years, there had been no dog at the homestead. That had been two years earlier. And, at best, the dull old cross-breed had never been any sort of a pal to Ray.

Now he found himself with a dog that was vibrant with life and brain and affection, that was even more eager to learn than was Ray to teach him. Boy and dog were inseparable. Day and night they were together. The collie slept on a rag mat at the door of Ray's bedroom, and was at his heels or romping in front of him all day. Ray named him Athos, after his worshiped Dumas hero.

Mr. Closser watched with concealed approval the way of the boy with the collie. He rejoiced to see that Ray was a born dog-handler and that he kept his temper and his patience in training his pet. Yet Ray's devotion to Athos worried the old man. He knew what a wrench it must be, some day, to the lad, to have the dog's rightful owners come in search of their lost thoroughbred.

The same thought sometimes clouded Ray's own happiness. But it did so less and less as the weeks passed and nobody came for Athos. Meanwhile, he was happier than ever he had been, and he and Athos grew daily to be closer chums.

During one of their woodland rambles—a mile or more beyond home and amid the rank forest which, to the north, rolls unbroken to the edge of Hoytsburg's outlying farms —they came upon a mild adventure. Boy and dog were swinging along the narrow path that wound through the woodland, Athos a few yards in advance of Ray.

Suddenly the collie checked his trot and stood with nostrils aloft, sniffing the still air. As he sniffed, the lips curled back from his white young teeth and the hackles on his back began to bristle.

He himself did not know what he smelled. But far back in his queer collie brain some long-dead ancestor's heritage whispered to him that he had caught the scent of a tribal foe. Wherefore he sniffed the harder and growled.

Ray noted his chum's odd change of demeanor, and instantly was as excited as the dog. He had the sense not to interfere, but stood waiting. Presently Athos dropped his nose to the ground and began to canter in a wide circle. The lad knew what this meant. His dog was once more reverting to ancestral tricks, to locate the smell that a vagrant puff of forest breeze had borne to him through the stillness.

Before the first half of the circle was complete Athos had found what he sought. His nose, close to the moist earth, told him that the creature whose scent he had caught had passed that trail.

Head still down, Athos galloped along this fresh trail, crashing through almost impenetrable thickets of hazel and witch elm and white swamp poplar, never swerving a hair's-breadth to either side nor pausing to verify the increasingly rank scent.

Almost at his tail crashed Ray Closser, risking a scratched face and a tumble in order to keep up with his questing dog. Thus the two forged their loud way through some fifty feet of dense copse. At the far end of this belt of undergrowth, they came out in a cathedral-like clearing, perhaps two hundred feet across, a natural glade carpeted with low huckleberry bushes and wild blackberry vines and white-man's-foot.

At the clearing's edge Ray halted in surprise. The dog kept on, trailing by sight now, and no longer by scent. In almost the center of the glade, alongside a rotting chestnut stump, something was thrashing about in the huckleberry bushes.

Here, months earlier, a farmhand had set a steel trap for foxes or for raccoons, or for whatever form of skin-bearing "varmint" might be lured by a lump of raw pork to set foot on its clumsily hidden spring. No such varmint had done so, a whisky-jack having flown deftly down and abstracted the meat without springing the trap.

For some reason the farmhand had neglected to come back for his futile snare. Rains had washed away the man scent from it. Leaves had blown across it, camouflaging its presence far more skillfully than could any human. So for months it had lain forgotten.

This morning a belated she fox, on the way back to her lair after a night's hunting with her quarter-grown cubs, had taken a short cut athwart the glade. Her left forefoot had missed the steel spring by an inch or less. Her left hind-foot had planted itself in the center of the pan. The trap had sprung.

The pain and shock had stunned her. For a fox is as high-strung and nerve taut, in its own way, as is its distant cousin, the collie. Then, coming to herself, she had struggled madly to get free. Rust and bad alignment had kept the antique trap's jaws from closing tight enough to snap her leg bone. But the serrated iron teeth were yet far too tight to permit of her breaking loose from their grip.

She had begun to quiet down to the strange fatalism of the Wild, when the scent and sound of dog and boy had made her crouch lower in abject dread.

Now that they had broken cover and could see her, she was roused to a fury of new endeavor. From side to side she flung herself, twisting, writhing, leaping, the rusted trap banging the ground behind her.

At her dashed Athos, all his hereditary instincts aflame. From time immemorial the fox and the dog have been mortal enemies, even as have been the dog and the wild

cat.   There is too much of the cat about the fox for the
dog to regard it with any natural tolerance.

Pluckily the vixen turned to the unequal combat.
Hampered by the trap and the chain, she none the less
ceased her useless efforts to get loose, and wheeled, snarling, to face the oncoming collie.   In gay excitement
Athos attacked.   Then, as he came within a few inches
of the pitifully defiant fox, he checked his rush and
stopped, irresolute.

Evidently he saw that his opponent was hampered and
could not well defend herself.   Even as many collies will
hold back from assailing a crippled or sick dog, so Athos
now abandoned his gleeful intention to do battle.

Head on one side and tail slightly awag, he stood looking inquisitively at the snarling little vixen so hopelessly
in his power.   Then he glanced back over his shoulder at
Ray, as though asking instructions from his human god.

Ray came forward, calling the dog back to him.   Like
Athos, his first eager excitement had turned to pity at
the spectacle of the plucky and fated beast before him.
Ordering Athos behind him and bidding him lie down,
Ray walked curiously forward to the stump.

As the boy drew near, the vixen shrank back.   Then
she gave a mad leap in the other direction, yanking the
chain and the heavy trap with her.   To the farthest limit
of the short chain she sprang in her effort to get away
from the oncoming boy.   The jump seemed to take her
last atom of strength, and of life as well, for she collapsed as the chain jerked her back, and she fell inert and
limp among the vines.

There she lay at full length, eyes shut, moveless.   Nor
did she stir as Ray stooped down and stroked her ruffled

fur. Compassion filled the boy's heart. She had been so game, so pathetically defiant! And that last supreme leap and the back jerk of the chain had apparently snapped her spine or her neck. She was lifeless.

Kneeling down, Ray felt for the trap jaws.

No sense in carrying her home for the sake of her pelt at this time of year. For in summer a fox's fur is "off prime" and of no cash value. In late autumn and in early winter such a skin as this vixen's would have brought from ten dollars to twelve dollars from any local fur dealer. The skin would then have been cured, and fitted with a few cheap snappers, and would have sold at retail for something more than sixty dollars, as a neckpiece.

But in that chicken-raising region there was a "bounty" of one dollar for the mask and ears of a dog fox and two dollars for those of a vixen, from the township Grange, at whatever time of year. So this vixen was well worth Ray's while. He spread out her fluffily limp body across his knee; and held it there with one hand while with the other he felt in his pocket for his knife.

As he did so, something far sharper than the knife blade pierced the fleshy part of his right hand, below the thumb. The "dead" vixen drove her razor teeth deep into the hand that held her. Instinctively Ray whipped back his lacerated thumb and started up. In the same fraction of a second there was a streak of rufous light across the clearing. The vixen, in one long jump, had landed far out of reach and was fleeing for cover in a lightning-quick scramble. Before Ray had gotten to his feet—before Athos had had a chance to spring up and give ardent chase—she had plunged into the thick leafage of the copse.

Ray took an uncertain step in pursuit. Then he stopped and stared goggle-eyed. For the cleared space seemed to his excited senses to be alive with whizzing little streaks of rufous color, all speeding frantically in the direction taken by the escaped fox.

The vixen's four cubs had been crowding whimperingly about their prisoned mother until the crashing of undergrowth and the scent of human and of dog had driven them to hiding. They had not deserted their luckless parent. But they had flattened themselves cleverly into the carpet of brambles and low bushes and rock-outcrops in the clearing.

Now, seeing the vixen take flight, they scurried after her.

Ray stared agape. Athos did not. With a dash and a deft scoop of the jaws he overtook and seized the rearmost cub of the four, at the very edge of the thicket. Ignoring the valiant snarls and murderous snaps of his prey, he bore his prize gleefully across the clearing to his young master.

Athos carried the cub by the nape of its furry neck, holding the squirming little creature daintily in his powerful jaws. In front of Ray the dog halted irresolute, the furious baby squirming tenfold harder than before and trying alternately to bite his captor and the boy.

Ray ceased sucking his torn hand and slipped out of his coat. Warily he wrapped the garment about the little fox, avoiding the pin-point teeth and muffling the infant's struggles in the folds of the coat. Then, with his new treasure, he started homeward, Athos bounding along in front and seeking from time to time to leap up and sniff at the writhing coat.

It had been a jolly exploit for both chums, if a painful one to Ray. But the boy did not heed the hurt. Always he had wanted a fox-cub to bring up. This was his chance to try certain training experiments an old trapper had once related to him.

Half an hour later, with thick leather gloves on his hands, Ray was fastening a strap collar around the cub's neck and chaining him to a kennel coop he had built for Athos and which the collie never used.

"There!" remarked the boy as he stood back and watched the fox's mad efforts to tear loose from the collar and chain. "In a few minutes you'll quiet down and be glad to lap that nice bread-and-milk. You'll be a lot happier here than if you were slinking out yonder in the woods, half starved and getting shot at by everyone who sees you. Your name is Ginger, because that's the color you are. In a couple of weeks you'll get to knowing that name. It didn't take me but an hour or so to teach Athos his name, but I guess collies are interesteder in learning than foxes are. Say, Athos! I pretty near forgot. Look here! *You're—not—to—touch—him!* Understand? *Leave him alone!*"

Athos understood. Thus had it been impressed on him not to chase the kitchen cat, nor to try to kill the Buff Orpington chickens which were Mr. Closser's chief pride in life, nor to harry the three calves in the paddock back of the barn.

But it had been a matter of small renunciation for the collie to obey these former prohibitions, compared with leaving alone this wild thing his nature urged him to destroy. However, as Ray repeated the command a second time, pointing alternately to the fox and to the dog,

Athos turned mournfully away, tail adroop, and went to lie down under the porch. And Ray knew the wise young dog would obey.

Thus began the domesticated life of Ginger, the quarter-grown red fox. Ray wasted no time before starting in to train him. As the boy had a way with animals and as he could control temper and impatience, the task was not as difficult as Ray had feared. Also it was interesting.

A fox is uncannily quick to learn—if he cares to learn. Indeed, there is no other animal with his natural brain and cunning and adaptability. Though sometimes he refuses to learn, yet oftener, with the right teaching, he learns with brilliant ease. And so it was with Ginger.

But if the fox learned from Ray, it was Ray who learned infinitely more from him. For example, he discovered that a fox is never natural and off guard in the presence of a human. A dog accepts a human as his god and lets his innermost character be known to his master. He has no secrets from him. But a fox will give no human the slightest inkling as to what is going on in his crafty brain.

Ginger obeyed Ray—at times—and even exhibited a certain affection for him. But Ray had a queer feeling that the fox was forever hiding from him his real nature and intentions and desires. There was an impalpable barrier between them that the boy could not break down.

Again, Ray learned that not only is a fox eternally on guard, but that the human who handles him must also be on guard. There is always the chance of a slashing bite or a snap for the wrist or the throat, even in moments of seeming friendly playfulness. By only one sign could Ray foretell these fierce onslaughts and avert them, and this sign he did not discover until more than one sharp bite had taught him how to look for it.

Ever he kept a furtive watch on Ginger's eyes. The eyes of a fox are slitted like a cat's. So long as those slits were visible, Ginger meant no harm. But as soon as the eye pupil began to wax round and to give forth a greenish glow, then danger threatened the luckless human who happened to be within reach of the vicious jaws. In this way alone could Ray foretell peril from his pet. In this way alone did Ginger betray any of his mental processes.

Let a stray chicken or sparrow venture within reach of the fox's chain, and murder followed almost sooner than Ray could follow the flash of the red body. But once when Ray's tame crow hopped inquiringly up to the very door of Ginger's coop, the fox paid no heed at all to the intruder. For a fox will not molest a bird of prey, nor so much as touch its dead body. Nobody knows why. Just as nobody knows why a fox, almost alone of all carnivora, loves to devour apples and grapes and why it revels in eating carrion, instead of merely rolling in it as does a dog.

As for Athos and Ginger, their mutual relationship was tolerant rather than cordial. Bit by bit they outgrew their first innate dislike for each other. In time they would even frolic together in puppy-like romps. But such romps were rare. As a rule there was scant association between the two distant relatives. Yet they were more friendly than otherwise. Only when Ginger undertook to snap or snarl at Ray did the dog fly at him in punitive wrath. Only when Athos herded away a bunch of heedless fowls from the radius of the long fox chain did Ginger growl at him in impotent rage. For the most part they got along comfortably together.

Then came a morning when Mr. Closser stood near the window of his bedroom, shaving. He saw Ginger fetch forth from his coop a bit of dry bread he had hoarded there from his supper. Crunching this bread between his teeth Ginger let its crumbs scatter loosely in every direction. Then he hopped up on the flat top of his coop and stretched himself out in the early morning sunlight as if for a snooze. Just as Mr. Closser was putting away his razor he saw one of his best Buff Orpington hens wander out in the dooryard in quest of food. Lured by the crumbs, she neared the fox kennel and began to peck.

Instantly the slumberous Ginger went into action. At one second he had been lying dead still on the coop roof. In the next second he had dropped with unbelievable swiftness on the plump hen, slaying her before she could squawk or so much as flutter. Then, glancing cunningly around to make certain he was not observed, he bore her body into his kennel.

Five minutes later a sullenly unhappy Ray was receiving a lecture on the folly of trying to tame the untamable, and was told how valuable was the slaughtered hen, compared with a miserable fox. Then his father retired to his own room to think the matter out. Mr. Closser did not believe in acting hastily. He must plan judiciously, beforehand, any sentence he might be going to impose.

Ray foreknew what that sentence was likely to be. He was certain his father would ordain that Ginger must die before the fox could wreak further damage, and that the skin's price must pay for the prize hen killed. The boy hurried out to the fox kennel. Ginger came forth to meet him, frisking innocently about his young master. Ray stooped down and patted him. Then, taking off the collar, he set the fox free.

Ginger pretended not to know he was loosened from that abhorrent chain. He gamboled the more gayly about Ray. Next he ran in a prancing circle about the boy. Then, as he began a second playful circle, he veered suddenly to the right and bolted for the distant woods. Athos made as though to give chase. Ray whistled the collie back to him.

"Let him go," he bade his dog. "It's better than to have to shoot him. But, gee! Look how he is streaking it! Running away from us, after all we've done for him. If we'd done half as much for any *dog,* Athos, that dog would stick to us all his life. Let him go. You and I are the best chums for each other, without any thieving rank-smelling fox to play with. Now let's go and tell dad; and I'll take my licking."

Twenty miles across country—twenty miles as the crow is supposed to fly and doesn't—at that minute, fifteen of the ultra-exclusive Cestus Country Club's members were busily organizing a hunt association. Five of the members spent much of their time in England. There they had learned to ride to the hounds and to love the stirring joys of fox hunting. Now they were forming a local hunt club, taking advantage of the country's rolling sweep of cleared fields and of the abundance of foxes.

A pack of hounds was imported at huge cost. A professional huntsman and two kennel men were imported at even higher cost. And correct "pink" (really "red") hunting coats were ordered at one of the few American tailors where such unfamiliar costumes can be turned out as satisfactorily as at Poole's. All that remained was the opening of the fox-hunting season. Imported hunters champed in the Country Club stalls. Members furtively questioned the huntsman or read all they could on hunt lore in the club library.

Marvin Heyde, the newly elected master of the hounds, was thrilled at his access to importance. He yearned for his first day in the field as commander of this time-honored sport. He was grateful that two seasons of inexpert riding to English hounds had taught him at least the rudiments of his professional duties as master.

On a brisk October morning—months after the escape of Ginger—the entire club assembled for its first hunt. Out rode the phalanx of red-coated sportsmen, their horses atingle at the bracing air and at sight of the hounds. The huntsman and his assistants raked copse after copse while the riders, at Marvin Heyde's direction, sat their fidgety horses, on the crest of a knoll, and waited.

At ten promising coverts the hounds drew back. The hunt, by this time, was some miles from the clubhouse. As they surged toward the eleventh covert the pack's leader gave tongue. With white tails waving, the twenty hounds sprang forward, hot on the trail. Into the copse they crashed—into it and through it. At the same moment the tremblingly watchful Marvin Heyde could see a wisp of yellow-red slip out of the copse at its far side and make off across a field toward the nearest patch of woods.

"Gone away!" bellowed Heyde, setting spurs to his mount. "Gone away! Yoicks!"

Shouting all the hunting terms he could call to mind, he spurred down the slope and in pursuit of the far-off fox. Already the pack had fought its way through the copse and was stringing out into the field, hunting by eye now as well as by scent. Fast they bore down on the fleeing fox. But the fox whipped through a great tangle of briers and thorn, in midfield, without so much as breaking his stride. The English-bred hounds, unused to this sort of obstacle, were checked while they plowed through or skirted the formidable mass of bramble. By the time they streamed out in pursuit once more, the fox had gained a long lead on the foremost of them.

Followed miles of chase which did all manner of things to both riders and dogs. The hounds were unaccustomed to the country. The riders, for the most part, were unaccustomed to fox-hunting. The fox was accustomed to traveling fast and warily. His was the advantage.

He led the chase at one time in a détour, and whizzed past the lair of a skunk, too swiftly for the den's occupant to get into action. The first few dogs were less lucky. Automatically, they dropped out of the chase, their sense of smell damaged beyond all immediate repair and their zest of battle gone. By the time the remainder of the pack could cast about and recover the fox's scent through the far more compelling and pervasive odor of the skunk, the fugitive had gained a full mile on them.

Later, when he seemed in fresh danger of being pressed too closely, he détoured again, and leaped high over the body of a half-waked and cranky porcupine. Not a single fast-bristling quill touched him. The hounds poured on in pursuit. Several of their front rank came in violent contact with the porcupine, which, in the confusion of the race, they mistook for their prey. They were undeceived in a hideously painful manner. Thus, five more of the dogs ceased to pursue. Three more were mired in a bog over whose alternate half-submerged logs the fox fled with ease. Other hounds lost the scent or lost their way or lost interest. A few survivors stuck stubbornly to their task.

The fate of the dogs was easier than that of the riders. At first Marvin Heyde had bawled over his shoulder:

"Don't ride over the hounds! Don't spoil your own sport, that way!"

There was no further need for such exhortation. The hunt had strung out like feathers in a gale. One by one, horses had pulled up, dead lame, or had sent their riders over their heads in refusing some stiff fence or ditch. Four steeds had mired down in the slough through which the fox had led the dogs. Now, Marvin Heyde and the huntsman and one lone member of the club remained within cheering distance of the three hounds which still kept on.

Thus far the fox had been the sole member of the party to get any fun out of the day's outing. But the fox himself was wearied. No longer did his whalebone muscles respond gladly to the strain put upon them. Run as he would—double as he would—trick as he would—he could not shake off the heavy-dewlapped, tick-faced leader of the pack, a veteran dog with the heart of a lion. Wherever the tired fox led the chase, that tireless hound was at his heels.

Mile after mile slipped past. Of the dogs, the tick-faced leader alone had survived their grilling ordeal. Of the riders, Marvin Heyde and the huntsman stayed in the

race. The huntsman remained because he was an inspired equestrian and well mounted. Heyde kept on, by
virtue of a grand horse and unbelievable good luck.

Spent, dizzy, panic-smitten, the fox put on a last burst
of speed. No chance to hunt for "earths" or for other
woodland refuge, with that inexorable hound hot behind
him and the two horsemen lumbering on in the rear. In
his extremity, the fox bethought him of a desperate
chance. He knew well where he was. He knew well that
there was a haven of safety for him a bare furlong ahead.
Not among his own kind, but among humans.

When Ginger had escaped from his loathed collar and
chain he had not expected to risk capture by going again
within five miles of the Closser homestead. But now the
memory of that safe kennel coop and the friendly Athos
and the protective young human master who had been so
kind to him—these things bulked large in his frightened
mind. Ray and Athos assuredly would protect him from
his pursuers. Later it would be possible to escape, as
before, from bondage. Just now the kennel seemed to
Ginger the safest and most desirable spot on earth.

Ray was coming home from high school, Athos having
run out to meet him at the top of the Closser hill.
Together they crossed the yard toward the kitchen door.
Halfway, Athos stopped, stiffening and lifting his head to
sniff the frosty air. Something had struck his hearing
and his nostrils at the same time. Ray, listening, heard
thumpy sounds in the patch of woods beyond the home
tract—sounds as of running and the splintering of twigs.

Then out into the open flashed a limping and bedraggled fox. Straight toward the boy and the dog he galloped. Athos, with a growl, ran to meet him. But before

he could catch up with the unafraid creature he dropped to a walk and began to wag his tail. Athos had recognized an old acquaintance.

Paying no need to the collie, Ginger pattered past him and up to Ray. He curled himself into a ball close between the astonished lad's feet, and snarled pantingly toward the patch of woods he had left.

Before Ray could speak or move, out from the trees lurched a big fox-hound, heavy of dewlap, ticked of face. Giving tongue, he made for the fugitive fox at a tired canter. Athos sprang forward to repel this canine intruder from the land he himself had been taught to guard so zealously.

He and the hound came together with a crash, midway in the dooryard. Then both lunged for an opening. The hound, angry at being balked when his prey was at last run to a standstill, was in no wise averse to giving battle to this much slighter dog. Growling, he launched himself at Athos. But Athos did not chance to be there when the heavy bulk reached the spot where he had crouched for a spring. The collie had slipped nimbly aside and had secured a grip on the side of the charging hound's neck.

To the ground rolled the two dogs in ferocious battle. Out from the woods pressed two horsemen and bore down on the warriors.

"View halloo!" croaked Marvin Heyde at sight of the fox cowering between the dumfounded boy's feet.

The huntsman wasted no time in words. Riding down on the dogs, he caught the bleeding hound by the nape of the neck and lifted him across his saddlebow. Athos leaped after his departing enemy, but Ray found voice to call him back. Obediently, though sore disappointed, the collie went over to his young master.

Ginger, seeing that the pertinacious hound was at last out of the running, oozed unostentatiously from sight around the corner of the house and thence to the woods on its far side.

Marvin Heyde came riding up to the boy and the dog. His glazed eyes, peering out of a red and dust-caked face, were riveted on Athos. His first hoarse words were:

"Where did you get that collie?"

With sinking heart Ray told him. This was the hour he had been dreading for more than six months.

"I thought so!" exulted Heyde. "I knew I couldn't be mistaken. That's my Elderkin Guardsman. I'd know him anywhere. I ought to. I bred him. I was taking him home, after the Ridgewood show, when I missed him out of my car. I advertised for him in the Paterson papers. I supposed he must surely have fallen out near there. I never thought he'd gotten as far as this or I'd have advertised in your—"

"Say!" broke in the boy, his voice wabbly but terribly eager. "Say! Athos has been my chum for more'n six months. He and I are the best pals there are. I—I don't know what either one of us'd do without the other one. Dad says he was worth one hundred and fifty dollars when he came here. If you'll take that for him, I'll pay you all the cash I have, and I'll come and work out the rest of it for you. How about it?"

For answer, Marvin Heyde shook his head contemptuously and whistled the dog to him. Athos stared calmly at the red-faced man, then walked back to Ray and stood beside the boy. The dog remembered Heyde. He remem-

bered him well. He recalled him as a semi-stranger who
had deigned occasionally to visit his own collie kennels
and who took no pains to make friends with his dogs.
Athos saw no reason to go to him.

At this insolent disobedience Heyde's temper went by
the board. It had been a wearying and painful and farci-
cally disappointing day. As its climax, his own collie
turned its back on him and went to this farm boy. With
riding crop upraised, Marvin Heyde pricked his horse
forward. With a swish the crop smote Athos across the
back. It was raised for a second blow, when the dog
sprang furiously at the rider. Athos had never before
been struck. The blow filled him with red rage. From
Ray he would have endured anything, but it was not on
the free list for a stranger to beat him.

Ray ran forward and dragged away the frantic dog.
As he did so the crop struck the boy full athwart the face.

He reeled back, then dropped the snarling collie and
whirled on the man who had struck him. But at the same
instant a hand thrust him aside. Mr. Closser had come
out of the barn, at first sound of the commotion. Behind
him ran his hired man. Now, with a look on his quiet face
that Ray had never before seen there, the old man was
accosting Marvin Heyde.

"In this state," said Mr. Closser, forcing his voice to
steadiness, "it is a serious matter to strike a minor. My
man and I can prove that you struck my son. We can
prove you did it, unprovoked. We can prove more. We
can prove you struck him when he was trying to keep
your own dog from tearing you. Also, we can prove that
you and that other man have committed willful trespass
in riding on my posted land. The brutal hitting of my

son will land you in prison, with any jury of fathers. The trespass suit will cost you more than the value of this dog."

Marvin Heyde sat glowering uncertainly. A vague idea that the boy was reinforcing the dog's assault on him had led Heyde to deliver that second blow. He had sense enough to realize now in what light a jury would regard the action. Ray looked up wonderingly into his father's bone-white face, his own face's sting and bruise forgotten. Athos tugged to get at the assailant of his young master.

"You say this dog is yours?" went on Mr. Closser. "My son thinks more of him than of anything else. I shall be willing to offer you a fair price for the collie, perhaps, when—"

"Dad!" cried Ray in ecstasy.

—"When my civil and criminal suits against you have been settled," continued Mr. Closser.

Marvin Heyde gurgled. He made as though to speak; then, with a twitch of the rein and a dig of the spurs, he galloped to the highroad and out of sight; the huntsman following.

"Son," observed Mr. Closser, watching them go, "you've got a new dog. His name is Athos. You never really owned him before, because there was always a chance the owner would come for him. That chance is gone. To-day, Athos is paid for. His owner—whoever he is—will never dare come back to claim him. If he does, he will have to identify himself. As soon as he is identified there will be a criminal suit and a civil suit for him to incur. And he knows it. They and the publicity will cost him, together, more than any dog is worth to him. Go and wash the blood off your face. Take Athos along with you."

VIII. Foster Brethren

BOBBY THERON called Thor his twin. For the big gray collie had been born on Bobby's twelfth birthday. Thor's mother, Lassie, had six other pups, born that day; pups for which Lassie's master, Colonel Theron, visioned bright futures as farm workers.

But six of the seven pups died—for no special reason—within twenty-four hours after they were born. A collie pup is the easiest or the hardest of all dogs to rear. Nobody knows why. A knowledge of the secret would cut down the price and quadruple the number of collies in no time.

It was no fault of Lassie's that six-sevenths of this litter died. She was a born mother. Once she had even carried a squalling baby kitten to her brood nest and insisted on bringing it up with some new-born pups. Now, she grieved pitifully over the six dead infants and she concentrated all her care on the seventh.

Colonel Theron had promised Bobby one of the pups. When six of them died, the colonel stuck to his word. He gave his son the only surviving puppy—the fuzzy gray youngster that was a throw-back to his merle grandsire.

The day was Thursday. Bobby had just begun the study of mythology at school. His teacher had told him that "Thursday" was derived from "Thor's day" and was named in honor of the Norse god of thunder. There was a terrific thunderstorm that morning. So Bobby accepted the omen and called his puppy Thor.

Among other devastative things wrought by that thunderstorm was the smashing of a giant oak, in the forest, a mile behind the Theron farm. This oak had ever reared its crest high above the neighboring trees. Bobby and his father were standing at an upper window of the farmhouse, watching the storm, when they saw it struck.

As soon as the sky cleared they walked out to get a closer view of the scene.

The oak had crashed down athwart the lesser denizens of the forest with the force of a falling tower, leaving a swath of shattered limbs. It had done more. Its trunk had smitten squarely against an overslanting outcrop of granite, smashing it and driving part of it into the earth.

From beneath this mass of broken stones issued a trickle of blood and the stifled moaning of some stricken thing. On the instant Colonel Theron and Bobby were feverishly at work hauling aside such of the rock particles as were not too much for their combined strength. With bare hands, and then using saplings as levers, they toiled. Presently they came upon what they sought and upon a sight that told its own story.

A huge black bear—one of the very few still left in that recently-cleared region—had chosen the leafy hole beneath the granite slant as her brood nest. Here she lay crushed and dying. Under her side lay a killed cub. At sight of the man and the boy the mother bear sought to rear her bloody head and shoulders in defense of her young. The effort was too much for her. She slumped back, dead.

But her futile motion had shown the onlookers a second new-born bear cub, hitherto hidden by his mother's head. This baby had somehow been wedged under a spur of slanting stone which did not crumble with the rest. He was unhurt—a puny and naked and blind and tiny morsel of life.

Bobby felt a lump in his own throat at the mother bear's instinctive attempt to shield her young, even in the moment of death. With this twinge of pity still stirring him, he stooped and picked up the one surviving cub and cuddled it gently under his coat.

"What are you doing that for?" asked his father, looking up from his calculations on the value of the dead bear's off-prime pelt and flesh. "It would be more merciful to knock him in the head. He'll starve without his mother."

"If Lassie would adopt a baby kitten, there's no reason she won't adopt a baby bear," answered Bobby. "She's so unhappy over her six puppies dying, that she'll maybe like to have this new baby to bring up."

Colonel Theron was on the point of forbidding such an absurd project. Then he remembered it was his boy's birthday and that Bobby's impulse of kindness was more or less commendable.

"All right," he assented. "Only, don't feel bad if Lassie eats him or if he starves. One of those two things is due to happen. I never heard of a dog nursing a bear."

"I did," said Bobby, eagerly. "I read it in one of those

old trapping books in the school library. If one dog did it, another one can."

He was right. After a doubtful preliminary sniff at the hairless little creature that reeked of the wilderness, Lassie's all-encompassing mother instinct asserted itself. She forbore to thrust away the hungry little thing which Bobby had laid close to her udder.

Thus it was that a black bear and a gray collie came to be foster brothers. Both throve apace under the nourishment that had been planned for seven ravenous pups. After the first few hours, Lassie did not seem to remember which of the two was her own baby and which was the wildling. She lavished on both alike her solicitous mother care.

If Lassie did not realize increasingly the difference between her nestlings, she must have been blinded by affection. During the first few days there was no vast divergence between the helpless little fellows, except that one looked like a blind and grayish rat, while the other looked like a rat that was not only blind, but hairless. Then, day by day, the change grew stronger.

At the end of eleven days, Thor could see. (In spite of tradition, a collie pup's eyes open oftener on the eleventh day than on the ninth.) At the end of three weeks he was stumbling clumsily around the brood nest on wavering feet. Also he was learning to lap milk and he was beginning to look less like a rat than like a dog.

But up to the fifth week the bear remained sightless and nude and utterly dependent on Lassie for everything. By that time Thor was weaned and was full equipped in a fuzzy coat of silver-and-snow. Patiently Lassie cared for the helpless bear, long after Thor had no further use for her except as a teacher and a playfellow.

Yet to Bobby Theron it seemed almost no time at all before the cub had taken Lassie's place as playfellow to the collie pup. Though the bear was slow to start growing, yet when once he had begun he made mighty advance.

Bobby named him Ursus. His teacher told him it was the Latin for "bear." The boy was at the exciting point of education when he made use of every interesting name or word he picked up at school.

Ursus and Thor were adoring pals to each other, never happy unless they were together. They romped and played by the hour, none too gently; getting into hot little gusts of temper when a pinch or a scratch or a tumble was over-vehement; battling doughtily for a moment or so, then forgetting their wrath in some new twist of the game.

It was pretty to see them roll over and over in a scrambling embrace or chase each other around the kennel yard. Neighbors used to drop in to watch the oddly matched playmates. The first time, presumably, that Thor realized his chum was not like himself was the day Ursus first tried to climb a tree.

The bear paused in a race around the yard and began gravely to shin up an oak sapling which grew there. Slowly and hesitatingly and right awkwardly he ascended the slender trunk. Thor watched with eyes of dumb amazement. Then he, too, rushed at the tree and tried to run up its side. A fall on his furry back rewarded the effort.

Breathless and bruised, he burst into falsetto barks of wrath and leaped upward again, this time for the bear. His milk teeth seized Ursus by the stumpy tail and hung on. Ursus struggled to maintain his new-found grip on the trunk. Then the twenty-pound weight was too much for him. Down he fell, atop of Thor. A fierce combat waged for several seconds, until both warriors chanced to see a cat mincing along just outside the yard's wire fence. With tacit agreement they abandoned their scrimmage and dashed harrowingly at her.

But that first climb was the forerunner of many such an ascent. Worriedly, Thor would lie at the tree-foot and watch the clumsy but sure progress of his chum toward the upper branches. Thus he would lie, in patient sorrow, till Ursus came slowly down to earth again, hind-quarters first, with much loud scratching of the tender bark.

In their rough-and-tumble play, bit by bit Ursus's increasing strength and size gave him an ever greater advantage over his collie friend. Also, he had a quite bewildering way of using all four feet as weapons as well as his teeth; while Thor—like other dogs—could rely only on his jaws for offensive work. At close quarters Thor was no match for the bear. But at footwork, and at flashing in and out, Ursus was his hopeless inferior. Thor discovered this. Nine times in ten he would dance around his gawky opponent, flashing in to nip the fat Ursus and then slipping safely back out of range of the bear's short arm swipes and futile bites.

The tenth time, it was another story. Once let Ursus get a grip on the collie or land a swinging blow on him, and Thor had not the remotest chance against the bear. But all their mock-fighting and rare flashes of temper were governed by mutual good-fellowship that astonished the human onlookers. The two youngsters had a deep and genuine love for each other.

For months the young bear lived happily enough in his kennel yard. Meanwhile his education and Thor's had begun. While Ursus spent all his time in the fenced inclosure, Thor spent more and more hours outside of it.

Bobby Theron had not only made a house dog of his big gray collie, but he and his father were teaching Thor to herd sheep and cattle. Not until he was a year old, and as fleet and wiry as a wolf, did they trust him to drive hogs. Not that he could not have mastered that duty as readily as sheep-and-cattle herding, but because of its peril to himself.

A hog is neither a safe nor an easy animal for a dog to manage. A drove of pigs, such as Colonel Theron kept in his east orchard and low bog lot, cannot be turned and controlled as can even the most recalcitrant cattle. A collie can learn with ease to avoid the flying heels or tossing horns of a cow, and to nip or bark her into line. A hog is different.

There is something latently murderous about an unpenned hog, especially a hog that is accustomed to root for a living and to roam at will. The tough hide is hard to hurt by even the sharpest nip. The teeth are rendingly terrible. There is a vicious devil lurking behind the red-rimmed little pale eyes.

Yet, when he was a little over a year old, Thor was taught hog-driving. He made a gay and gallant job of it, though in the bottom of his stout heart he loathed the task. Instinctively he seemed to realize its stark danger, and the fate that would he his if he should slip or lose his balance on the slimy bog footing, when a hog or a group of hogs chanced to turn on him, as often happened during a single drive from marsh to pen.

The life of a farm collie, in those days, on a big farm

in the new-cleared region, was no flowery bed of ease.
But Thor reveled in it all—except in the hog-driving.

Bobby was busy, in his own few spare hours, educating
Ursus. But the bear's education was purely ornamental.
Bobby had a gift with animals. He had the knack of
making them understand what he wanted them to do, and
then, as a rule, of being able to make them do it. This
with no cruelty or flare of anger, but by dint of gently
firm patience.

For instance, he taught Ursus to stand up and beg, to
turn around, at command, on his hind-legs; to roll over,
to wrestle, to do a score of other simple tricks. It was
a pretty sight to watch the boy put the huge brute through
his paces, with Thor standing at one side, his head cocked
critically, and with the bear enjoying the performance as
much as did either of the others.

So things went on for the first eighteen months of
Ursus's life. In all that time it had never once occurred
to the captive bear that he was not free. But one day, in
trying to slap a bumble-bee that had alighted on the wire
of his yard, Ursus made a rent in the netting that a man
could have walked through.

He crawled out through the ragged and jagged aper-
ture and made his way to the road. There he encountered
a passing farmer, whose horses promptly ran away.

The farmer was thrown out and hurt. He threatened
suit and he made a complaint to the selectmen of the
township. True, Ursus had been caught and returned to
his yard within five minutes of his escape. But the mischief was done. Colonel Theron was notified officially
that he was maintaining a dangerous wild animal and he

was instructed either to shoot the bear or to place him in safe confinement.

Accordingly, Bobby and his father rigged up an empty box stall as a cage for Ursus, knocking out enough of the barn wall at one side of the cage to make a barrier of heavy stakes. These stakes were less than a foot apart. The bear could not possibly slip through them, though Thor could and did wriggle his own lithe bulk in and out of the cage at will.

In this cramped space Ursus discovered for the first time that he was a prisoner. His collie chum could come and go at will. The bear could not. This knowledge and the lack of exercise and advancing maturity combined to sour the captive's temper.

It is always so with a tame bear. Let him be brought up with the wisest and most friendly care, the time will come when the wilderness will reclaim her own—when he will forget he is a pet and become a menace. It is so with every wild animal. He is man's servant only on sufferance and for a limited time. Soon or late he will escape or he will attack.

Luckily for Bobby Theron, the bear escaped before he could so far forget his fondness for his master as to attack him.

For perhaps two months Ursus sulked in that miserable stall-cage, with only Thor's companionship and Bobby's occasional visits to amuse him. As the spring farm work was at its height, Bobby was able to spend little time with him. Thor, too, was always at Bobby's heels. The lonely Ursus moped; then by degrees he grew savage.

One night he tried to break or bite the tough hickory

bars of his cage in two. Failing, another idea came to him. He shambled across to the stall door. Unable to push it down, he stooped, hooked his claws under it, and lifted it bodily from the hinges. One thrust of the shaggy black shoulders and he was loose in the barn. A second mighty shove burst the rotting lock on the barn's outer door.

Ursus ambled through to freedom. The night was moonlit. The nearby forest was full of alluring smells and softly whispering invitation. Head down and big body swaying, Ursus lurched across the acres of cleared ground toward the woodland where he had been born.

Never had he been forced to find one mouthful of food for himself. Yet, before he had advanced a furlong into the forest, some instinct made him halt and turn over a rotting log. From beneath it he scooped a handful of fat white grubs and ate them with a delight he had never felt for his farm food.

Thus it was that Ursus returned to the wild; mysteriously able, as have been hundreds of other forest-born creatures in like situation, to forage richly for himself and to keep out of the way of humans.

Next morning Bobby was keenly unhappy at his pet's departure. He had grown fond of the clown-like animal whose puny life he had saved nearly two years earlier. Colonel Theron did not share his son's unhappiness. He was relieved that Ursus had solved his own problem by escaping.

The bear had been a useless and expensive luxury at the thrifty homestead. There was always danger, too, of his getting his owners into trouble with the law. Bobby was so attached to him that the colonel had not liked to suggest the bear be killed for his rather valuable pelt.

A century earlier the colonel's grandfather had founded a tidy little fortune by purchasing black bear skins from Indian trappers and selling them to exporters. In those days there was an insatiable demand for such fur. No fewer than twenty-five thousand black-bear pelts had been sent yearly, from this country, to England alone.

Well, Ursus was gone. That was all there was to it. Presently Bobby reconciled himself to his loss. He and Thor were the only two that had cared for the bear. Bobby had other things to think of. Yet it puzzled him that Thor showed no greater sorrow over his beloved chum's vanishing. The collie did not seem to miss Ursus at all; though, on the farm, they had been inseparable.

The reason Thor did not grieve for losing his pal was that he had not lost him. He knew perfectly well where Ursus was. Before daybreak on the morning after the bear's escape, the collie, in his patroling of the farm, had come upon his scent.

He had followed it and had caught up with his friend as Ursus was completing the robbery of a bee tree. He and Thor feasted happily, side by side, there in the gray dawn, on giant hunks of sticky honeycomb, undeterred by the assaults of such few bees as followed their treasure from its broken hollow limb to the ground below.

Scarce a day passed when Thor did not find time for a romp or a hunt with Ursus in the forest. Always it was ridiculously easy to pick up the bear's trail and to find him. Ursus was delighted to be found. Often he lurked for hours at the very edge of the woods, hoping his scent might attract Thor to him—as usually it did.

To Ursus, the humans at the farm and the life he himself had led there were growing vague in memory. He felt the natural distaste for them that is the heritage of woodland creatures. Existence in the food-rich forest was an endless joy. He had no mind to jeopard it by letting any human catch sight of him or by revisiting his old home.

But Thor was different. Ursus loved the collie that had been his foster brother and his daily playmate. Perhaps it was the far-back strain of the wild, hidden in every collie, that made the bear continue to hanker for the companionship of the dog. In any event, the chumship increased rather than diminished.

True, there were things about this new Ursus which puzzled Thor; as when, in late autumn, he found the bear one day chewing and swallowing great mouthfuls of pine needles and hemlock twigs.

Ursus was soggy with fat at this season—the fat which was to carry him alive through the long cold season of hibernating. Now he was gorging the evergreen food which was to stuff his stomach throughout the hungry months—the stuffing which he would eject disgustedly from his mouth on the first warm day of very early spring.

On another daybreak Thor trotted to the woodland and caught Ursus's trail, as usual. It led him through the bitter cold and driving snow to a shale hillock against whose southerly base lay a big windfall.

Daintily the collie made his way over the fallen trunk to a low-apertured little cave behind it, completely hidden from casual view. In the back of the cave lay Ursus, huddled in a corner and as motionless as the dead. In vain did Thor sniff at him and even paw his fat sides to awaken him.

His chum was asleep and would not or could not be

roused. But he was alive. Thor was not worried. Only he felt strangely lonesome as he trotted back to the farm and to his day's work.

Again and again during the long icy winter Thor made his way to the cave behind the windfall. Something seemed to tell him that his comrade would come to life again.

One muggy dawn in early April, when the forest was adrip and misty with unseasonable heat, Thor neared the windfall in time to see Ursus crawl atop it. The bear was nauseated, bone thin, weak as a sick cat. Together the chums ranged the woods for food that morning, but at a snail's pace. And so recommenced their forest friendship.

One day when Ursus had been gone for perhaps two years, Colonel Theron rode in to the village courthouse as witness in a land-boundary case. The hired man was busy in the south mowing, nearly a mile from the house. Bobby—now nearly sixteen—set off, across lots, to join the man, Thor, as ever, at his heels.

The boy's course took him alongside the tight-fenced bog meadow where rooted at this season some twenty of the Theron hogs. Bobby paused to note with surprise that not a hog was in sight. Closer inspection showed him the reason.

At the forest side of the meadow some uneasy pig had rooted away at the bottom rail of the ancient fence until the wormy wood had split asunder. The pig had tried to wiggle through the opening. The leverage of his tough back had broken the rail above. That was enough. He had blazed a path that any hog might follow.

Indeed, every hog had followed it. All twenty had rioted through the gap and into the lush forest beyond. Not one was in sight, though a blind puppy might have followed the drove's devastating trail into the heart of the woodland.

Had Colonel Theron been at home he would have let the hogs root there in the mast and the mold all day, and then would have had Thor round them up and drive them back to their pen in late afternoon when they should be tired and full of food.

But Bobby had all the conscientious energy of his father, without the latter's long experience. The hogs had gotten away. Perhaps, like Ursus, they might never return nor be found. At the very least, there was strong chance they might double, and emerge in the field of young corn just to northward. They must be gotten back into their meadow and into the pen.

Bobby whistled to Thor, who was sniffing interestedly at a woodchuck hole. Pointing to the trampled swath through the undergrowth, the boy commanded:

"Get 'em, Thor! Round 'em up!"

With no outward sign of reluctance, the collie bounded forward on his unpleasant duty. Bobby ran close behind him. The two entered the woods and plunged deeper and deeper into them, following the unmistakable trail of the runaway hogs.

Thor soon left Bobby behind in the chase. The running boy put on a new burst of speed as he heard the dog begin to bark. He could read the meanings of his collie's various barks as well as he could read print. This was the har-rowingly nagging bark wherewith Thor was wont to start cattle or hogs from their grazing as he began to round them up.

Out through the trampled undergrowth ran Bobby, hot and panting. He was at the edge of an oak glade on whose every side arose the bushes and saplings in an almost impenetrable wall. The glade's moldering fallen leaves were wet and greasy from last night's rain.

Scattered through the cleared space were the twenty strayed hogs. Glumly greedy, they had been munching the half-decayed mast. At Thor's clamorous summons they lifted sullen heads, in no way minded to be interrupted at their feast.

The dog was not interested in their likes and dislikes. His job was to cluster them and start them homeward. This he prepared to do in true business-like fashion. His flying feet sent up swirls of sodden leaves behind him as he darted among the hogs.

Crankily, most of them obeyed his threatening summons. A half dozen of the largest and oldest paid no overt attention to him, but grouped themselves a little closer together and pretended to go on eating.

Too excited to realize that this was not a promising sign, Bobby ran at the six, while Thor was herding the less recalcitrant majority of the bunch toward the path they had blazed when they entered the glade. Straight at the sulking brutes the boy ran, shouting. Closer the six pressed to one another.

As Bobby was almost upon the nearest of the half-dozen—a lean old tusker whose furrowed sides told of many battles and victories—the hog wheeled about and charged him.

In astonishment at such an unlooked-for move, Bobby slid to a standstill. His heels slipped on the greasy mold in his sub-conscious effort to halt. Up went his feet and down went the rest of him, full in the path of the charging hog.

At sight of the lad's fall the other five members of the group joined ferociously in their leader's onslaught upon the helpless human. Bobby, by instinct, rolled quickly aside, in time to miss the gouging tusks and razor hoofs of the first assailant by little more than a hair's-breadth.

But before he could get to his feet the six were at him.

As he had fallen he had cried out in dismay. That involuntary cry prolonged his life. Thor, herding the rest of the drove, had whirled at sound of it.

Now, as the six rushed in, a silver-and-snow catapult landed among them from nowhere in particular, snarling, snapping, slashing.

No longer had Thor any use for the finesse which had been taught him as part of his education as a herder. His master was down. These grunting devils were pressing in, avidly, to rip him to pieces. It was a moment for stark action.

With a wild-beast roar, the collie threw his furry bulk between the struggling boy and the hogs.

As he sprang, he slashed clean through the forward-thrusting pink snout of the nearest tusker, and in the same motion he flung his sixty pounds of weight athwart the head of the second. He was stabbed to the rib-bone for his daring. Giving no heed to the deep flesh wound, he hurled himself forward and back and sidewise among the galloping hogs, to fend their charge from Bobby.

Not all Thor's fierce war prowess nor all his generalship could have stayed that porcine avalanche for more than a fraction of a second. But a fraction of a second was long enough for the nimble boy to get his own legs under him and leap up.

With his back to a tree whose trunk was far too thick

for shinning, he braced himself for the oncoming murder wave. As he had risen he had snatched away a heavy stick that lay within reach of his clawing hand. With this he smote a mighty blow across the eyes of the tusker that was all but upon him.

The blow numbed Bobby's arm to the elbow. It jarred the hog to a brief halt. It broke the past-worthy cudgel in three pieces.

And now down upon the vainly battling boy and dog swept the six hogs. Bobby, with back braced against the tree, kicked with all his football prowess at the lowered heads. The collie rent and tore and slashed as he was forced backward against his master by the sheer weight of the forward-jostling hogs.

Thor knew well that he could take to his heels and leave this crew of murderers a mile behind him. But he would not run and leave Bobby there.

The lad, at his own first step, realized that his ankle had turned under him as he fell, and that it was either sprained or broken. Flight was out of the question. The best he could do was to keep his back to the tree and kick his hardest, for such few seconds as might remain before the blood-mad hogs should pull him down.

Then all at once appeared a giant figure infinitely taller than himself, that ranged close beside the boy. It had advanced from the near-by wall of undergrowth at unbelievable speed. Out of the corner of his eye Bobby could glimpse it in blurred fashion. Some one had come to reinforce or rescue him. His heart throbbed at the relief.

But Bobby Theron was wholly wrong. The newcomer had not arrived thus opportunely for the sake of rescuing him. The newcomer had no interest whatever in rescuing him. So far as the newcomer was concerned, the hogs might have torn the boy to fragments and eaten him.

No, it was Thor the rescuer was seeking to aid. It was Thor and Thor alone.

Rooting for grubs near the edge of the glade, Ursus had caught the scent of his chum. But with it was a faintly remembered human scent, as well. Wherefore the bear did not shamble forth as usual to greet his pal. Then, a second or so later, Ursus had heard the collie's stark battle roar. He had smelled spilled blood, too—his chum's blood. That was all the incentive Ursus needed.

The hog leader's rush banged Thor up against Bobby's knees before the collie could elude it. As the tusker gouged for the momentarily pinioned dog's throat, a vast black paw descended from just above, falling with the speed of light and the force of a pile-driver. Its five curved claws stood out distinct from one another, like a quintet of saber blades.

Down slumped the hog leader, with a skull crushed as by a sledge hammer. But already the second hog was tearing for Thor's throat. With a swiftness that had an oddly leisurely look Ursus gathered the pig in his short arms, lifting him aloft and cuddling him for an instant to his hairy breast. Then he let his victim slither to the ground, with four broken ribs and a snapped foreleg.

Without waiting for further preliminaries, Ursus waded luxuriously into the fray. His first two encounters had not consumed two seconds of time between them. The four other hogs were still trying to push past one another's impeding bodies, to the slaughter of the trapped boy and the dog. Just as they succeeded in doing so Ursus strolled among them with his clown-like gait and solemnly, swaying black head.

He made no attempt at self-defense, but received unheedingly the impact of one hog's body against his middle and the crunch of another's overshot jaws on his haunch.

At the same time he aimed a gravely careful blow with each uplifted forepaw. A hog crumpled into the slime with a broken back. Another rolled over with a crushed shoulder-blade.

Then for the first time Ursus seemed to note that he was assailed amidships by the two remaining pigs of the stricken sextet. With true comedian effect he swung aloft the hog that was tearing at his haunch, and he flailed the squirming body down, with much precision and with supernatural strength, upon its colleague.

It was all over before Bobby Theron could get his breath or realize fully what miracle had befallen him. Panting, the boy stared down at the swathes of dead and crippled hogs in front of him. Then he stared up at the towering form of his one-time pet. He tried to speak or to move. But he could not.

Ursus was paying no attention to him. After sniffing at each of the moveless or spasmodically twitching hogs on the ground, he dropped on all-fours and waddled over to Thor.

Lovingly he touched noses with the bleeding and breathless collie. The contact seemed to assure Ursus, somehow, that his chum was not dangerously hurt. His comical little eyes roved to the remaining fourteen hogs, bunched in terror at the far end of the glade.

Rearing his mighty frame once more onto his hind-legs,

Ursus walked majestically toward them. But he did not go far.

At the bear's second forward step each and every one of the fourteen spun about, with a deafening chorus of squeals, and tore homeward through the undergrowth. Nor did they check their panic flight until they reached their own meadow and crowded one another noisily for precedence under the broken fence into the only sanctuary they knew.

Bobby could have sworn there was a glint of happy mischief in the bear's eyes as he watched that headlong stampede.

Again Ursus and Thor touched noses; the collie's plumed tail wagging happily. Then the bear waddled slowly back into the undergrowth.

Thor made as though to follow him, but presently checked himself and came back to Bobby's side, looking wistfully up at his human god for whose sake he had just deserted the four-footed chum to whom he owed his life.

Bobby stooped and petted the collie's classic head. Then he stared blankly at the shambles in front of him. Then his eyes roved toward the swaying underbrush which marked the leisurely passage of the departing Ursus. Half aloud, the bewildered lad babbled:

"Yet—yet they say the—the *Jungle Book* isn't true! I guess India hasn't got much on the U. S. A. when it comes to—to Mowgli stuff!"

IX. Love Me, Love My Dog

IF Bobby Theron had been born in a circus, instead
of on a farm, he might have made a name for himself
as a tamer and trainer of wild animals. To him, as
to scarce one human in a thousand, was granted the Scriptural gift of "authority over the beasts of the field." He
had a natural way with animals.

When he was only twelve he undertook to bring up
and train a bear cub he and his father found in the forest.
He succeeded, too, until the bear's wilderness nature took
him back to the woods where he was born and to the free
life from which Bobby had tried to wean him.

The boy had attempted, with unusual success, to tame
and civilize other denizens of the woodlands. But ever
his pets had gone back to nature when the hot blood of
maturity overcame their fondness for their adopted mode
of life.

For this is the law of the Wild: no creature of forest or
of jungle, save the dog alone, will continue always to
serve and to associate with man, of its own accord.

208

Bobby Theron was no fool. He had learned many things during his twenty-two years. But this one basic truth he could never be made to believe. Nor did repeated failures teach it to him.

Our story begins with a very brief prologue; a prologue whose action occurred in Bobby's nineteenth year.

The lad and his great gray collie, Thor, were coming back to Colonel Theron's farm, from the distant village, one morning. They took a short cut through the thick belt of woodland which lay between the settlement and a corner of the farm. The region was still so new to man that there were unbroken miles of forest rolling back from the valley's rich farms into the uninhabited mountains behind. An arm of this forest encircled the farm on two sides and lay between its southern end and the village.

Midway in their progress through the woods, Bobby noticed Thor's tulip ears prick and Thor's classic muzzle begin to sniff the still air. Then to the ears of the lad himself came a light and intermittent beating sound on the soft leaf carpet, a few rods ahead. It was like the thump of a rabbit's hind-feet in fight or play. But rabbits were not enough of a novelty to rouse such keen interest in Thor.

So Bobby pressed on, noiselessly, through an intervening thicket, in quest of the sound. Thor was for darting ahead, but a motion of his master's index finger brought him back to heel, quivering with excitement.

In another few seconds Bobby was peering out into a handkerchief-sized clearing. The open space was the scene of a duel.

One of the combatants was a fat copperhead snake,

dirty of checkered coat and abhorrent. The other was a spotted fawn, perhaps two months old.

Like the pig, the deer is the snake's ancestral enemy. This fawn had been wandering dolefully through the woods in search of a mother that had been shot by a meat-hunting surveyor, the night before. Reaching the tiny glade, he had beheld the copperhead sunning itself.

At once hereditary instinct had made the baby deer attack this foe of his race. Hereditary skill taught him how to do it. Darting forward, the fawn had sprung straight up in air, and had come down with all four sharp hoofs bunched on the spot where the snake had been lying.

But the snake shrank out of the way and struck venomously for the descending clump of feet. The deer did not wait for the deadly fangs to reach their mark. Nimbly he sprang aside, and then came back to his bunch-hoofed attack.

Twice and three times he and his enemy repeated this attack and counter-attack of theirs before Bobby arrived on the scene. The boy and the dog stood transfixed by the odd spectacle. The fawn was far too interested to note their presence. But the snake saw or heard or smelled the newcomers.

Avoiding one more impact of the four sharp little hoofs, the copperhead swung its arrow-shaped head to one side toward these possible enemies. For the briefest instant it flashed its head aside, but that instant was enough for the fawn.

Down came one of the pronged forefeet with incredible speed and with perfect accuracy. The fight was over. With cut and broken back the copperhead writhed uncoiled amid the leaf mold, a reek as of crushed cucumbers fouling the sweet morning air.

A low growl was born far down in Thor's furry throat. At the sound the fawn spun about. His fighting blood up, he faced the collie, lowering his dainty head as for a charge.

"Back, Thor!" said Bobby, almost in a whisper.

The unwilling dog obeyed, as always he had been taught to obey the lightest order of this adored young master of his. Bobby moved forward quietly, coming to a halt barely six feet away from the fawn. Then he held out his hand.

The average fawn learns in babyhood to avoid man; to flee from sight or scent of him; to crouch so low in the grass as to be invisible. All this he is taught by his mother and by instinct.

Yet, as every veteran woodsman knows, there are fawns, newly deprived of their mothers, which will approach man fearlessly and will even follow him like puppies. The loss of the dam, the bewilderment, the loneliness, the longing for friends and protectors—these drive away the hereditary dread of humans.

It was so now. For a second the baby deer stood irresolute. His ears were pricked forward. His great dark eyes were fixed in shy wonder on this first human he had ever seen. Then slowly he advanced toward the inviting hand.

He sniffed it, then licked it timidly. Bobby let the fawn lick his palm for a moment. Then, avoiding any sudden motion, he passed his hand over the soft ears, rubbing them gently. Thence he stroked the quivering shoulders, talking soothingly to the baby. Under his caress, the quivering ceased.

Bobby rummaged in his pocket with his free hand and presently brought forth a crust of bread, none too clean and exceedingly stale. This he offered to the fawn. The youngster sniffed it, then very daintily proceeded to nibble it. The salt in it was a delight to him. He nuzzled Bobby's hand for more.

"Thor!" called the lad, adding the injunction, "Easy!"

Thor understood. "Easy" had been the command, fifty times, when he was herding ewes and new-born lambs. The collie came forward softly and stood by Bobby's side. At Thor's approach the fawn started away. But as the big gray dog did not fly at him and as Bobby continued to talk to him in that pleasant low voice and to rub his ears, he came to a standstill, his instinctive fear allayed.

"Heel, Thor!" said Bobby, after he had found a second morsel of bread and fed it to the hungry fawn.

Turning, he strolled off toward home. Without any hesitation the fawn trotted along beside him, the great dog bringing up the rear.

It was thus a trapper friend of Colonel Theron's had told Bobby of luring a motherless fawn to camp; there to become a pet. The boy had ever been eager to try a like experiment. Now, bearing in mind the trapper's tale, he was following its precepts.

At the clearing, where the forest gave place to the rich plowed acres of Colonel Theron's farm, the fawn paused again, but only for a second. Then, with no show of fear, he followed Bobby across the field and an orchard and almost to the very doorstep of the house.

The lad turned in at the open gate of a temporarily

unused chicken yard. The fawn followed into the wire inclosure with its half-grown peach trees and its trickle of running water in a corner tub. He was thirsty from his battle and from his long walk through the heat. Trotting across to the tub, he drank avidly. By the time his thirst was slaked, Bobby had left the yard and had closed and latched its gate.

When Colonel Theron came home an hour later he found the fawn munching happily an armful of new-cut lush grass, and Bobby sitting on the ground of the chicken yard beside him.

"Another pet!" grunted the colonel. "And the worst one of the lot."

"The worst?" echoed Bobby, chagrined at his father's greeting. "Why, he's the prettiest, gentlest, friendliest—"

"They all are," said the colonel. "I—"

"Let me tell you how I got him," cut in Bobby.

When the story was finished, Colonel Theron's comment was: "If you'd killed the fawn and brought home the copperhead alive, you'd have had a safer pet."

"What do you mean?" asked the boy, scenting a joke in the disgusted tones.

"If you had had to live in the backwoods as I did— in the days when backwoods were really backwoods," answered his father, "you'd know that a deer is the deadliest and most dangerous brute anywhere in this part of the country. They've got soft eyes and they're nice to look at. But they're devils, at heart, every one of them. I'd rather take my chances with a wounded bear than with a wounded deer. Any expert hunter would."

"But—"

"As for *pet* deer—well, the stupider a wild beast is, the

more dangerous he is. Look at that fawn's head—look at any deer's head. It's too small, in comparison with its body, for any real brain space. But it's not too small for deviltry."

"Deviltry?" scoffed Bobby. "With those eyes? Why, he—"

"I was reading a piece in the paper, last week. It was written by the man at the head of the Zoo in New York City," went on Colonel Theron. "He's supposed to know wild animals from the ground up. I guess he does, too, from the way he writes. In this piece he says a woman asked him once if a sweet little fawn would be a safe pet for her child. He says he told her a sweet little Bengal tiger would be just as safe a pet. And he's right."

The lad's face was sullen with disappointment as he looked down at the fawn, which had stopped eating grass and was nosing shyly at his hand for another piece of bread. Colonel Theron noticed the look.

"I'm not forbidding you to keep him," said he. "You're pretty near a grown man now; not a kid. I've warned you. If you want to gain your own experience, go ahead and gain it. Keep him, if you like. But, mind you, you're responsible for any harm he does."

"Thanks, sir," said Bobby. "And I'll guarantee he won't do any harm. Why, he's just a baby! A friendly baby, at that."

"So were Judas Iscariot and Benedict Arnold, at his age," replied his father, drily.

The next three years turned Bobby from a lanky youth of nineteen to a muscularly lean man of twenty-two. They rounded out the tenth year of Thor's busy life, leaving the

big collie still mighty and active and increasingly wise.
They developed the spotted little fawn into a huge and
tawny stag.

The deer seemed a living refutation of Colonel Theron's
warning. He was as friendly and as gentle as on the day
Bobby lured him home. His owner named the beautiful
creature Morven, from a character in a Scottish romance
he had read.

Morven's nominal home was still the wide chicken yard
and the shack that had been put in one corner of it for
a shelter. But for the most part, he roamed the farm at
will. He would follow at Bobby's heels like a dog, coming
at the young man's whistle, rummaging in his pockets for
food, laying his antlered head lovingly against Bobby's
arm, to be petted.

Thor alone failed to make friends with the stag. From
the first, the gray collie and the gold-brown deer had not
gotten on well. Obedient to Bobby's order, Thor had left
Morven severely alone. The deer, by ancestral instinct,
had never sought to make friends with the dog. The two
refused to associate on any terms. There was no war
between them, but a mutual avoidance.

But if Thor was not numbered among Morven's ad-
mirers, Hilda Blake most emphatically was.

Hilda was the new teacher at the district school that
stood almost on the county line, midway between the village and the Theron farm—a small school for the benefit
of outlying families in the new-cleared valley. She was
boarding at Colonel Theron's.

By the time Hilda had been boarding there one month
of the first fall term, Bobby was deliriously in love with
her. His parents saw the situation at once, mask it as

Bobby tried to. But they were not displeased. In that back-country region men and maids married early. Moreover, Hilda was a sweet and strong and rather pretty girl, and they both liked her. If she guessed at Bobby's infatuation, she gave no sign. Nor could he guess as to her feelings toward himself.

Hilda used to spend hours of her spare time in sketching Morven. She was thrilled at the stag's stately beauty and she was proud that he made friends with her so soon. Indeed, he obeyed her as readily as he obeyed Bobby, and he seemed even fonder of her. When she was through sketching him she would go into his yard to pet him and to feed him the crusts of bread he loved.

But from the first, Hilda was afraid of Thor. She knew nothing of dogs. The big collie's friendly advances seemed threatening. When he sought to lay his classic head on her knee, as the family sat together on the porch or in the living room, in the evenings, she shrank involuntarily away from him.

Knowing the Therons' love for the dog, she tried to hide her fear and aversion. She succeeded in doing so, deceiving everyone except Thor himself. The collie, with the queer sixth sense of his breed, recognized at once the girl's dislike. Wistfully he sought to overcome it by his own friendliness—he who was not wont to make friends with strangers.

Failing, he let her alone, never obtruding himself on her notice and forbearing to accompany her, as at first, on her walks to and from school. The great dog grieved over her aversion for him. All his life he had been loved and had been made much of. At sight, he had taken a strong liking to Hilda Blake. He had tried hard to make friends with her. He could not understand this distaste for him, any more than he could understand her fondness for Morven.

Being a collie aristocrat, he did not keep on pestering her with overtures of chumship, but kept out of her way. Only when she walked or talked with Bobby did Thor remain willingly in Hilda's presence. Not even her disapproval could keep the collie far from his master's side.

It was the day before Thanksgiving—a half-holiday at the district school in preparation for the next day's whole holiday. As soon as the midday meal was over, Bobby set forth to the lower corn-field to pick out the biggest pumpkin there, for the next day's pies. This was an old custom in the Theron household. From the time he could toddle, Bobby had always gone to one of the corn-fields on Thanksgiving eve for the best pumpkin.

To-day he asked Hilda to go along with him on the traditional errand. A little later in the afternoon, he and she, as well as his parents, were going to drive to the village to a Harvest Home festival.

Bobby and the girl made their way over the sere and frost-blackened meadows, toward the corn-field. Thor trotted gayly ahead of them. The two humans spoke little during the quarter-mile walk. They had reached the stage in courtship where words are prone to be few and constrained, lest too much be said.

"I wish we had let Morven out of his yard and brought him along," observed Hilda, idly, at last.

"We have Thor," Bobby reminded her. "He and Morven don't hit it off very well. If Morven had come along, Thor most likely would have stayed behind. He's worth fifty of Morven."

"In what way is he worth fifty of him?" she challenged, nettled at this slight to her favorite. "He isn't half as beautiful. And he—"

"He's handsomer than any deer that ever happened," contradicted Bobby. "And he has a million times more sense. Why, Thor has as much sense as any man! He—"

"He looks it!" she commented, mischievously, nodding toward the collie.

A belated or a hardy annual flea had chosen that moment to bite Thor just behind the ear. The dog sat down in the dead weeds and began to scratch with much unctuous vigor. Now, never was there a dog of any breed that looked at his best when in the pursuit of fleas. Thor's head was thrown back. His jaws were parted in an idiotic and vacuous grin as he scratched his itching neck. He had the aspect of a wide-smirking idiot.

Bobby noted all this. He was unreasonably vexed at Hida's mischievous tone and smile. He spoke sharply to the dog. Instantly Thor gave up the delights of flea-scratching and came trotting obediently to his master, wondering at the latter's abrupt tone.

As he passed by Hilda the dog brushed accidentally against her skirt. She drew the skirt a little to one side at the contact.

"What's the matter?" asked Bobby.

"Why," she explained, laughingly, "he couldn't get rid of the flea by scratching it, so he was trying to rub it off against my dress."

"He was not!" declared Bobby, failing to regard her words as jocose and resenting their faintly contemptuous tone. "Bobby is as thoroughbred in his manners as he is in blood. He'd never—"

"I'm sorry I objected to his doing it," she said, in mock meekness. "If I'd known how you'd take it, I'm quite sure I'd have consented to let him make my unlucky skirt the repository of *all* his fleas. I—"

"You speak of him as if he was some kind of vermin," objected Bobby. "Thor's the whitest chum and the best collie in this state. I told you how he tried to save my life from that bunch of angry hogs when I was a kid. And you've seen for yourself how wise he is. Don't you like him at all, Hilda?"

"No," she said, stung to frankness by his half-arrogant manner. "If you must know, I don't. If ever I have a home of my own, there won't be a collie or any other kind of a dog in it. That's one thing I'm going to insist on."

"There's something mighty wrong about people who don't want dogs around them!" said Bobby, her words and their implication cutting him to anger. "I never knew anyone who was all right who didn't like dogs."

"Thanks!" she made sarcastic answer. "Then I am content to be all wrong. If I have to have a horrid flea-some dirty dog around me all the time, to be all right, I'd rather be wrong."

"Well," retorted Bobby, sulkily, "you've sure got your wish. If you haven't the brains to appreciate a grand dog like Thor—"

"I'm afraid I haven't even the brains—or perhaps the taste—to appreciate Thor's master," she interrupted, hotly, as she stopped in their walk. "If you don't mind, I'll go back to the house now, and let you get the pumpkin by yourself. You can't really enjoy being with a girl who isn't normal and who is all wrong and who has no brains. Good-by."

She turned and was gone before he could find a fitting reply to her unexpected blaze of temper.

Yes, it was an utterly absurd and inexcusable squabble, this first quarrel of theirs. And like most quarrels, it had grown out of nothing at all. The school children, in anticipation of their holiday, had been unusually exasperating this morning, and Hilda's ordinarily calm nerves were frayed. Bobby, in blundering defense of his loved dog, had said far more than had been his intention.

Mutual infatuation, in its half-formed state, had done the rest. Never yet was there a lovers' quarrel that was logical or even interesting, to any sane mind. Never was there one which did not seem as tragic as an earthquake and as ferociously eloquent as a Cicero oration, to its participants.

Bobby stamped on, scowling. Thor sensed there was something amiss with his master. The collie whimpered softly and sought to thrust his nose into Bobby's cupped palm. For once, the man rebuffed the caress of his dog. But the touch roused him to surly speech.

"She hates you, Thor!" he declaimed. "And she doesn't want to be with *me,* either. She— Oh, let her go! We're better off without her, both of us."

When Bobby returned to the house with the haphazard-chosen pumpkin, Colonel Theron and his wife were in the carryall, waiting to start for the Harvest Home.

"Hilda's got a sick headache," reported Mrs. Theron. "She says she doesn't feel up to coming with us. She's going to lie down till supper-time."

Bobby took his place in the carryall without comment on the girl's defection. His parents noticed his scowl and his silence, and they glanced amusedly at each other. They had reached an age when lovers' quarrels can be regarded as something less hideously devastating than a world war.

Thor galloped in front of the horses, in delight at the prospect of a run. But Colonel Theron ordered him back to the porch. There had been a "mad-dog scare" at the village, a few weeks earlier. Nervous folk were still in the habit of reaching for their guns when a galloping dog passed their homes. Thor would be safer where he was, besides serving as guard to the almost deserted farm.

Reluctantly the collie obeyed the injunction. Head and tail adroop, he made his way to the back porch and there laid himself down with a thump, on the mat, sighing as he put his head between his outspread forepaws. He was unhappy. With the queer psychic sense of a collie, he realized that something had happened to sadden and anger his master. Also, he himself was forbidden to go on this pleasure jaunt with the people who were so dear to him. Life was not joyous.

Thor was not the only denizen of the farm to find existence irksome, that day. In her room upstairs Hilda Blake looked dolefully after the departing carryall and wished she were dead. All men were brutes. Bobby Theron was the most inexcusably brutal of them all. She was glad she had found out his true character before it was too late. As proof of her gladness, she began to cry.

A third resident of the Theron farm was in even less enviable mood than were Hilda and Thor. This third malcontent was Morven, the giant stag.

For weeks—indeed ever since the birth of the hunter's moon—the stag had been increasingly restless and nerve-racked. Of late this strange irritation had settled into a brooding anger against everything and everybody. As in

the case of every tame deer and almost every other prisoned wild thing, there was born at last in his cramped
brain a murder craving. He had no more grudge against
one human than against another. But his stifled instincts
fairly screeched to him to *kill!*

It had been a busy season on the farm. Nobody, recently, had had time to take special note of the captive deer
or of his possible moods. The hunting season was on, in
the forests beyond. Wherefore, Morven had been kept
cooped up in his yard, lest he stray to the woodland edge
and be shot. Close confinement had fed his murder lust
tenfold and had added to his hatred for everything and
everybody.

Presently Hilda dried her eyes, telling herself very
determinedly that the best man on earth was not worth a
single tear from her eyes. Also, that Bobby Theron was
by far the worst of men. To take her mind from her woes,
she glanced about for something to do. On the table lay
her almost finished sketch of Morven.

She gathered up her drawing materials and made her
way downstairs and out of the house. On the steps she
all but stumbled over the recumbent Thor. Favoring him
with a look of disgust, she went on until she came to the
chair she had placed in front of Morven's yard. There
she seated herself, arranging her drawing board and opening her crayon case.

On her approach and at her friendly salutation, the stag
lifted his head and stared morosely at her. Then he
hoisted a mass of straw bedding on his antlers and shook
it savagely about the yard. His pronged left forefoot
began to scrape the frost-hardened ground.

Hilda smiled at this exhibition of supposed playfulness.

As the stag resumed his pose of staring sourly at her, she began to sketch.

But, in his cranky tossing about of the bedding, Morven had shaken a matted swathe of it across his own shoulders. There it stuck out like some grotesque wing, marring his symmetry.

It annoyed Hilda to see it there. It took her mind from her sketching. It blurred the correctness of the shoulder lines. After waiting for a few moments for it to tumble off of its own accord, she got up, still carrying the drawing board, and went into the yard to remove the straw wisps.

A hundred times Hilda had gone fearlessly and safely into the inclosure. Now, engrossed with her unhappy thoughts, she did not observe anything new in her pet's demeanor.

Hitherto, the stag had come forward to greet her and to nuzzle her pockets for bits of bread. Today, as she opened the wire gate and went in, leaving it open behind her, Morven did not look at the girl.

Anyone versed in the ways of tame deer would have taken warning from the fact that he turned away his antlered head and would not meet her eye, also from the fevered pawing of his forefoot.

But Hilda did not notice. Carelessly she went toward him, the drawing board swinging in one hand, the other hand outstretched to pick off the offending bunch of straw.

Too quickly for her to realize what had happened, the stag spun about and charged her. If she had been three feet farther away from him, the assault must have ended in instant murder. But she was almost touching him as he wheeled. Instinctively she raised both hands to fend him off. The left antler missed her. The right smote resoundingly against the broad surface of the basswood drawing board.

The stout board was split in two by the impact. The girl's slender body, which it had shielded, was driven backward as from a catapult, clean through the open doorway of the pen. Hilda fell in a heap on the frozen ground, just outside the inclosure, half stunned and with the breath knocked clean out of her.

In the fraction of a second before Morven's horns had hit the drawing board Hilda had cried out in alarm. The terrific blow had cut short her breath, and the cry as well. But the sound had reached the drowsy dog, and so had its stark appeal.

Morven drove his antlers at the smashed drawing board that lay in front of him. He seemed to regard it as part of his victim. He tossed high one half of it, and demolished with a single hoof blow the other half.

Then he saw the huddled and half-unconscious body of the girl lying just outside the open gate of his pen. The stag lowered his head and charged.

No need now for close-quarters work, with a chance of missing. This was a clean dash, with perfect aim, and express-train speed and force behind it. A single toss of his serried prongs would hurl the light body high and far. Then there would be time for the rare luxury of ripping the sprawled figure to ribbons with fifty hacking hoof cuts, and of tossing it again and again. Eyes bloodshot and nostrils scarlet, the stag launched himself in his charge.

Hilda saw him coming. She could not stir, even were there time, which there was not. For the moment her muscles were paralyzed by the shock to nerve and to flesh. She shut her eyes. But in the same movement she opened them again.

Something silver-and-white had flashed across her line of vision. The silver-and-white whirlwind had hurdled her fallen body and was in midair, headed straight for the open doorway of the deer pen.

The stag thundered forth through the opening, head down. As his horns scratched against the posts of the narrow gate he was aware of a red-hot anguish in his tender nostrils, and of a sixty-four-pound dynamic weight that jerked his head and shoulders to one side.

It was all finished in a breath. More than once Thor had done the same thing—as had centuries of his ancestors—in deflecting the rush of a cross bull or an infuriated steer.

The stag's momentum carried him out of the yard and far ahead. But the sidewise jerk and weight at his bleeding nostrils swung him a little to one side from the straight line of his rush. His scooping horns and his homicidal hoofs missed the panic-stricken girl by barely an inch.

There had been scant margin. All of Thor's strength and weight and skill had not been able to swing the charging brute farther aside. But the charge had failed.

Rearing, the stag wheeled, shaking the dog loose and trying to strike Thor's nimbly flashing body with his flailing forefeet. Thor dodged nimbly the hoof blows, any one of which must have killed him outright.

Back to the attack rushed Morven. The girl had been able to rise to a sitting posture and she was trying to force her numbed body to its feet. The stag saw. The sight made him forget the harrowing collie and his own rent nostrils. Again he charged the half-recumbent Hilda.

But before he could get fairly into motion, the great gray dog was upon his haunch. Thor's terrible eyeteeth were driving deep into the stag's hip muscles. Thor's sixty-four pounds of whalebone weight were hanging impedingly from Morven's left thigh. With such a handicap, the charge could not be effective. The dog first must be shaken loose.

With a wheel of his body and a backward toss of his antlers, Morven tore free from the gray demon that assailed him so furiously. Thor dropped to earth, bruised, and with his shoulder scored by an antler graze.

Morven whizzed back to the demolition of the girl. But Hilda's young vigor and her scattered wits had returned sufficiently to enable her to stagger forward to the doorway of the pen, a few feet in front of her. Through this she reeled, swinging shut and latching its thick wire door behind her, just as the stag's antlers crashed against the barrier, nearly ripping it to pieces.

The stout latch had caught as the door swung shut, but the force of Morven's charge snapped it like rotten wood. The upper hinge tore loose. The door sagged on one hinge. Morven drew back to throw himself against it once more.

Hilda pressed against the inner side of the broken gate, bracing her feet in a futile effort to stop the avalanche which was about to be hurled against it. Well she knew she would have no hope of escaping, once the gate should be down.

But, as the stag drew back, Thor was at him again, slashing clean through the torn nostrils, slipping eel-like out of the way as the punitive forefeet struck killingly at him.

In practically the same motion the collie dove beneath the stag, slashing deep into the hairy white underbody.

The double move served the turn which Thor had planned it should. In torture and in a blind fury, Morven abandoned his rush for the swaying gate and turned to demolish the dog he had always hated.

Morven whirled on the collie. But the collie was not there. Years of cattle driving had taught Thor many things. Ancestral battles of wolves with deer were teaching him still more things, by instinct.

As the stag rushed, Thor dodged to one side. The stag was after him with hurricane speed. But few are the animals whose pace can cope with that of a collie. Again Thor slipped under the rushing stag and again he slashed deep into the underbody. This time a deflected kick sent him rolling over and over.

With the swiftness of light Morven was at the collie. But even as he fell Thor had tucked his feet under him. The raking antlers missed him by a hair's-breadth, and the tormented nostrils of the deer received another deep slash.

Blindly enraged as a baited Spanish bull, Morven tore after the dodging dog. When a bull did this, Thor was wont to gallop away, just in front of the lumbering creature, leading the bull whithersoever he cared to. But he knew these tactics would not serve with anything so fleet and so versed in the wiles of the forest as is a full-grown stag.

Thus, the dog doubled and doubled again, trusting to his smaller size and litheness to enable him to outmaneuver his big enemy. In a straightaway run he knew he would stand no chance against such a pursuer.

It was a pretty sight—though to the watching girl it was horrifying—this game of hide-and-seek with death which the gray collie was playing. The antler graze on Thor's shoulder was sending down a trickle of dark-red blood over the silver-and-snow of his coat. A nearly avoided hoof blow had opened the big vein in the dog's right ear and had scraped the side of his face. Yet he fought gayly on.

At nearly every wheeling maneuver he managed to rake some portion of his foe's anatomy. Morven was a mass of superficial wounds.

Then, as he slipped aside from the charging brute once more, the collie sought to hamstring his enemy. His teeth found their mark in the hind-leg where runs the thick tendon that has been the goal of so many wolves. But as he swung aside from the hind-hoofs and before his jaws could drive through to their mark, he slipped upon a smear of Morven's blood on the frozen ground.

It was a matter of almost no time at all for the collie to recover clawingly his threatened balance. But it was a matter of still less time for the stag's antlers to catch him, sidewise, and send him whizzing bodily through the air.

The collie brought up against the sagging gate's wires. The impact was lessened greatly by the wires' springiness and by the elasticity of the girl who was braced against the other side of the gate. Therefore the dog's ribs were not broken, nor were any other bones, although the breath was driven out of his lungs with a panting grunt.

The shock sent Hilda reeling back. The gate sagged halfway open, and the dog's falling body slithered through into the yard. Instantly Thor was on his feet, though staggering from the shock. Instantly, too, Hilda sprang to shove shut the crazy one-hinged gate, as a flimsy barrier against the murderous stag.

She was too late. Thor knew she would be too late, for he sprang protectingly in front of her as Morven rushed the gateway.

The stag's antlers clove through the half-closed opening to wrench away the only impediment between him and his prey. Thor sprang upward. The terrible curved eye-teeth of the collie struck deep into the momentarily exposed throat of the stag.

Up flashed Morven's forefoot, and down again, to exterminate the gray devil that was gripping his throat. But the foot smote only the thick wooden bar that formed the bottom of the gate. The gate's top bar and its torn wire were already stranded on the wide antlers.

Morven plunged and thrashed madly to free himself of the incumbrance that hampered his horns and his right forefoot. While he struggled, a convulsive shudder swept through him. Thor's saber teeth had shorn their way through the stag's jugular. The collie's wolf ancestry had told him what to do. He had done it.

Bobby Theron had a miserable time on the way to the Harvest Home. Reaction had set in, and he wanted to bite out his own tongue when he recalled the things he had said to Hilda. Lover-like, he magnified them, in fancy, to unforgivable insults. Because they were unforgivable, he resolved to go back and implore forgiveness.

With a mumbled excuse, presently, he jumped out of the slow-jogging carryall and started homeward, across lots, at a run. November dusk was beginning to close in as he reached the farmhouse. There he came to an abrupt halt. Some one was crying, very softly. Aghast, Bobby peered around the corner of the house.

There, on the back porch, crouched Hilda Blake. On the mat was Thor, his head cradled in the girl's lap. She was bathing his flesh wounds with witch hazel and a handful of her own best handkerchiefs. Between applications of the lotion, she was stroking the classic silver head and crooning in a sob-choked little voice:

"I—I said *horrid* things about you—you—you glorious old hero, you! And you're the dearest dog in the world. And—and you saved my life, when—when you knew I—I hated you. And—I love you, Thor! I love you almost— almost as much as—as I love HIM! And I've—I've been awful to you both. I—I— OH!"

The crooning merged into a cry of amaze. A man had strode forward from the corner of the house and swept her up from the floor—close against his breast.

X. A Glass of Milk

GIL Tanner sat eying the long glass of fresh milk with some such look as he might have been expected to cast on the same quantity of rat poison. Then he blinked up drearily at the white-aproned girl who had just handed it to him.

There was covert inquiry in his eyes, as well as glumness. Much he desired to know whether or not she despised him as thoroughly as he despised himself and as Lafe Hewitt openly despised him.

But in Kay Leonard's level gray eyes there was no expression that he could read, beyond a patient waiting for him to drink the milk and give her back the glass.

"All right," he said, presently. "I'll just sip it slowly, and when it's empty I'll set it down here beside me. Don't bother to wait for the glass. I'll bring it in when I come."

"That's what you said this morning," the girl reminded him. "I happened to look out through the kitchen window, a minute later, and I saw you pouring it into Napoleon's tin dish. He lapped up every drop of it. Does he lap up every drop of every glass of milk you're supposed to drink, Gil?"

For a moment the man's pallid face reddened and he scowled. Then he broke into a rueful grin.

"I might have known it was too good to last!" he grumbled. "If it wasn't for Napoleon, here, I'd have died from a surfeit of glasses of milk, a week ago. I hate it, and he loves it. Every drop of it helps to make him bigger and fatter and stronger. He needs strength. I don't. The sooner I drop out of life, the better pleased I'll be."

He stooped painfully forward as he spoke, and rumpled the fluffy ears of a plump collie pup that lay at his feet, looking expectantly up at him and at the brimming glass of milk. Gil did not meet Kay's eyes. Which was lucky for his self-respect. For an angry scorn leaped from their cool gray depths.

"You have no right to say such things!" she blazed. "The sooner you drop out of life the better pleased you'll be? I'm ashamed of you, Gil! Honestly, I am. Here your mother and all the rest of us are doing everything we can to build up your health and make things pleasant for you and help you forget what you've been through. And you pay us by giving the milk to the puppy and by wishing you were dead!"

"Why shouldn't I?" he countered, miserably. "What use am I, to myself or to anyone else? Maybe you think it's fun to be boosted out on to this porch every morning and lugged in again every night, and sit here all day, paralyzed from the waist down! To sit here like a dead one; while all the rest of the world goes hustling on around me and sound men are doing the work that meant everything to me! Why shouldn't I wish I was dead? What is there to live for? I—"

Ashamed of his own babyish outburst, he fought for self-control and for a fresh grip on his racked nerves.

"What is there to live for?" she repeated, as his complaint was choked into surly silence. "There's everything to live for. Your mother, for one thing. She worships you. This farm, for another thing. This farm you brought to life again when it was sour and worn out and tumbling to decay. There's *everything* to live for, Gil. And you know there is, if only you'll let yourself think a minute. Just because you've had a setback, it's no reason why you should talk in that cowardly way. The doctor says your best chance to get well is to build up your strength and your general health. That's why he prescribed the four glasses of milk-and-egg a day, along with the rest of the diet and the treatment. Yet you won't even help yourself or help us help you. You sit there, unhappy, and letting yourself get weaker and more forlorn every day. You feed the nice fresh milk to that puppy, and—"

"Oh, suppose we take the rest of my sins for granted!" he broke in on her gravely sad reproof. "I'm sorry I was so cranky and babyish, Kay. Forget it, won't you? Here—I'll do penance. Watch me."

He lifted the pint glass to his lips and drank it down in a succession of gulps. The puppy, his furry head on one side, watched pathetically this unkind vanishing of his expected feast. Gil handed back the glass to Kay, then stooped again and patted Napoleon's head remorsefully.

"Sorry, Nap," he apologized. "But I had to do something to atone for snarling like a sick bear. And you've

had two glasses of it already to-day, besides your regular
meals.   There was a raw egg whipped up in each of them,
too.   I guess you won't starve to death before supper-
time."

He forced a whimsical grin to his white face as he looked
up at Kay.

"Doesn't that make up, a little bit, for my acting like
a cross kid?   I hate the measly stuff.   I hate it worse
than ever, with those raw eggs beaten in it.   I used to
think I liked milk, but since it's been stuck at me, with
eggs in it, four times a day, I wish there wasn't a cow
or a hen left on earth.   Do I get forgiven, Kay?"

He asked the question lightly, but there was a thread
of deeper feeling in his tired voice.   The girl did not
answer.   She turned away quickly and went indoors, leaving him there.   Gil could not know she had turned aside
so hurriedly to hide a hot mist that had sprung upbidden
to her eyes, at his tone and at the brave smile he essayed.

Left alone, Gil Tanner stared morosely after her.

"Gee!" he muttered to himself, the pain in his voice no
longer disguised.   "She's as sick and tired of me as Lafe
Hewitt is.   What in blazes is there left that cares for me
and that doesn't think I'd be better out of the way?"

As though in answer to his question, a tawny-and-white
collie dog emerged from under the porch vines where she
had been dozing.   Stretching her dainty body fore and
aft, she came mincing up the steps and across to Tanner's
armchair.   Pausing there, she laid one white little forepaw on his knee and peered up in troubled pity into his
face.   Instinctively she seemed to know her worshiped
master was unhappy, and she was seeking to comfort him.

Roughly the man caught her classic head between his two palms.

"Nance, you've answered the question!" he told her, a catch in his voice. "I was just asking myself if anyone would care if I was out of the game. And along comes the only thing on earth that thinks as much of me, now that I'm a cripple, as she did when I was sound. Thank the good Lord, a man's dog is the one thing in this rotten world that hasn't got the sense to know when he's down and out or to act as if he was something the cat had dragged home from the swamp!"

Nance seemed to sense a compliment to herself in his mumbled words. For she wagged her plumed tail with much vigor, and whimpered delightedly, far down in her throat. Her puppy, Napoleon, came lumbering up to her for a romp. Disdaining him, Nance placed both paws on Gil's knees and tried to lick the man's sorrowful face.

Absent-mindedly, Gil patted her, his eyes straying across the broad fields he had reclaimed from worthlessness—fields which no longer knew his wise and loving personal care. To his morbid fancy, the farm was beginning to lose some of the brightness and prosperity to which his tireless work had brought it.

Ten years earlier Gil had been called home from the agricultural college through which he was working a way. His shiftless father had died, leaving to his only son the farm and the care of his widowed mother. It had not been a promising heritage. The elder Tanner had scorned modern methods of farming and had sneered at Gil for insisting on taking the agricultural-college course.

"I suppose you'll come back here and try to teach me how to run the place," he had said to the boy, in fine sar-

casm. "Well, you needn't do it. Because I won't listen
to you. I know more about farming than any college can
teach. I ought to. Haven't I worked out three farms, in
my time? And haven't I pretty near worked this one
out? College, hey? Bunk!"

The nineteen-year-old boy had thrown himself zealously
into the task of saving the dying farm from utter worthlessness. The attempt had been cruelly hard and dis-
couraging. But bit by bit he had succeeded. The waste-
lands grew rich again. The ramshackle buildings were
replaced by new. The mortgages had been paid off. In
less than ten years the farm was on a well-paying basis.
Modern methods, wisely and unwearyingly applied, had
wrought wonders.

Gil had felt that at last he was out of the woods. Now
he could find time to think of his own happiness. And
that happiness was centered around one woman—Kay
Leonard, daughter of his prosperous next-farm neighbor
—a girl who had also been like a daughter to Gil's own
widowed mother. For two years Tanner had been increasingly deep in love with her. But until the farm
should be prospering and his own mother well provided
for, he had felt he had no right to tell her of his love.

Then at last all obstacles had been cleared away. Gil
had told himself he could enter into his reward for the
years of grinding toil and worry. He planned to go to
Kay's home on the evening of her return from a month's
visit to a school friend, and to ask her to share his brighten-
ing fortunes with him.

On the morning of that day he was hard at work with
his hired man, shingling his newly built hay barracks, when
he slipped and pitched headlong on to a pile of stones that

had been left there as material for piers to go under a projected water tank.

He had been carried, senseless, into the house. There the two local physicians had wrought over him until the concussion of the brain was cured.

Then and only then did they discover that he was paralyzed from the hips down.

When Gil emerged from his sick-bed it would have been hard to recognize him as the upstanding young giant of a month before. He had been known as one of the strongest and most athletic men in the county. His face had been tanned by sun and wind to a light mahogany. His mighty hands had been as calloused as rawhide. Now he was pale, and his eyes stared big and bewildered from above bony cheeks. His hands were white and soft.

He had been wont to take a standing jump, from the ground, clear over the back of his tallest work-horse. Now his legs dragged, useless, and he was helped out on to his porch armchair between his grieving hired man and his brawny cousin, Lafe Hewitt.

Mrs. Tanner had sent, post haste, for Lafe, when Gil was stricken. He was the nearest of kin and she turned to him in her fright, although he and Gil had disliked each other with a growing intensity ever since they had fought as children.

Lafe's farm adjoined Gil's, on the side farthest from that of Kay Leonard's father. Somewhat to his surprise, Gil found, on his convalescence, that Lafe had consented to Mrs. Tanner's foolish plea that he take over the working of the Tanner farm, as well as of his own, on shares, until Gil should be well again or until some permanent arrangement could be made.

Accordingly, Lafe Hewitt was in and around the house much of the time. He made no secret of his contempt and scorn for the helpless owner of the home, nor did he mask his own contemptuous disregard for such orders or advice as Gil gave for the running of the farm. Confused, sick, stricken, Tanner had no energy nor power to combat this disregard.

But when he found that Lafe was spending all his spare minutes in seeking Kay Leonard's society, apathy gave way to impotent rage. Kay was at the Tanner house every day now, helping Mrs. Tanner and trying to make herself useful to Gil. Thus Lafe's vigorous if ponderous courtship came hourly under the anguished attention of the cripple.

Gil found himself increasingly wretched, in mind and body. The first bewildered numbness was passing, and the hideous facts of his condition waxed daily clearer to his tormented soul.

The giant strength in which he had reveled, and by whose aid he had dragged the farm back from ruin to prosperity—from the waist down this strength was gone. His legs were powerless of motion or even of supporting his hundred-and-eighty pounds of muscular weight. What profited him the trained energy of his upper body, if paralyzed legs were to fetter him forever to a chair?

The farm had been his life ambition. Another was in charge of it now, and was more and more openly flouting its owner's wishes in regard to its management. In his peaceful and friendly career Gil had known but one hatred. That had been for his hulking cousin, Lafe Hewitt. From birth he and Lafe had been as savagely antagonistic as cat and dog.

Never had he trusted or been able to tolerate Hewitt. Wherefore he had avoided him for years, as far as he could in so small a neighborhood. Now he and his home were at the mercy of the enemy.

True, Gil could have exerted his legal authority and canceled the arrangement made by his mother, thus ridding himself of Lafe's presence and domination. But that would have left the homestead without an efficient active manager, at the busiest time of year and at the most important period of the farm's new lease of life. Labor was practically impossible to find at this season. Gil's hired man was a well-meaning fool who could do halfway efficient work only when some one was forever at his elbow, guiding and urging him. There could be no hope of making him carry out correctly a daily set of orders issued from a porch chair.

No, Lafe was a necessary evil, unless the farm were to be allowed to go back to ruin and unless the season's half-finished work were to collapse. He must be endured— for the present, at least.

Yet all these mishaps were as nothing to the heartsick invalid, in comparison to the loss of Kay Leonard. Gil could not ask her to cast in her lot with a hopeless cripple, to bind herself for life to a physical wreck like himself. His golden dreams lay withered and dead about him. He had lost forever his chance of marrying the only woman to whom his heart had ever gone out in love. Compared with this crowning tragedy, the rest of his griefs mattered nothing. It was this which racked his nerves and ripped at his heart and made him yearn morbidly to die.

Yet he set his teeth and faced the black future as best he might. It was only once in a while that his stoic resolve slipped beyond his control, as it had done just now in his talk with Kay.

Thus he sat to-day, gloomily staring out across his smiling fields and absently caressing Nance's silken head.

There was queer comfort to him in the silent adoration of this little collie of his. He had bred and trained her, and she had been his eagerly efficient helper on the farm, doing brilliant work as a herder and driver of sheep and cattle and as a guard.

She had rejoiced to obey his slightest orders, and to go far afield in all weathers to round up sheep from the hill grazing grounds and drive them to the fold or to bring in the cows from the farthest pasture at milking-time. Nance had made herself useful in a hundred ways. Best of all, she had been his loyal chum. He had counted on training her leggy pup, Napoleon, to follow in her steps as a farm-helper. And now . . .

From the first, Nance had refused flatly to obey Lafe Hewitt or to do a lick of work for him. Indeed, she had taken at once an aversion to the interloper. She made no secret of her dislike for him. She had gone further. In some odd way she seemed to have discovered that Lafe was now in charge of the farm. Wherefore—as other highly sensitive collies have done, before and since—she dropped her workaday duties. She spent all her time as near to Gil and his invalid chair as she could place herself.

True, at Gil's command she would leave him and go to and from pasture with the livestock. But when a bunch of yearlings had rubbed down a panel of fence in the ten-acre lot and galloped clumsily toward the truck garden, all of Lafe Hewitt's yelled orders and profane exhortations, and those of the hired man, could not budge her one inch toward the rescue. With all a collie's natural insolence, she had turned her back on the bellowing men and had walked off, with flattened ears and stiff tail, to the porch where Gil sat.

Lafe detested the scornfully aloof little dog that showed such open contempt for him.

To-day, as Gil and Nance sat side by side on the tiny veranda, with Napoleon stalking imaginary bears under the legs of the chair and of the table beside it, Lafe came stamping across the dooryard from the barns. Big, powerfully awkward, he swung along sulkily, his face glooming afresh as he caught sight of his cousin and the collie.

"I'm sending those twenty wethers to Paterson on the two-fifteen freight," announced Hewitt. "Sim and I are starting for the station with them now. They're as wild as jack rabbits. Nance will have to drive them for us. If Sim and I try it, it'll take us two hours to get there. Give her the orders when Sim runs them out of their pen, presently."

"I told you to wait till the six-fifty-three freight, this evening," answered Gil. "It's too hot, in the middle of the day, for them to take a mile hike to the station and then have that two-hour ride in a red-hot freight car to the yards. I want them to start in the cool of the afternoon. Then—"

"And *I'm* wanting them to start now," said Lafe, unheeding. "I don't aim to be an hour late for my supper by traipsing all the way to the station and back, with them, at six o'clock. They're going now."

"They're going at six o'clock," corrected Gil, speaking

with what calmness he could. "Those were my orders. At that time I'll tell Nance to drive them for you. Not now."

Lafe shrugged his wide shoulders and grinned down on his cousin with amused disgust.

"Those are your 'orders,' hey?" he mocked. "Well, my own orders are that the sheep go *now*. And while we're jawing about 'orders' get one thing clear in your thick head: You've talked a lot about 'orders' and about what *you* want done or don't want done, ever since I've been here. I guess you've seen how much I care about what you want or don't want. I'm running this bum farm on shares, for you. And I aim to get my share. I'm not going to lose good cash by obeying a lot of fool orders. I know what's best to do, and I'm going to do it, whether you like it or don't. Get that, here and now."

In spite of the sneering dominance of his words, Hewitt kept his gruff voice at too low a pitch to penetrate indoors and perhaps reach Kay's ears, where she was humming to herself as she worked in the kitchen. Gil noted this, and his hard-held temper began to fray. Not daring to trust his own self-control, he kept silence, his hands clenching in helpless wrath.

Tanner's silence served to sting Hewitt to fresh illtemper, for he thought he sensed in it a tinge of the superiority which Gil always had felt toward him. Lafe's unshaven lip curled, showing his eyetooth beneath it.

"And while we're still jawing about orders," he hurried on, his voice low-pitched, but increasingly furious, "get this, too: I don't take orders from a has-been that's eating his head off and doing nothing to pay his own way. I'm a he-man. I don't let myself be bossed by a measly cripple. If you don't like it, see how you can run your farm without me."

Gil Tanner's eyes blazed black in a drawn white face. His upper body shook as with an ague. In the instant's tense stillness both men could hear Kay's soft voice through the kitchen window as she sang over her work. Lafe, stung by his cousin's persistent silence, glared about him for new fuel to his anger. His eyes fell on Nance.

The dog was standing midway between the men, glancing worriedly from one to the other. With a collie's strange sixth sense, she knew this loathed outsider was somehow making her worshiped master unhappy. She resented it, to the bottom of her loyal collie soul. Yet, as no physical attack had been made upon Gil, she was at a loss how to defend him.

"Then, that mangy mutt of yours," pursued Lafe, hotly, "it's time to come to a showdown about her, too. She's as much dead wood as you are. She won't work. She won't mind a thing I tell her to do. What this farm needs is a good wide-awake dog that'll handle the stock. Not a slinky beast that spends all her time loafing around your chair. I'm on shares here, and I'm going to get my full share. No rotten dog is going to eat good money of mine. That goes for her puppy, too. They've got to be got rid of, the two of them, and I warn you I'm going to get rid of them."

Napoleon had tired of chasing hypothetical wild beasts around the table legs. Now his youthful attention was attracted by Lafe's rumbling voice. Still at an age when he deemed the whole world friendly, he ambled forth from under the table and made a playful dash at Hewitt's muddy boots.

Lafe smiled in grim anticipation. Calculating the distance to a nicety, he drew back one foot and awaited the onrush of the play-seeking puppy. Already Hewitt was anticipating with cranky relish the kick which should smash the fluffy little body against the side of the house, and thus not only vent his own ill-temper, but perhaps rid the farm of one of those extra mouths that ate away at his share of the farm profits.

A swift move of Gil's arm attracted his notice. The foot hung poised, without delivering the kick.

For Gil had snatched up from the table a heavy plated-silver vase—it had been a wedding gift to his mother—in which Kay Leonard was wont to keep fresh wild flowers on the table beside the invalid chair. Tossing out the handful of white and yellow daisies, Gil in the same gesture poised the heavy vase upward and behind his head.

Small wonder that Lafe paused in his punitive mission! From the boyhood days when Gil had been star baseball pitcher of his rural township, Hewitt had known with what incredible force and accuracy the cripple had been able to hurl any missile, from a ball to a rock. There could be no doubt, now, as to Gil's intention. The men were not eight feet apart. The two-pound vase, flung from that mighty arm, and at such range, could not fail to do frightful damage.

Not a word did Gil speak. There was no need for words. Lafe drew back, almost cringingly, his tanned face working. Napoleon seemed to realize at last in some vague way that he would be safer under his master's chair than in such close proximity to this foot-waggling and grumbling outlander. So, scampering sidewise, he ran under the chair, and from between Gil's knees yapped defiance at Hewitt.

Nance had swung about, facing Lafe, her dainty body braced, her teeth showing. A growl shook her furry throat. Lafe looked from her to the invalid, and he hesitated. Still without a word, Gil lowered his arm. Holding out the vase in his right hand, he curled his fingers about its shining surface.

Then, as Lafe watched, those fingers grew white and splayed by the dumb effort of their grip. Slowly the solid sides of the vase began to dent and to sag. Hewitt stared as if hypnotized.

Followed a slight crackling sound. The heavy receptacle crumpled itself into a crushed ball of silver leaf and pewter. No longer was it a graceful vase, thick and heavy. It was two pounds of shapeless and writhen and wrecked metal.

Lafe looked on, spellbound. Compared with this supreme exploit of a rage-impelled giant grip, the mere bending of a horseshoe was petty. It was an exhibition of strength that not one man in a thousand could have achieved. Behind the action lurked its stark warning to Hewitt—a warning that was a million times more potent than all the shouted threats on earth could have been.

"You won't come within reach of my arm to get at Nance or Napoleon," said Gil, in a curiously muffled voice. "Now get back to your work. Those wethers go on the six-fifty-three. That's all."

Still dazedly awed by what he had seen, Lafe paused irresolute, then slouched away. Gil tossed the ruined vase into the dooryard shrubbery and slouched back into his chair, sick with miserable apprehension. Nance, as be-

fore, sensed his unhappiness. Again she placed her fore-
paws on his lap and tried to lick his brooding face.

"Old girl," muttered Tanner, his hands on her head,
"he'll get you. He'll *get* you, and he'll get Nap, besides.
I know him. I've scared him for a minute. But when
he begins thinking it over he'll hate me fifty times worse
than he ever did, because I've been able to best him. Here
in this chair, Nance, with my legs dead, I've been able to
send him slinking away—buffaloed. That isn't on the
free list. I know him. I know what he'll do. He'll
never forgive it, Nance. And he'll get back at me, the
first time he gets a chance. He won't dare do anything
to *me,* to pay me off. He's scared to come in my reach.
But he'll do it by killing *you.* He knows that'd hurt me
worse than if he was to paralyze the rest of me, old girl.
Good Lord, Nance! What am I going to do to keep you
safe from him? There isn't a thing I *can* do. He's
bound to get you. To be shackled into a chair, like this,
and not be able to do a thing to save my chum—!"

Nance whined softly and pressed her head against his
arm, petting at him with one loving forepaw.

"If I tell Kay or mother," he went on, talking to the
dog as if to some fellow-human, "they can't protect you
from him. He'll just say he was joking. He'll say he
wouldn't hurt you for the world. Then some morning
you'll be found dead from poison. So will Nap. . . .
Lafe Hewitt will be pretty near dead, the same day,
Nance, if I can get my hands on him. But he'll be too
crafty to let me do that. He—"

"What are you and Nance talking about?" asked Kay,
laughingly, from the kitchen door.

"I was telling her," lied Tanner, "that I wish you'd take

her over to your house, when you go, and tie her up there
and keep her for a while. Will you?"

"Why, Gil!" exclaimed the girl. "You'd be horribly
lonesome without Nance. You know you would. Whatever put such a crazy idea in your head?"

"I—I've been reading about farm dogs being poisoned,
hereabouts," answered Gil, lamely. "And I figured
Nance might be safer, for a month or two, if she was over
at your place, where she wouldn't get a chance to run
around so much and maybe get hold of poisoned meat.
How about it?"

"You poor boy!" soothed Kay. "Sitting here with
nothing to occupy your mind, you let yourself get brooding
on all sorts of impossible horrors. Nobody's going to
poison a friendly little dog like Nance. Nobody could
help being fond of her. Could they, Nance? As for
tying her up for a month, that would be as cruel to her
as—"

"As for me to be tied by the legs to this chair?" supple-
mented Gil. "Not necessarily. For she'll be with *you*
most of the day, while I only see you for a stray minute
or so every now and then. I—"

He checked his harmlessly gallant speech. That sort
of talk had no place in the mouth of a man whom no
woman could now look on as a possible suitor or even as
an admirer. The girl did not answer at once. Indeed,
she seemed waiting for him to continue, and she seemed
almost disappointed that he did not. When he did not
go on, she laughed uneasily; then she said:

"Your mother and I are going to drive down to the
village in a few minutes. I'm going across home now for
the car. I am going to take her to the King's Daughters

meeting. Then I'm going to get some things she wants at the store and bring them here. I'm going back for her at four o'clock and bring her home. Do you want anything before we go? Or do you want anything at the store?"

"No, thanks," he said, listlessly, sinking back into his usual apathy.

"Then I'll get your glass of milk ready," she went on, "and leave it out here on the table for you. You'll remember to take it at three o'clock, won't you? *Please* do, Gil!"

Half an hour later Gil Tanner watched her drive out of the yard with his mother. He replied as naturally as he could to her gay wave of farewell. Then he eyed disapprovingly the brimming pint glass of fresh milk, with a raw egg beaten up in it, which she had left on the wicker table within his reach.

For a few minutes the hot silence and peace of the summer day settled down over the porch. The bees droned drowsily in the flower borders. Napoleon, sprawling asleep in the shade of Gil's chair, chased innumerable squirrels and rabbits through the dales of dreamland. Nance lay snuggled close against Gil's feet. The sick man leaned back, relaxed and brooding.

Then from the fold behind the barn came a confused bleating of the twenty wethers penned there in readiness for the trip to Paterson market.

Instinct made Nance prick her tulip ears at the untoward sound. Jumping to her feet, the trained farm dog cantered off, around the side of the barn, to learn the cause of the disturbance.

The commotion had been made by Lafe Hewitt. After

dumb and ever more angry brooding, for an hour, Lafe's plan had been formed—the plan whereby he could wreak full revenge on Gil for cowing him, and, incidentally, could rid himself of Nance. The departure of the two women aided him and gave him an immediate chance for what he sought to do; for their going left the house empty. Sim, the hired man, was at work in a far field, out of call.

Lafe made his few simple preparations without loss of time. Then he tossed a handful of pebbles into the fold. The wethers, nervous at the unwonted confinement, ran bleating and huddling away from the noisy fusillade. In another few seconds Nance came bounding around the side of the barn.

As she rounded the corner she all but collided with Lafe. He dropped a noose rope over her head, yanking her off her feet. Then, eluding the fiercely snapping jaws, he tucked her struggling head under one arm and slipped over her jaws an impromptu rope muzzle he had just made. A dog has but one set of offensive weapons— namely, its jaws. Muzzle those and your dog is one of the most helpless animals in existence.

Gil sat wondering at the meaning of the commotion in the fold, yet certain that Nance could rout whatever stray dog or other creature had caused it.

Then around the corner of the barn appeared Lafe Hewitt, coming toward him.

By a rope Lafe was dragging the struggling Nance. Helplessly the collie was hanging back and trying to rid herself of the muzzle. With the stout rope Lafe was yanking her painfully along. In his free hand he carried a large tomato can.

Near the bottom of the porch steps, ten feet away from

Gil, he came to a halt, grinning obliquely up at the indignantly questioning invalid.

"This seems a good time to get rid of Nance's fleas," remarked Hewitt, airily. "Your mother was complaining at breakfast that Nance keeps scratching them, and she said we ought to give her a bath. Well, a feller told me it's good to soak a dog's coat in gasoline, to rid it of fleas. So—"

"It is not!" flashed Gil. "Let her loose."

"Oh yes, it is," smilingly denied Lafe. "So I aim to do it. That's why I caught her. That's why I filled this can with gasoline. I aim to rub it into her coat, from nose to tail, right here and now. But—well, when I get it all rubbed in, I'm going to light my pipe. If the match should just happen to drop on to her coat when it's all soaked with gasoline—"

A yell, as of physical pain, from Tanner, broke in on his drawling words. Lafe looked up at him, his grin wider than ever.

"Did you say something?" he asked, with exaggerated politeness. "Nope? Well, there's no vases to sling at me now, I take notice. That milk glass don't weigh anything. I'll take my chances at dodging it. I thought maybe it'd amuse you to see your nice pet get her gasoline bath. So I brought her out here to give it to her. Besides, here, she's far enough from the barn and the house, so she won't set fire to anything."

He stooped, set down the can, and tied the rope, short, to the stout stem of a syringa bush. Then he reached again for the can. Nance looked imploringly at her master. Hitherto this human god of hers had stood between her and all harm. She could not understand why he sat there, quietly, and let Lafe Hewitt maltreat her. But her entreating gaze brought no response from the tensely crouched cripple in the chair. Gil's eyes were aglare. He was panting, as if from a long run.

"Of course," went on Lafe, picking up the can, "I'll have to tell your mother and Kay that it was an accident— me letting a lighted match fall on her just when I'd soaked her in the gas. It'll be my word against yours, Gil. And your mother said, only yesterday, that your mind hadn't ever seemed quite right since that crack on the head you got. She said you're always imagining things. Well, this'll be one of the things you'll have imagined. I brought Nance out here to get rid of her fleas. And if she burns up, it was an accident. Your mother'll take my solemn word for it. Kay will, too. Kay thinks anything I say or do is just about right, anyhow, I guess. I—"

He paused, the can suspended above the squirming collie. The first few drops fell on Nance's burnished tawny coat.

Then through the air swished something that spread itself like a wind-blown white handkerchief.

Gil had caught up the brimming glass of milk and had flung its contents, with all his might, straight at his cousin's face.

Too late Hewitt was aware of the sudden action. Into his eyes cascaded the best part of a pint of milk, in which was whipped a raw egg.

He dropped the can, to clap his hands to his blinded eyes. The gasoline spilled broadcast over the grass, soaking harmlessly into the ground. Lafe gouged at the sticky fluid, swearing and stamping. With his first clear glimpse through the film of egg-stiffened milk he saw the upset gasoline can.

For a moment he stood there, stanching the rivulets of milk that trickled down his distorted face. Then, with a single baleful glare at Gil, he picked up the empty can and strode away.

"Oh, Nance," groaned Tanner, in answer to the frantic pleading in his loved dog's eyes, "that's all I could do to stop him. This table doesn't weigh anything. It wouldn't hurt him. He's gone to fill that can with more gas. He—"

Around the barn corner reappeared Hewitt. With one hand he was still scraping the milk-and-egg from his face. In the other he bore carefully a full can of gasoline.

"There's gallons more of gas in the tank," he informed Gil, cheerily. "So you didn't cost me anything but my time. Maybe I can afford that, for the fun of watching your fool face while she's doing her fireworks stunt. Now then—"

Slowly and with meticulous care he began to pour the fluid over the collie's beautiful coat, disregarding her futile struggles at the end of the cruelly short rope. Into her fur he rubbed the stuff as he poured.

At last he was through with the anointing. Laying down the empty can, he surveyed the drenched and trembling Nance. Then, wiping his hands on the grass, he drew from his pocket a card of matches. The collie never once had taken her imploring gaze from Gil's convulsed face. There was more than appeal in her look. There was deathless trust in Gil's power to save her from this man who was ill-treating her.

Hewitt struck a match. A vagrant gust of summer

wind blew it out before it was fairly alight. Dropping it, he selected another. This he struck more cautiously, holding out his big hands as a shield against the breeze.

He paused a moment, to view with genuine satisfaction the helpless writhing and twisting of Gil Tanner in his imprisoning chair.

Then, as the second match ignited, God vouchsafed His miracle.

Gil, tugging and fighting impotently for motion, lurched drunkenly to his feet. A single wavering step carried him off the porch to the ground. Another stride bore his swaying body to his cousin.

It was done in the merest fragment of time, the slippered feet soundless on boards and grass. Lafe Hewitt looked up, amazed, from his task of making the match stay alight. As he did so, two terrible hands seized him by the throat. The match fell to the ground where another breeze gust put it out.

Aghast, nerveless from astonishment, Lafe felt himself shaken as Nap might have shaken a dish-rag. Then, his throat swollen and bruised, he was flung back against a wide porch post with a force that well-nigh broke his bones.

"Put up your hands!" gasped hoarsely the giant who confronted him. "Will you fight or do I have to kill you with your hands down?"

As in a dream, yet warned by the blaze in the other's eyes, Lafe sought to throw himself on guard. In the same instant a human avalanche was upon him.

Hewitt was a strong man and a redoubtable rough-and-tumble fighter, withal. Yet against the demoniac prowess of his opponent his strength and skill were as a child's.

Blow after blow crashed past his guard. His head and his back thudded rhythmically against the broad post as Gil drove home one hammer punch after another to face and to heart and to wind.

Under that awful fusillade Hewitt's knees buckled. He slid downward. But Gil would not have it so. Holding him upright against the post, by one hand pinioning his throat, Tanner continued to slug murderously and with frightful efficiency with his other fist.

At last he let go. To the ground slumped the senseless and hideously beaten Lafe. Nor, for another five weeks, would he stand upright and move about as before. The scars on his battered face he was to carry for the rest of his days. His ruptured stomach and shattered jaws were to make food a lifelong torment to him.

Over him towered his swaying conqueror. The rage mists were still red and swirling before Gil's bloodshot eyes. He knew nothing, thought nothing, remembered nothing, except that he had wreaked ample vengeance on the brute who had sought to torture his dog to death and who by that spectacle had sought to inflict on the crippled Tanner a torment worse than mere death.

Through the roaring in the conqueror's ears came the whimper of his tied and muzzled collie. Absent-mindedly, Gil crossed to where she was tied and set her free, unbinding her roped jaws. Around him in an access of delirious happiness frisked Nance. He bent to pet her soaked and gas-smelling coat. Then of a sudden he stood upright. His eyes had fallen on the overturned armchair on the porch.

And he remembered.

Later the local doctors and the specialist from Paterson

explained the miracle in long words which the happy man scarce heeded. They said there were hundreds of similar cases in America's medical annals, and thousands in the history of the war. Concussion of the brain had caused temporary paralysis to the lower part of the body. There had been no "true paralysis," merely a brief loss of muscular control. The gradual building up of the system, followed by the tremendous mental and nervous shock of Nance's impending torture, had reformed the interrupted communication between the motor nerves and the lower spine and legs. There were innumerable precedents for the lightning-quick cure.

But Gil Tanner was not interested, then or ever, in the scientific explanation of his healing. All he knew or cared was that he had changed in a flash from a life-wrecked cripple to his former athletic self.

Awed, he stared long at the overturned chair, heedless of the happily scampering dog, heedless of the groaning and inert body sprawling amid the porch flower borders.

Then, slowly, awkwardly, he knelt down, there in the hot summer sunshine, and prayed his heart out in thanksgiving to God.

At last he got to his feet, rejoicing reverently in his new-found power of sensation and of movement. He went over to the bruised and bloody hulk that groaned so lamentably amid the crushed flowers of the porch border. Lafe Hewitt had come to his senses and was in dizzy agony.

Gil went to the barn, still walking swayingly on his unaccustomed legs. There he rang loudly on the gong nailed against the barn door. After some time, in answer to the summons, his hired man appeared from the distant field where he had been working. Ignoring Sim's blithering astonishment at sight of him on his feet and so far from the porch, Gil said, curtly:

"Get the runabout. I'll help you lift him into it. Drive him down to Doc Colfax's. Doc will patch him up better than anyone else can. Then he can take him down to the Paterson Hospital. Anyhow, I want him off my farm. Hurry up."

Sim had departed in the second-hand little car, with the moaning and gasping fight sufferer propped painfully alongside him. Nance had been sent repeatedly into the horse pond, after thrown sticks, to wash some of the gasoline out of her coat. Gil was walking back toward the house. Then it was that he caught sight of another car turning in at the lane from the highway—a car driven by a tall girl in white.

When Kay Leonard came up the porch steps she found Gil huddled low in his armchair. At his feet lay happily a soaking-wet and gas-smelling collie. Nap, with harrowing growls, was pursuing a black beetle across the porch boards.

At sight of the girl Tanner glanced up. "Back already?" he asked.

"Yes," she made answer, adding, solicitously, after a keen look at him: "Are you feeling worse? Your face is all flushed! And—and your eyes look so—so different! Are you sure you haven't any fever?"

"No," said Gil, trying to sound as spiritlessly glum as of late. "No. I'm all right. If I look queer, it's because I've been trying to get up my courage to say something that—that it scares me to say. Will you listen to it, Kay?"

Wondering, half frightened, she continued to look down at the big body huddling there so helplessly. Then—

"There's not any hope that you'll answer the way I'd give my life to have you answer, dear," continued Gil, forcing himself to meet her eyes as he spoke. "I know that. But I can't keep my mouth shut any longer. You must have known for a couple of years how much I loved you, sweetheart of mine. I figured I'd have the right to tell you about it and ask you to—to marry me, when the farm was clear and on its feet. Then I got smashed up. And I knew no girl would want to tie herself for life to a cranky cripple. So I didn't say anything. But I'm saying it now. Kay, there isn't a chance, is there—there isn't a chance that you'd be willing to marry a worthless dead one like me—is there? Tell me. Don't be afraid of making me unhappy, dear."

For a long moment she continued to look down into his imploring eyes, with that same cryptic wide-eyed gaze. Then, suddenly, she stooped and gathered his head in her strong young arms.

"Oh, Gil!" she sobbed, holding him close. "I was so afraid you'd be silly enough not to ask me. And then I'd have had to ask *you*. And—and I'd have hated to! But I know I'd have done it some day. I *know* I would! I—"

"But don't you know what it will mean to marry a cripple that can't even take a step or get out of his chair?" cried Gil, when he had drawn the sobbing girl to his breast. "Don't you? Do you realize what it will mean to waste your whole life slaving for a man who is more like a log than a human?   Do you?"

"I don't realize anything except that I'd rather be married to you, helpless, than to any well man on earth!" she declared, her grave reserve flown to the four winds. "Oh, can't you understand, Gil?   I'm not going to marry you for *your* sake or because I'm sorry for you!   I'm doing it because I'd be wretched without you.   I'm doing it because I'm selfish.   And I—"

She broke off with a cry of stark wonder.

For, with almost no effort at all, her lover was rising to his feet.   She stared back, incredulous.   No longer swaying, but walking firmly, he came toward her, his arms outstretched.

"I'm sorry you had set your heart on marrying a paralytic," he said, gathering her to him.   "Because you can't. You've got to marry *me*."

XI. The Hero-Coward

I

T BEGAN when Laund was a rangily gawky six-months puppy and when Danny Crae was only seven years old. Danny had claimed the spraddling little fluff-ball of a collie as his own, on the day the boy's father lifted the two-months-old puppy out of the yard where Laund lived and played and slept and had a wonderful time with his several brothers and sisters.

On that morning Ronald Crae ordained that the brown-and-white baby collie was to become a herder of sheep and a guard of the house and farm. On that morning seven-year-old Danny announced that Laund was to be his very own dog and help him herd his adored bantams.

Now Ronald Crae was not given to knuckling under to anyone. But he had a strangely gentle way with him as concerned this crippled son of his. Therefore, instead of the sharp rebuke Danny had a right to expect for putting his own wishes against his sire's, Ronald petted the wan little face and told Danny jokingly that they would share Laund in partnership. Part of the time the puppy should herd the Crae sheep and do other farm work. Part of the time he should be Danny's playfellow. And so it was arranged.

A year earlier a fearsome pestilence had scourged America, sending black horror to the heart of ten million mothers throughout the land, and claiming thousands of little children as its victims. Danny Crae had been brushed but lightly by the hem of the pestilence's robe. He did not die, as did so many children in his own township. But he rose from three-months' illness with well-nigh useless legs that would scarcely bear his frail weight.

Quickly he learned to make his way around, after a fashion, by means of double crutches. Slowly but with unswerving steadiness he was beginning to get well. Complete recovery was to be a matter of a year or two. But it was certain.

Small wonder his usually dominant father did not veto any plan of his stricken child's! Small wonder he skimped the hours of herd-training for Laund, in order to leave the puppy free to be the playmate of the sick boy!

In spite of this handicap, young Laund picked up the rudiments, and then the finer points, of his herding work with an almost bewildering swiftness and accuracy. Ronald Crae was an excellent trainer, to be sure; firm and self-controlled and common-sensible, if a trifle stern with his dogs; and a born dog man. But the bulk of the credit went to the puppy himself. He was one of those not wholly rare collies that pick up their work as though they had known it all before and were remembering rather than learning.

Crae was proud of the little dog. Presently he began to plan entering him sometime in the yearly field trials of the National Collie Association, confident that Laund would be nearer the front than the rear, in that stiff competition.

Then, when the puppy was six months old, Crae changed his opinion of the promising youngster—changed it sharply and disgustedly. It happened in this wise:

Of old, Danny had rejoiced to go afield with his father and to watch the rounding up and driving and folding and penning of the farm's sheep. Now that he was able to move only a little way and on slow crutches, the child transferred his attention to a flock of pedigreed bantams his father had bought him and which were the boy's chief delight.

Like Ronald, he had a way with dumb things. The tame bantams let him handle them at will. They ate from his wizened fingers and lighted on his meagerly narrow and uneven shoulders for food. Then it occurred to him to teach Laund to herd and drive them. Luckily for his plan and for the safety and continued tameness of the little flock of chickens, Laund was as gentle with them as with the youngest of his master's lambs. Gravely and tenderly he would herd them, at Danny's shrill order, avoiding stepping on any of them or frightening them.

It was a pretty sight. Watching it, and Danny's delight in the simple maneuvers, Ronald forgot his own annoyance in having to share a valuable puppy's valuable training time with his son.

One day Danny and Laund sat side by side on a rock, back of the barnyard, watching the bantams scramble for handfuls of thrown feed. Among the flock was a tiny mother hen with a half dozen downily diminutive chicks. Anxiously she clucked to them as she grabbed morsel after morsel of the feast and tried to shove the other bantams aside to give place to her babies where the feed was thickest.

As the last of the flung grain was gobbled, the flock dispersed. Most of them drifted to the barnyard. The mother hen and her chicks strayed out toward the truck garden, some fifty feet in front of where the boy and the dog were sitting.

Of a sudden the tiny mother crouched, with a raucously crooning cry to her children, spreading her wings for them to hide under. As they ran to her a dark shadow swept the sunlit earth. Down from nowhere a huge hen hawk shot, like a brown feathery cannon ball, diving at the baby bantams and at their frightened dam.

"Laund!" squealed Danny, pointing to the chicks.

The six-months puppy leaped to them. He had no idea why he was sent thither or what he was supposed to do. He did not see the swooping hawk. Never had he seen a hawk, though hawks were plentiful enough in that mountain region. But he noted the flustered excitement of the hen and the scurrying of the golden mites toward her and the alarm in Danny's loved voice. Wherefore he bounded alertly into the arena—to do he knew not what.

As a matter of fact, there was nothing for him to do. As he reached the hen something dark and terrible clove its way downward, so close to him that the air of it fanned his ruff.

A chick was seized and the hawk beat its way upward.

Instinctively Laund sprang at the bird before its mighty pinions could lift it clear of the earth. He leaped upon it right valorously and dug his half-developed teeth into its shoulder.

Then all the skies seemed to be falling, and smiting Laund as they fell.

A handful of feathers came away in his mouth as the hawk dropped the mangled chick and wheeled about on the half-grown puppy that had pinched its shoulder.

The drivingly powerful wings lambasted him with fearful force and precision, knocking him off his feet, beating the breath out of him, half blinding him. The hooked beak drove a knife gash along his side. The talons sank momentarily, but deep, into the tender flesh of his underbody.

It was not a fight. It was a massacre. Laund had not time to collect his faculties or even to note clearly what manner of monster this was. All he knew was that a creature had swept down from the sky, preceded by a blotty black shadow, and was well-nigh murdering him.

In a second it was over. Even as Danny yelled to the bird and as he gathered his crutches under him to struggle to his feet, the giant hawk had lurched away from the screeching and rolling puppy; had snatched up the dead chick, and was beating his way skyward.

That was all. On the recently placid sunlit sward, below, a frantically squawking hen ran to and fro amid five piping and scurrying chicks, and a brown collie puppy wallowed about, waking the echoes with his terror yelps.

In all his six months of life Laund had known no cruelty, no pain, no ill-treatment. He had learned to herd sheep, as a pastime to himself. He had not dreamed there could be agony and danger in the fulfilling of any of his farm duties.

Now, while still he was scarcely more than a baby—while his milk teeth were still shedding—before his collie character could knit to courage and tense fortitude—he had been frightened out of his young wits and had been cruelly hurt and battered about—all by this mysterious and shadow-casting monster from the sky.

Through his howling, he was peering upward in shuddering dread at the slowly receding giant hawk. Its blackness against the sun, its sinister sweep of pinion, its soaring motion, all stamped themselves indelibly on the puppy's shocked brain. More—the taste of its feathers was in his mouth. Its rank scent was strong in his nostrils. Dogs record impressions by odor even more than by sight. That hawk-reek was never to leave Laund's memory.

The pup's wails and Danny's brought the household thither on the run. Laund was soothed and his hurts and bruises were tended, while Danny's own excitement was gently calmed. The doctors had said the little cripple must not be allowed to excite himself, and that any strong emotion was bad for his twisted nerves.

In a few days Laund was well again, his flesh wounds healing with the incredible quickness that goes with the perfect physical condition of a young outdoor collie. Apparently he was none the worse for his experience. Ronald Crae understood dogs well, and he had watched keenly to see if the pup's gay spirit was cowed by his mishandling from the hawk. As he could see no sign of this, he was genuinely relieved. A cowed dog makes a poor sheep herder and a worse herder of cattle.

Crae did not tell Danny what he had feared. If he had, the child could have given him a less optimistic slant on the case. For more than once Danny saw Laund wince and cower when a low-flying pigeon chanced to winnow just above him on its flight from cote to barnyard.

It was a week later that Laund was driving a bunch of skittish and silly wethers across the road, from the home fold to the first sheep-pasture. Outwardly it was a simple job. All that need be done was to get them safe through the fold gate and out into the yard, thence through the yard gate out into the road, thence across the road and in through the home pasture gate which Ronald Crae was holding open.

It was one of the easiest of Laund's duties. True, there was always an off chance of the wethers trying to scatter or of one of them bolting down the road instead of into the pasture.

But the young dog had an instinct for this sort of thing. Like the best of his ancestors, he seemed to read the sheep's minds—if, indeed, sheep are blest or cursed with minds— and to know beforehand in just what direction one or more of them was likely to break formation. Always he was on the spot, ready to turn back the galloping stray and to keep the rest from following the seceder.

To-day, he marshaled the milling bunch as snappily and cleanly as ever, herding them across the yard and to the road. On these wethers he wasted none of the gentleness he lavished on heavy ewes or on lambs. This, too, was an ancestral throw-back, shared by a thousand other sheep-driving collies.

Into the road debouched the baaing and jostling flock. As ever, they were agog for any chance to get into mischief. Indeed, they were more than usually ready for it. For their ears were assailed by an unwonted sound—a far-off whirring that made them nervous.

Laund heard the sound, too, and was mildly interested in it, though it conveyed no meaning to him. Steadily he sent his wethers out into the road in a gray-white pattering cloud. Through the yard gate he dashed after them, on the heels of the hindmost, keyed up to the snappy task of making them cross the road without the compact bunch disintegrating, and on through the pasture gateway where Crae stood.

As his forefeet touched the edge of the road, a giant black shadow swept the yellow dust in front of him. The whirring waxed louder. Frightened, gripped by an unnamable terror, Laund glanced upward.

Above his head, sharply outlined against the pale blue of the sky, was a hawk a hundred times larger than the one that had assaulted him. Very near it seemed—very near and indescribably terrible.

A state forest ranger, scouting for signs of mountain fires, glanced down from his airplane at the pastoral scene below him—the pretty farmstead, the flock of sheep crossing the road, the alert brown collie dog marshaling them. Then the aëronaut was treated to another and more interesting sight.

Even as he looked, the faithful dog ceased from his task of sheep driving. Ki-yi-ing in piercing loudness, and with furry tail clamped between his hind-legs and with stomach to earth, the dog deserted his post of duty and fled madly toward the refuge of the open kitchen door.

Infected by his screaming terror, the sheep scattered up and down the road, scampering at top speed in both directions; dashing anywhere except in through the gateway where Ronald Crae danced up and down in profane fury.

The plane whirred on into the distance, its amused pilot ignorant that he was the cause of the spectacular panic or that a fool puppy had mistaken his machine for a punitive hen hawk.

After a long and angry search Laund was found far under Danny's bed, huddled with his nose in a dusty corner and trembling all over.

"That settles it!" stormed Crae. "He's worthless. He's a cur—a mutt. He's yellow to the core. If it wasn't that Danny loves him so, I'd waste an ounce of buckshot on him, here and now. It's the only way to treat a collie that is such an arrant coward. He—"

"But, dear," protested his wife, while Danny sobbed in mingled grief over his collie chum's disgrace and in shame that Laund should have proved so pusillanimous, "you said yourself that he is the best sheep-dog for his age you've ever trained. Just because he ran away the first time he saw an airship it's no sign he won't be valuable to you in farm work. He—"

" 'No sign,' hey?" he growled. "Suppose he is working a bunch of sheep near a precipice or over a bridge that hasn't a solid side rail—suppose an airship happens to sail over him, just then, or a hawk? There's plenty of both hereabouts, these days. What is due to happen? Or if he is on herd duty in the upper pasture and a hawk or an airship sends him scuttling to cover a mile away, what's to prevent anyone from stealing a sheep or two or what's to prevent stray dogs from raiding them? Besides, a dog that is a coward is no dog to have around us. He's yellow. He's worthless. If it wasn't for Danny—"

He saw his son trying to fight back the tears and slipping a wasted little arm around the cowering Laund.

With a grunt, Ronald broke off in his tirade and stamped away.

More than a month passed before he would so much as look at the wistfully friendly puppy again or let him handle the sheep.

With all a collie's high sensitiveness, Laund realized he was in disgrace. He knew it had something to do with his panic flight from the airship. To the depths of him, he was ashamed. But to save his life he could not conquer that awful terror for soaring birds. It had become a part of him.

Wherefore, he turned unhappily to Danny for comfort, even though his instinct told him the boy no longer felt for him the admiring chumship of old days. Laund, Danny, Ronald—all, according to their natures, were wretched in their own ways, because of the collie's shameful behavior.

Yet, even black disgrace wears its own sharpest edge dull, in time. Laund was the only dog left on the farm. He was imperatively needful for the herding. He was Danny's only chum, and a chum was imperatively needful to Danny. Thus, bit by bit, Laund slipped back into his former dual position of herder and pal, even though Ronald had lost all faith in his courage in emergency.

A bit of this faith was revived when Laund was about fourteen months old. He was driving a score of ewes and spindly-legged baby lambs home to the fold from the lush south mowing. There was a world of difference in his method of handling them from his whirlwind tactics with a bunch of wethers.

Slowly and with infinite pains he eased them along the short stretch of road between the pasture and the farmstead, keeping the frisky lambs from galloping from their fellows by interposing his shaggy body between them and their way to escape, and softly edging them back to their mothers. The ewes he kept in formation by pushing his head gently against their flanks, as they sought to stray or to lag.

Even Ronald Crae gave grudging approval to strong young Laund coaxing his willful charges to their destination. Try as he would, the man could find nothing to criticize in the collie's work.

"There's not a dog that can hold a candle to him, in any line of shepherding," muttered Crae, to himself, as he plodded far behind the woolly band. "If he hadn't the heart of a rabbit there'd be every chance for him to clean up the Grand Prize at the National Collie Association field trials next month. But I was a fool to enter him for them, I suppose. A dog that'll turn tail and run to hide under a bed when he sees an airship or a hawk, will never have the nerve to go through those stiff tests. He—"

Crae stopped short in his maundering thoughts. Laund had just slipped to the rear of the flock to cajole a tired ewe into rejoining the others. At the same moment a scatterwit lambkin in the front rank gamboled far forward from the bunch.

A huge and hairy stray mongrel lurched out of a clump of wayside undergrowth and seized the stray lamb. Crae saw, and with a shout he ran forward.

But he was far to the rear. The narrow byroad was choked full of ewes and lambs, through which he must work his slow way, before he could get to the impending slaughter.

Laund seemed to have heard or scented the mongrel

before the latter was fairly free from the bushes. For he shot through the huddle of sheep like a flung spear, seeming to swerve not an inch to right or to left, yet forbearing to jostle one of the dams or their babies.

By the time the mongrel's teeth sought their hold on the panicky lamb, something flashed out of the ruck of the flock and whizzed at him with express-train speed.

Before the mongrel's ravening jaws could close on the woolly throat, young Laund's body had smitten the marauder full in the shoulder, rolling him over in the dust.

For a moment the two battling dogs rolled and revolved and spun on the ground, in a mad tangle that set the yellow dust to flying and scared the sheep into a baaing clump in midroad.

Then the two warriors were on their feet again, rearing, tearing, rending at each other's throats, their snarling voices filling the still afternoon air with horrific din.

The mongrel was almost a third larger than the slender young collie. By sheer weight he bore Laund to earth, snatching avidly at the collie's throat.

But a collie down is not a collie beaten. Cat-like, Laund tucked all four feet under him as he fell. Dodging the throat lunge, he leaped up with the resilience of a rubber ball. As he arose, his curved eyetooth scored a razor gash in the mongrel's underbody and side.

Roaring with rage and pain, the mongrel reared to fling himself on his smaller opponent and to bear him down again by sheer weight. But seldom is a fighting collie caught twice in the same trap.

Downward the mongrel hurled himself. But his adversary was no longer there. Diving under and beyond the larger dog, Laund slashed a second time, cutting to the very bone. Again he and his foe were face to face, foot to foot, tearing and slashing, the collie's speed enabling him to flash in and out and administer thrice as much punishment as he received.

The mongrel gained a grip on the side of Laund's throat. Laund wrenched free, leaving skin and hair in the other's jaws, and dived under again. This time he caught a grip dear to his wolf ancestors. His gleaming teeth seized the side of the mongrel's lower left hind-leg.

With a screech the giant dog crashed to the road, hamstrung, helpless. There he lay until Crae's hired man came running up, rifle in hand, and put the brute out of his pain with a bullet through the skull.

For a mere second Laund had stood panting above his fallen enemy. Then seeing the mongrel had no more potentialities for harming the flock, the collie darted among the fast-scattering ewes and lambs, rounding them up and soothing them.

In his brief battle he had fought like a maddened wild beast. Yet now he was once more the lovingly gentle and wise sheepherder, easing and quieting the scared flock as a mother might calm her frightened child.

"Laund!" cried Ronald Crae, delightedly catching the collie's bleeding head between his calloused hands in a gesture of rough affection. "I was dead wrong. You're as game a dog as ever breathed. It's up to me to apologize for calling you a coward. That cur was as big and husky as a yearling. But you never flinched for a second. You sailed in and licked him. You're *true* game, Laund!"

The panting and bleeding collie wagged his plumed tail ecstatically at the praise and the rare caress. He wiggled and whimpered with joy. Then, of a sudden, he cowered to earth, peering skyward.

Far above flew the forest ranger's airplane, on the way back from a day's fire-scouting among the hills. With the shrill ki-yi of a kicked puppy Laund clapped his tail between his legs and bolted for the house. Nor could Crae's fiercest shouts check his flight. He did not halt until he had plunged far under Danny's bed and tucked his nose in the dim corner of the little bedroom.

"Half of that dog ought to have a hero medal!" raged Crae to his wife as he stamped into the kitchen, after he and the hired man had collected the scattered sheep and folded them. "Half of him ought to have a hero medal, and the other half of him ought to be shot for the rottenest coward I ever set eyes on. His pluck saved me a lamb this afternoon. But his cowardice knocks out any chance of his winning the field trials, next month."

"But why? If—"

"The trials are held at the fair grounds, the second day of the fair. There's dead sure to be a dozen airships buzzing around the field, all day. There always are. The first one of them Laund sees, he'll drop his work and he'll streak for home, yowling at every jump. I'm due to be laughed out of my boots by the crowd if I take him there. Yet there isn't another dog in the state that can touch him as a sheep worker. Rank bad luck, isn't it?"

So it was that Laund's return to favor and to respect was pitifully brief. True, his victory prevented the Craes from continuing to regard him as an out-and-out coward. But the repetition of his flight from the airship all but blotted out the prestige of his fighting prowess.

The sensitive young dog felt the atmosphere of qualified

disapproval which surrounded him, and he moped sadly. He knew he had done right valiantly in tackling the formidable sheep-killer that had menaced his woolly charges. But he knew, too, that he was in disgrace again for yielding to that unconquerable fear which possessed him at sight of anything soaring in the air above his head.

He lay moping on the shady back porch of the farmhouse, one hot morning some days later. He was unhappy and the heat made him drowsy. But with one half-shut eye he watched Danny limping painfully to the bantam yard and opening its gate to let his feathered pets out for a run in the grass.

Laund loved Danny as he loved nothing and nobody else. He was the crippled child's worshiping slave, giving to the boy the strangely protective adoration which the best type of collie reserves for the helpless.

As a rule Laund was Danny's devoted shadow, at every step the fragile little fellow took. But at breakfast this morning Crae had been delivering another tirade on Laund's cowardice, having seen the collie flinch and tremble when a pigeon flew above him in the barnyard.

Danny had seen the same thing himself, more than once. But, now that his father had seen and condemned it, the child felt a momentary disgust of the cringing dog.

Wherefore, when the little fellow came limping out on the porch between his awkward crutches and Laund sprang up to follow him, Danny bade him crossly to stay where he was. With a sigh the dog had stretched himself out on the porch again, watching the child's slow progress across the yard to the bantam pen.

Danny swung wide the pen door. Out trooped the bantams, willingly following him as he led them to the

grass plot. Supporting his weight on one of the two
crutches—without which he could neither walk nor stand
with any steadiness—he took a handful of crumbs from
his pocket and tossed them into the grass for his pets to
scramble for.

Laund was not the scene's only watcher. High in
the hot blue sky hung two circling specks. From the
earth they were almost invisible. But to their keen sight
Danny and his scuttling chickens were as visible as they
were to Laund himself.

The huge hen hawk and his mate were gaunt from long-
continued foraging for their nestlings. Now that the
brood was fledged and was able to fend for itself, they
had time to remember their own unappeased hunger.

For weeks they had eaten barely enough to keep themselves alive. All the rest of their plunder had been carried to a mammoth nest of brown sticks and twigs, high in
the top of a mountain-side pine tree; there to be fought
over and gobbled by two half-naked and wholly rapacious
baby hawks.

To-day the two mates were free at last to forage for
themselves. But food was scarce. The wild things of
woods and meadows had grown wary, through the weeks
of predatory hunt for them. Most farmers were keeping
their chickens in wire-topped yards. The half-famished
pair of hawks had scoured the heavens since dawn in quest
of a meal, at every hour growing more ragingly famished.

Now, far below them, they saw the bevy of fat bantams at play in the grass, a full hundred yards from the
nearest house. True, a crippled and twisted child stood
near them, supported by crutches. But by some odd in-

stinct the half-starved birds seemed to know he was not formidable nor in any way to be feared.

No other human was in sight. Here, unprotected, was a feast of fat fowls. Thrice the hawks circled. Then, by tacit consent they "stooped." Down through the windless air they clove their way at a speed of something more than ninety miles an hour.

One of the bantams lifted its head and gave forth a warning "chir-r-r!" to its fellows. Instantly the brood scattered, with flapping wings and fast-twinkling yellow legs.

Danny stared in amazement. Then something blackish and huge swept down upon the nearest hen and gripped it. In the same fraction of time the second hawk smote the swaggering little rooster of the flock.

The rooster had turned and bolted to Danny for protection. Almost between the child's helpless feet he crouched. Here it was that the hawk struck him.

Immediately Danny understood. His beloved flock was being raided by hawks. In fury, he swung aloft one of his crutches and brought it down with all his puny strength at the big hawk as it started aloft with the squawking rooster in its talons.

Now, even in a weak grasp a clubbed and swung crutch is a dangerous weapon. More than one strong man—as police records will show—has been killed by a well-struck blow on the head from such a bludgeon.

Danny smote not only with all his fragile force, but with the added strength of anger. He gripped the crutch by its rubber point and swung it with all his weight as well as with his weak muscular power. The blow was aimed in the general direction of the hawk as the bird left ground. The hawk's upward spring added to the crutch's momentum. The sharp corner of the armpit crosspiece happened to come in swashing contact with the hawk's skull.

The impact of the stroke knocked the crutch out of Danny's hand and upset the child's own equilibrium. To the grass he sprawled, the other crutch falling far out of his reach. There he lay, struggling to rise. One clutching little hand closed on the pinions of the hawk.

The bird had been smitten senseless by the whack of the crutch-point against the skull. Though the force had not been great enough to smash the skull or break the neck, yet it had knocked out the hawk's consciousness, for a moment or so. The giant brown bird lay supine with outstretched wings. Right valorously did the prostrate child seize upon the nearest of these wings.

As he had seen the first hawk strike, Danny had cried aloud in startled defiance at the preying bird. The cry had not reached his mother, working indoors, nor the men who were unloading a wagon of hay into the loft on the far side of the barn. But it had assailed the ears of Laund, even as the collie was shrinking back into the kitchen at far sound of those dreaded rushing wings.

For the barest fraction of an instant Laund crouched hesitant. Then again came Danny's involuntary cry and the soft thud of his falling little body on the grass. Laund hesitated no longer.

The second hawk was mounting in air, carrying its prey toward the safety of the mountain forests; there to be devoured at leisure. But, looking down, it saw its mate stretched senseless on the ground; the crippled child grasping its wing.

Through the courage of devotion or through contempt for so puny an adversary, the hawk dropped its luscious burden and flew at the struggling Danny.

Again Laund hesitated; though this time only in spirit, for his lithely mighty body was in hurricane motion as he sped to Danny's aid. His heart flinched at sight and sound of those swishingly flapping great wings, at the rank scent and at the ferocious menace of beak and claw. Almost ungovernable was his terror at the stark nearness of these only things in all the world that he feared—these flying things he feared to the point of insane panic.

Tremendous was the urge of that mortal terror. But ten-fold more urgent upon him was the peril to Danny whom he worshiped.

The child lay, still grasping the wing of the hawk he had so luckily stunned. With his other hand he was preparing to strike the hawk's onrushing mate. The infuriated bird was hurling itself full at Danny's defenseless face, heedless of the ridiculously useless barrier of his outthrust fist. The stunned hawk had begun to quiver and twist, as consciousness seeped back into its jarred brain.

This was what Laund saw. This was what Laund understood. And the understanding of his little master's hideous danger slew the fear that hitherto had been his most unconquerable impulse.

Straight at the cripple's face flew the hawk. The curved beak and the rending talons were not six inches from Danny's eyes when something big and furry tore past; vaulting the prostrate child and the stunned bird beside him.

With all the speed and skill of his wolf ancestors, Laund

drove his curved white tusks deep into the breast of the charging hawk.

Deep clove his eyeteeth, through the armor of feathers and through the tough breast bone. They ground their way with silent intensity, toward a meeting in the very vitals of the hawk.

The bird bombarded him with its powerful wings, banging him deafeningly and agonizingly about the head and shoulders, hammering his sensitive ears. The curved talons tore at his white chest, ripping deep and viciously. The crooked beak struck for his eyes, again and again, in lightning strokes. Failing to reach them, it slashed the silken top of his head; well-nigh severing one of his furry little tulip ears.

Laund was oblivious to the fivefold punishment the very hint of which had hitherto been enough to send him ki-yi-ing under Danny's bed. He was not fighting now for himself, but for the child who was at once his ward and his deity.

On himself he was taking the torture that otherwise must have been inflicted on Danny. For perhaps the millionth time in the history of mankind and of dog, the Scriptural adage was fulfilled and perfect love was casting out fear.

Then, of a sudden, the punishment ceased. The hawk quivered all over and collapsed inert between Laund's jaws. One of his mightily grinding eyeteeth had pierced its heart.

Laund dropped the carrion carcass; backing away and blinking, as his head buzzed with the bastinade of wing blows it had sustained and with the pain of the beak stabs.

But there was no time to get his breath and his bearings. The second hawk had come back to consciousness with a startling and raging suddenness. Finding its wing grasped by a human hand, it was turning fiercely upon the child.

Laund flung himself on the hawk from behind. He attacked just soon enough to deflect the beak from its aim at the boy's eyes and the talons from the boy's puny throat.

His snapping jaws aimed for the hawk's neck, to break it. They missed their mark by less than an inch; tearing out a thick tuft of feathers instead. His white forefeet were planted on the hawk's tail as he struck for the neck.

The bird's charge at Danny was balked, but the bird itself was not injured. It whirled about on the dog; pecking for the eyes and lambasting his hurt head with its fistlike pinions.

Heedless of the menace, Laund drove in at the furious creature, striking again for the breast. For a few seconds the pair were one scrambling, flapping, snarling, and tumbling mass.

Away from Danny they rolled and staggered, in their mad scrimmage. Then Laund ceased to thrash about. He braced himself and stood still. He had found the breast hold he sought.

For another few moments the climax of the earlier battle was re-enacted. To Danny it seemed as if the bird were beating and ripping his dear pal to death.

Beside himself with wild desire to rescue Laund, and ashamed of his own contempt for the dog's supposed cowardice, Danny writhed to his feet and reeled toward the battling pair, his fists aloft in gallant effort to tear the hawk in two.

Then, as before, came that sudden cessation of wing-beating. The bird quivered spasmodically. Laund let the dead hawk drop from his jaws, as he had let drop its mate. Staggering drunkenly up to Danny, he tried to lick the child's tear-spattered face.

In the midst of the annual field trials of the National Collie Association, the next month, a gigantic and noisy airplane whirled low over the meadow where the dogs were at work. If Laund heard or saw it, he gave it no heed.

He went unerringly and calmly and snappily ahead with his tests; until he won the Grand Prize.

He saw no reason to feel scared or even interested when the airship cast its winged shadow across him. A few weeks earlier he had fought and conquered two of those same flappy things. He had proved to himself, forever, that there was nothing about them to be afraid of.

XII. Collie!

GLAMIS found the cabin, with no difficulty at all;
though twelve years had passed since his last visit
to it or to the virgin wilderness in whose center it
stood.

He found it and he made it habitable and stocked it
with emergency provisions. Then he settled down to a
mode of life once very familiar to him.

From boyhood, he had known the outdoors and every
detail of camping and of living off of the wilderness. All
this as a diversion, and as a change from the city life whose
activities claimed him for ten months of the year. But
now, when the results of those same activities made him a
fugitive from the law, he turned to forest life as a refuge,
and not as a diversion.

The oil-lands swindle, which he had fathered, was exposed. It was a matter for federal prison, not for mere
state penitentiary. And Uncle Sam has a bothersome way
of sticking to the trail of federal criminals. Wherefore,

Glamis hit on the one hiding-place likely to outwit his trailers.

The ports were watched. He knew that. Moreover, his crime was extraditable. Hence, Canada was closed to him. All his known haunts were shadowed. But—well, along the semi-trackless wilderness from eastern Maine to western New York, close to the Canadian line, there were thousands of square miles of wild forest-and-lake country. Scattered through it, in those days, were hundreds of woodsmen—hunters, trappers, petty farmsteaders, guides, and the like. They minded their own business. The outer world meddled with them not at all, except when the season for moose or for salmon lured well-to-do tourists to the fringe of the wilderness hinterland.

Were a "city chap" to invade this region and restore a tumbledown cabin and set up housekeeping there and become a permanent inhabitant, the news would spread among the back-country folk. In time it would seep all the way from Bangor to Buffalo and presently to the authorities.

But nothing of the sort happened.

A bronzed and unshaven fellow, who spoke English with a strong French *habitant* accent when his glum taciturnity could be broken through at all, slouched into White Timber, from the direction of the border, one day. He bought a wisely chosen supply of provisions and utensils from the White Timber storekeeper, to whom he gave a smudgily penciled note of introduction from Jean Baptiste Louvremont, a former guide. That was all—except that the Canadian newcomer had taken squatter occupancy of the decrepit Louvremont cabin, six miles back from White

Timber, and that he paid cash and kept to himself and
very evidently was a life-long woodsman.

There was nothing about such an advent to rouse talk
or even a passing interest. The tidings did not travel.
Nobody was interested in the hermit-like man who picked
up a fair living by his traps and his rifle, and who discouraged intimacy. There were many such in the backwoods fastnesses. The hermit called himself "Grau," and
a weekly paper, printed in French, came to him by that
name, from Quebec.

If any of the neighbors recalled that a spruce New
Yorker had saved Jean Baptiste Louvremont from drown-
ing in No Bottom Lake, some years earlier, assuredlly
none of them connected this frowsy trapper with the tour-
ist. Indeed, few of them recalled the long-departed guide
at all. Louvremont had left the White Timber country
for his birthplace, near Quebec, on coming into a little
legacy, and neither his backwoods cabin nor his backwoods
friends had seen him since.

His tracks covered, Hugh Glamis was leading the free
life he had always craved. Even though it was a bare
and rugged life at times, and starkly lonesome all day and
every day, it was a million times better than a federal
prison. In another five or six years, the government
might give him up for dead or as hopelessly lost, and
then, with the secretly invested bundle of cash he had
saved from the wreck of his hopes, he might be able to
start his financial life afresh; in Montreal or Buenos
Aires or Mexico City.

In the meanwhile he was as secure from arrest as though
he were on the planet Mars. Not for naught had he planned every move of this sort, from the very first days when

a crash had begun to seem possible. Each step was cleverly safeguarded.

This story begins on a day when a ferocious spell of heat had gripped the late spring wilderness. The air hung pulsing, stifling, burning, over the suffering world. The sun rode like a copper ball in the sky. The moon was red and bleary. The clouds had forgotten how to water the thirst-sick earth. Nature panted in an agony of heat and drouth. All this, at a season when, wontedly, the woodlands were fresh and dewy and when all the universe smiled.

Black flies made life a horror for every breathing thing. So did mosquitoes and "no-see-'ems" and the like. The insect tribe alone rejoiced in this period of hot misery.

Word went forth from the forest wardens, bidding folk use every precaution against the Red Terror of fire. Men went about their duties right dourly. The wilderness animals were as worn of temper and as frayed of nerves as were their human superiors.

At four o'clock one morning, at the latter part of this heat spell, three denizens of the hinterland set forth to find food. Of the trio, one was a cow moose, shaggy, black, hideous. Leaving her shapeless calf in a dense thicket where the June flies would be less likely to torture it than in the open, she plodded lakeward for a dawn-time feast of watergrass and for a wallow in the ice-cool shallows before the rising sun should turn these shallows lukewarm and wilt the brief freshness from the lakeside herbage.

At about the same time Hugh Glamis turned out of his tumbled cot, sleepless and mosquito-bitten. Rod in hand, he sought the lake edge for enough fish to vary his wonted ham-and-flapjack breakfast. On a muggy morning like this, the thought of a fresh-broiled lake trout was more appetizing than that of a soggy meal of salt meat and sourdough.

The third member of the food-seeking trio was a gray and gaunt and wild-cat-tempered she wolf, whose late-born litter of three had been abiding under a windfall at the edge of an inshelving ledge of rock. The heat and the comparative lateness of their birthtime and the hordes of winged pests—these had not been aids to health for the trio of newborn wolves.

Two of them had sickened and died before they were a week old. The third now, at the age of four weeks, was husky enough, though too lean. But the deaths of his two brethren had done queer things to the dam's always overstrung nerves, and had made her savage beyond even the wont of wolf mothers.

Also, it had made her unduly anxious to get enough food to suckle properly this last and only cub of hers. Hence, of late, she had been taking chances which normal lupine wiliness would have forbidden. Morbidly courageous, she ranged everywhere and anywhere for meat.

Otherwise—even after drawing blank in her night's food-hunt—she would have had too much caution to start from her lair by dawn light, in quest of the baby moose whose scent came so fresh to her from the nearby thicket. For baby moose do not roam alone through the forest at dawn. They are attended by mothers who are as formidable to child-stealers as they are repulsive to look upon.

The wolf slunk noiselessly along—a silent shadow scarce denser than that of the departing night. Straight to the thicket she made her way. So deftly did she enter the copse that scarce a leaf stirred. Yet, rounding a corner of the trail, twenty yards below, Hugh Glamis had the merest fleeting glimpse of her brush tip, as it vanished among the lower branches.

At the distance and by such faint light, the man could not be certain what he had seen. Quickening his pace, his moccasined feet as noiseless on the soft trail as the she wolf's, he walked toward the spot whence he had seen the fleeting flicker of whitey-gray fur.

A tiny breath of breeze shook the dead stillness of the air. There was just enough of it to send warning to the nostrils of the moose that a wolf was nearing the copse where her gangling baby lay hidden. Almost at the brink of the lake she wheeled, and plunged with ungainly speed toward the thicket. At the fourth or fifth bound, her canter changed to a charge. For from the leafage came to her flapping ears the sound of a terrified and pain-wrung bleat.

The she wolf had sprung on the gawky calf.

Before the gray thief could fairly sink her curved tusks into the shambling little victim's throat, a brown-black thunderbolt burst through the tough copse stems and down upon the marauder.

The wolf dropped her prey and flashed to one side, with the bewildering speed of a cat, in her instinctive effort to avoid the furious charge. But it is easier for a galloping moose to tear through a thicket hedge of stout bush-stems than for a sideways-jumping wolf. The intruder caromed against a bunch of stiff boughs that threw her backward and out of her stride. Before she could recover herself the moose's spear-like forefoot smote her glancingly.

Beneath that fearful blow, her right shoulder-blade and

the leg beneath it were broken like rotten wood. To the earth tumbled the wolf mother, screaming once with torment as she fell. But, wolf-like, as she went down she rolled to one side. Thus the pair of battering forefeet missed her, clean. And on the instant she was up and away, scurrying through the impeding thicket stems on three legs, the fourth leg trailing like a dead thing. The moose thundered along in vengeful chase.

Now, with anything like an even chance, there is no wolf that cannot escape at will from a moose. But here these chances were anything but even. In the first place the thicket hindered the wolf's every step. Yet its toughest branches were as gossamer to the giant pursuer. In the second place, one cannot run as fast or dodge as well on three legs as on four.

At the copse edge the moose's forefoot caught the wolf on the hip. There was a snapping sound. Over and over on the ground the back-broken creature rolled, shrieking. The moose, in midcharge, caught sight and scent of the man standing not thirty feet away.

She halted, irresolute, too ragingly angry to retreat at once, but too wary by nature to continue the chase. With splayfeet pawing up great clods of forest loam, and with ugly head lunging, she hesitated.

The wolf, ceasing to roll and howl, caught sight also of the man. And she did a most amazing thing. Getting her legs under her as best she might—half rolling, half crawling—she made off at right angles to her former course, her snakelike wrigglings getting the broken-backed sufferer over the ground at an astonishing rate of speed.

Twice she peered over her crumpled shoulder at the

horrendous black foe behind her. At the second of these terrified glances her bloodshot eye fell on Glamis, standing spellbound, within ten feet of her. The moose took a plunging step forward. The wolf gave one final agonized scramble and vanished under the near-by windfall.

The moose's incipient charge halted a second time, as sight and scent of the man counterbalanced her insane maternal rage against the wolf. And—old-time hunter and forest dweller as he was—Hugh Glamis stood movelessly staring at this close-up of raw woodland passions. But only for an instant did the queer stage-wait endure.

Then, from under the windfall the stricken wolf reappeared. Feebler now, and scarce able to make her tortured muscles obey her dying commands, she emerged from her refuge. Again she eyed the pawing and snorting moose.

Then, unfalteringly, she writhed across the short stretch of clearing, straight toward the man. She seemed to realize that Glamis's presence held her murderous enemy in check, Also, goaded by her infinitely greater dread, she seemed to have lost entirely her race's innate fear of man.

As he gaped, open-mouthed, Hugh saw the wolf was carrying something between her slavering jaws. The "something" was a fuzzy, yellow-gray creature, perhaps twice the size of a rat. It twisted and whimpered in the unsteady grip of the dying mother. Focusing his eyes in the dim dawn light, Glamis saw that the morsel was a baby wolf.

The anguished mother wolf, feeling death close upon her, had wriggled her painful way to her lair, and had taken thence her whelp. Perhaps she reasoned that a moose has as keen scenting powers as has a wolf and that the moose mother might smell out and kill the helpless baby, once its dam were dead.

Perhaps, too, she was merely moving the whelp to some safer hiding-place, and chose to pass close to the man in doing so, that his presence might protect her and her off-spring from attack by the furious moose. It is not for humans to try to fathom the deeper instincts of the wild, especially when those instincts are made preternaturally sharp by the approach of death. One can only relate the facts as they stand.

Up to the gaping man crawled the back-broken and crushed mother wolf. To within a yard of his motionless form she came. Then her jaws relaxed. Out of their cavernous grasp rolled the shapeless wolf pup. It rolled to Glamis's feet and lay there, whimpering and twisting in baby impotence.

The mother, as her mouth opened, cried out and lay flat on her stomach. Glamis saw at a glance that she was dead. The moose saw it, too, and her own red rage departed, leaving only the ancestral terror of humans. With a bellow of fright the huge creature whirled about and disappeared crashingly through the undergrowth.

Glamis stood blinking after her. Then he looked at the mangled gray body of the mother wolf. Last of all, his blank stare fell upon the whimpering infant at his feet. And he began to mutter, dazedly, to himself.

"Brought the pup straight up to me—to—to protect!" he mused, incredulously. "Trusted me to save it from that filthy cow moose! Trusted *me*—a—a *man!* Lord! It doesn't make sense!"

To Glamis there was but one solution to what had hap-

pened. He believed that the wolf, dying, and in fear
lest the whelp also be slain, had cast aside her hatred for
his race and had brought her adored baby to him for protection. To the death, she had trusted him—had trusted
Hugh Glamis, whose financial record showed him worthy
of nobody's trust.

At the fantastic thought a mist swam for an instant before the man's shrewd eyes. Then, frowning, he shook
himself back to sanity.

This dead wolf and her miserable cub represented
two dollars apiece in "bounty money" back at White Timber. This, apart from such slight sum as the mother's
trampled pelt might bring. Appraisingly, Hugh ran his
eye over the dead mother. Then, lifting one moccasined
foot, he prepared to drive his heel into the shapeless head
of the orphaned wolfling. Four dollars was four dollars,
there in the hinterland. And he had won it without a lick
of work. He had won it, in addition to seeing a mighty
entertaining forest drama enacted.

Then, down came his heel. But it came softly to earth,
instead of smashingly down upon the baby wolf's skull.
Something was at work on the over-lonely man's imagination and perhaps on his heart as well.

No one likes to know the whole world distrusts him.
This had not been a pleasant thought to Glamis, in the
long months of solitude. And now, he had been trusted—
"to the death," he told himself again. And by a wolf.
He had heard that animals' instinct is a surer guide than
human logic.

His own world—the world of men and of finance—had
branded him as an outcast. Wasn't it possible perhaps,
that this creature of the wilds had had clearer vision into

his character? And now, was he going to treat that trust as he had treated the trust of his business associates? Was he going to prove unworthy even of this?

(Yes, solitude and nerve-strain had done odd things to Glamis's power of reasoning; as to those of many another solitary and hunted man!)

Long he stood there, glowering down at the ground and sometimes mumbling disjointedly to himself. The dawn smiled into red sunrise and the forest around him took on a myriad wondrous dancing lights and shadows. The bird songs were in full chorus. The pulsing of heat could be seen in the open spaces ahead. And at his feet whined and whimpered and wriggled the helpless baby wolf.

At last, as though half ashamed of himself, he stooped down and ran his calloused hand gently along the fuzzy back of the tiny woodland orphan. Instantly the baby's whimper merged into a really creditable snarl. A double set of needle-like little milk teeth were driven into Glamis's thumb.

The man jerked back his pricked hand. Again his heel was raised to end the foolish scene. But, as before, he set his foot softly to the ground again. A grin crept over his sullen face. This ridiculous wisp of life had not feared him. Powerless against his strength, it had not cringed, but had fought back, right valorously, at the supposed assailant. That was true pluck. The outcast's heart warmed still further toward the wolf baby.

Presently, Glamis had made up his mind. It was characteristic of the man that his decisions, once formed, were changeless. Lifting the dead mother wolf in his arms, he carried her to the windfall and shoved her stiffening body in through the opening of the lair. Then, taking off his cotton shirt, he threw it over the snarlingly battling young-ster. He picked up the squirming bundle and set forth for his cabin.

Ten minutes later, his hands incased in tough leather gloves, he was offering a saucer of condensed milk and heated water to the rebellious cub.

Naturally, the whelp had no idea what to do with the food, and its angry kicking upset the saucer all over the cabin's fairly clean floor. In no impatience at all, Glamis heated and mixed a new dish of milk and water.

As he did so, he recalled a boyhood memory of a litter of motherless collie pups he had brought up by hand, and he began to review the various stages of such feeding.

All his life, Hugh Glamis had been a dog man. It had not been the least of his griefs that the flight into exile had forced him to give up his kennel of thoroughbred collies. He had heard of the strange resemblance between collie and wolf, and he resolved to bring into play his collie-train-ing experiences in the rearing of this wolf whelp he had adopted.

First of all, taking the growling baby by the nape of the neck, he stuck its nose gently into the warm milk, then let go of the prisoned head. Disgustedly, the cub pulled back from the contact. But a few drops of milk had ad-hered to nose and lips. By instinct the youngster began to lick these off, and, finding they were food, it made some-what less resistance at the second immersion of mouth and muzzle into the saucer. The third time . . . the cub approached the saucer, unbidden, and nuzzled at its con-tents. Within a half hour the pink little tongue was lap-ping vigorously and happily at the warm milk.

"That's so much gained," commented Glamis, proud

of the lesson's success. "Now after this you'll know how to lap it up. You'll do it pretty footlessly and sloppily for a day or two, till you get the full hang of it. But if I feed you often enough you'll get all you really need to keep you alive. And now you and I are going to have a chat, Wolfie. If I left you to your own devices or kept you in a pen, you'd grow up, all right. But you'd grow up a wolf. And a wolf is one of the meanest things the Almighty ever yet turned out.

"So I'm going to keep you here in the cabin and try to humanize you. In the first place, you're going to forget you started out as a wolf. You're going to be a collie. And you're going to be my chum. Lord knows I need one! As a first step, we're going to call you Collie. That's going to be your name. In another month, I expect you to know it and to come when I call you 'Collie.' Understand?"

This was quite the longest speech Glamis had made in a year, and he felt a vague satisfaction in being able to talk again, as freely as of old and without the carefully acquired French-Canadian accent.

He set about, diligently, converting an old dry-goods box into a roomy and comfortable bed for his new pet. Then, when Collie had eaten much and showed signs of drowsiness, the man picked him up, carefully, and held him on his lap. The whelp snarled and snapped, but not with the former zest. Warm food had done its work. The shock of first contact with mankind was gone. And there was something namelessly comforting in being cuddled and talked to and rubbed behind the ears. There was a charm about the human voice, as ever to puppies.

"That's better!" approved Glamis as, after less and less

snarling, the baby consented at last to lie sleepily supine under the caressing hand. "Now, Collie, before I put you to bed I'm going to tell you something more about your education. If you'd been left to yourself, out yonder, and if your mother had lived—do you know what you'd have grown into?

"You'd have grown into a wolf. That means you'd have had a tucked-in stomach and that your tail would have spent all its time between your hind-legs, tucked in as tightly as your stomach itself; and your coat would have been mostly burrs and scratches; and your eyes would have been shallow and yellowish and furtive.

"You'd have been a skulker and an outlaw—like—like —well, never mind who—and you'd have been as mean as dirt. Now, you aren't going to be any of those things. You're going to be a collie dog. And if there's anything whiter and finer and more of a chum than the right kind of collie dog—well, I've never seen it.

"A collie is the cleverest dog alive. Where does he get his brains? He gets them from his wolf ancestors. Well, if that's true, then a wolf must have about all the brains there are. And *this* wolf is going to be trained to use his brains, to make himself a collie and not a varmint. I— There! You've gone to sleep. Right at the best part of my lecture. Now for bed."

He laid the baby on a tangle of soft blanket at the bottom of the box, and left him there for a snooze.

Oddly happy and amused, Glamis went about his own morning chores. The devil of lonesomeness seemed to have departed from the shack. Life had a new interest. It was almost good to be alive.

So began a period of genuine pleasure for the fugitive.

With all the zest of an unemployed active man, and with all the skill of long years as a canine-trainer, Hugh threw himself into the task of making Collie forget to be a wolf and learn to be a dog. This was the easier, of course, by reason of the pupil's youth and lack of anything but instinct to bind him to the wolf family. He had no memories to warn him; nothing but the ingrained feelings of his forbears to tell him that man and wolf are foes, and under human friendliness this was wearing away.

From the age of one month to two months a well-nourished wolf pup more than doubles in weight and increases still more rapidly in intelligence. At nine weeks, Collie was another creature from the paunchy but thin morsel of fuzz and bone and savage temper which had come to the cabin in Hugh Glamis's shirt.

Thanks to such non-lupine dainties as condensed milk and broth-soaked biscuit and the like, he was as round as he was long, and he had grown most amazingly. Thanks to daily and hourly association with a wise master, he had lost practically all his furtive ways and his sullenness and distrust. He would roll and romp by the half-hour with Hugh. Head on one side, he would sit at Glamis's feet for an endless time, listening to the companionable voice droning friendlily at him.

More as a game than as a task, Collie had begun to learn the meanings of certain simple words and simpler tricks. Glamis had not been wrong in attributing brains to wolves. But not even Glamis had realized the uncanny swiftness wherewith a rightly taught young wolf can pick up an education. Not the cleverest of Hugh's long line of collies had learned with such ease and eager intelligence as did this foundling. It was a joy to teach him. At five months old he was better educated and wiser than is the average yearling dog.

Hugh Glamis was not given to deeds of unselfish kindliness. Nor had he spent all this time on Collie's training from mere altruism. The wolf's bewildering wisdom and ease of learning had delighted the man. It was no duty, but a positive joy, for an animal man to train such a pet. And in the course of the training there stole into Hugh's bitter heart a depth of affection for Collie, such as never had he been able to feel for even his favorite dogs. Man and wolf grew to be stanch comrades. And by reason of this the wolfling learned the faster and became daily the more humanized.

It was not until Collie was six months old that he saw a man other than Hugh. Then, one sourly cold gray morning in late autumn, a trapper named Brace chanced to round the trail leading to the cabin. The wind was in his face and did not send forth his scent or light footsteps as a herald of his coming. Thus he arrived in view of the dooryard unnoted. There he stopped in stupid astonishment at sight of the hermit-like "Grau" sitting on a chopping block, in seeming converse with an overgrown young wolf. As Brace still gazed, unbelieving, he saw Hugh fumble in his pocket for something, and then heard him say in a conversational tone to his weird companion:

"I left my tobacco pouch on the table, inside, Collie. Go get it for me."

The wolf turned, scampered indoors, and came back instantly, carrying between his teeth a dirty leathern bag. Up to Hugh he trotted, and was about to drop the pouch into the lazily outstretched hand when, from a corner of his eye, he beheld the trapper.

On the instant Collie dropped the bag and spun about, head lowered, fangs bared, hackles abristle, to face the intruder.

Thanks to Hugh's training, he had lost the inherent lupine fear of man, but he had not had a chance to lose his race's hatred for humans in general. To this stranger he offered deadly challenge.

Before Brace had chance to whip his rifle to his shoulder or even to take a snap shot from the hip, Collie had flown at him. Noiseless, terrible, lightning swift, the wolf charged. Glamis's sharp cry of *"Collie! Back!"* reached him just as he was launching himself for a throat spring; yet, obedient as ever to his god, Collie dropped to earth and sulkily retraced his steps to Hugh's side. Yet, always, as he went, he looked obliquely over his shoulder at Brace, and he snarled hideously at him.

"I catch 'im, a bebby," explained Hugh, in his best *habitant* accent. "I make 'im—wot you call it?—pet. He gentle. Vair good. See, he mind. *T'accouche-toi,* Collie!"

Never before had Collie been addressed in French. Never before had he heard his master speak so mincingly. Yet well did he understand the simple gesture of the forefinger that went with the words, and he dropped to the ground, obedient, at Hugh's side. Not once, however, did he take his distrustful eyes from Brace; nor did he abate that snarl of utter hatred.

And thus passed off Collie's first meeting with any man other than his master. But that meeting was to have far-reaching results.

The fact that an obscure backwoodsman had made a pet of a wolf was not of any tremendous interest in that

wild region, where raccoons and foxes and even skunks
had been pressed into a like service. True, one or two
neighbors dropped in at the cabin during the next few
months, to verify Brace's report and to see for themselves
the wolf that behaved like a dog. But as the taciturn
Glamis did not encourage the visits or offer the slightest
hospitality to his unbidden guests, the curiosity-seekers
were not many, nor did they come thither often.

Collie showed a diminution of surprise as he saw man
after man, but no slackening of hostility. Even as there
are many one-man dogs, so, in greater measure, this was
a one-man wolf. He had learned Glamis was not the only
man in the wilderness, but he could not learn to tolerate
the others. Nor did Hugh want him to.

Once, when Glamis was off on a round of his traps—
having left Collie at home on account of a cut foot—he
returned to the cabin in bare time to save the life of a
forest ne'er-do-well who had come snooping around the
supposedly deserted shack and whom Collie had hurled
to the floor. As Glamis ran up, shouting, the wolf had
just gained a death grip on the tramp's throat, and with
difficulty was made to relinquish it. That story spread,
too, and thenceforth Glamis's cabin was as safe from petty
thieves as though it had been a police station.

For two years thereafter, man and wolf lived right contentedly together in the silences of the wilderness. The
cabin was off the beaten trail and seldom were its occupants molested.

Sometimes, in the endless winter evenings, when the
dry snow, gale-blown, scratched hungrily at the windows,
and the world lay white and dead under the horrible chill
of the north, other voices would add themselves to the

screech of the wind. These were the voices of the wolf pack, swirling past, in search of hard-hunted food.

At such times Collie would jump up from the scrap of rag rug where he sprawled dozingly at Glamis's feet. He would tremble all over, while strange yellow glints showed from his wistful eyes.

Again, in late March, while the forest lay black and dripping and the days waxed longer and the nights less deathly cold, there would be scurryings of light feet on the trail beyond, and the whisk of running bodies through the sodden undergrowth. Then Collie's wistfulness would brim from his eyes and he would whimper softly, looking alternately from Glamis to the door. For this was the mating season for the wolf folk; the season when the pack split up into pairs at first breath of far-off spring.

On one such eager night Hugh walked to the door and flung it wide. Then he stood aside and watched. Across the threshold and out on to the clearing sped Collie. The eerie low mate howl quavered from his shaggy throat. For perhaps a hundred yards he flew onward, like a gray shadow.

The man spoke no word; made no motion. Yet the deep lines at his mouth corners set themselves in a cast of grim unhappiness. At the end of the hundred yards Collie's sweeping stride broke and slackened. The wolf came to a hesitant standstill. Then, with something like a human sob in his throat, he trotted back to his master and lay down, quivering all over, at Glamis's feet.

Across the man's face came the first smile that had brightened it in many a long month. He had thrown down the gage of battle to the wilderness, for the love and loyalty of this wilderness comrade of his. And he had won.

Stooping, he flung both arms about the great wolf, and hugged him. Then, ashamed of the unwonted caress, he went back indoors, Collie at his heels.

Next week a sheep was killed at a White Timber farm, ten miles distant. It was unquestionably the work of a wolf, and an irate farmer trudged ten miles to Glamis's cabin to demand satisfaction. Nor would he credit Hugh's solemn assurance that Collie had not been out of his master's sight at any time for a single hour. Another farmer, a few miles farther away, suffered similar loss, during April, and made like complaint. And again Hugh had much difficulty eluding dire punishment for his chum.

"It's the beginning of the end, Collie!" he told his four-footed worshiper when they were alone again. "Those sheep were killed by a wolf. You're a wolf. So they figure you must have done it. They forget these woods are full of wolves—wolves that killed sheep, hereabouts, years before you were ever born. If it keeps up, they'll make trouble for us. That means we'll have to move. I don't care to show up in a backwoods court and have a hundred people staring at me. Some of them might remember that my picture was scattered pretty freely through the police stations and village courtrooms, from Canada to Miami, a couple of years ago. We must be ready to light out, any time, now. If Brace hadn't blundered in here on us, that time, and blabbed about it, nobody'd need know anything about you."

But Brace did more, to bother the two. Varying his trade of trapper by acting as guide for tourists, he chanced to mention, one night at a campfire, that a Frenchie, about five miles north, had a tame wolf that minded as well as any collie pup. Two bored members of the party wanted

to see the queer pet.   One of them especially, a professional photographer, foresaw a salable picture, and
begged Brace to take him to the cabin.   Brace consented,
though none too willingly, and he insisted that the camera
be kept in the background.   Grau, he said was a cranky
cuss and mightn't like to be snapped.

Next day the tourists, under the convoy of Brace, dropped in at the cabin just as Glamis was about to start for
the lake.   Hugh received them glumly enough and he
strove by sheer ungraciousness to shorten their visit.   He
succeeded.   They did not stay staring at him and at the
snarling wolf more than five minutes.   So great was
his annoyed effort to freeze them off, Glamis took no
special note of one of the party who hung around modestly
in the background, with something that looked as if it
might be a fish-creel all but covered by the mackinaw he
carried over his arm.

Four weeks later a news syndicate carried in all its
fifteen Sunday papers a rotogravure enlargement of
Hugh Glamis's photograph as he stood scowlingly in front
of a wilderness cabin, with an equally inhospitable giant
wolf sitting beside him.

On the day after this picture was printed a government
agent called on the photographer for what scant information he could give.   On the following day a trio of federal
officers set out for the region in which their quarry had
hidden himself so successfully for nearly three years.

Now the wilderness does strange things to the minds
and instincts of those who live long enough and wisely
enough in its borders.   At three o'clock on an early summer morning Hugh Glamis woke.   He woke wide.   He
woke breathlessly tense.   Through every atom of him

pulsed a sensation of warning. He could not account for it. It was pure instinct. For nothing tangible or visible or audible had awakened him. Of this he was sure.

The night hush was still on the forest. As Hugh lay there, ears astrain, nerves taut, he could hear the first cockcrow from the far-off farm of his nearest neighbor. Then through the hush came the first triple flute-notes of a thrush. A robin's "laugh" took up the call. Minute by minute, the rest of the bird folk awakened, to pour forth their gloriously joyous thanksgiving hymn to the God who had kept them safe throughout the forest night. The blue-black oblong of the cabin doorway softened to ashy gray. Dawn was at hand.

Angry at himself for his queer nervousness, Hugh lay still, listening for he knew not what and striving for calm. Then he stirred restlessly. At once Collie was on his feet. Leaving his mat in the doorway, the wolf trotted eagerly across to his master's bunk, placed his two forefeet on its edge, and thrust his cold nose loving into Hugh's face. His bushy tail was awag. His round eyes were glowing with loving welcome. So, daily, it was his custom to greet Glamis's awakening. Ever he would lie still until a stir from the bunk told him Hugh was awake.

To-day the greeting found but absent-minded response from Glamis. Carelessly he stroked the great head and shoulders of his pet. Then, getting up, he started for the spring, for his morning wash. Collie gamboled along gleefully at his side. Together they traversed the hundred yards from cabin to spring. Then, as he reached the water, Hugh looked ruefully down at his own empty hands.

"I'm so rattled—all about nothing at all—that I clean

forgot my towel," he told Collie, speaking to the wolf, as always, in the way he would have spoken to a fellow-human. "Run back and get it for me. Towel, Collie. *Towel.*"

Understanding perfectly—for this was by no means the first time he had been sent by his absent-minded master on the same errand—the wolf galloped to the house. Once, halfway, he paused, and sniffed doubtfully at the air. But the light dawn wind was running at right angles between spring and cabin, and, beyond an impalpable suspicion, it told him nothing. Glamis, seeing him pause, called out to him to hurry on. Collie obeyed.

Into the cabin he ran, and on into the shed at the back where hung the grimy towel. Standing on his hind-legs, he proceeded to pull it down from its nail. At the same instant Hugh Glamis lifted his face, dripping and gasping, from its deep plunge into the ice-cold water of the overflow tub beside the spring. He had heard something—or sensed something—that set his nerves athrob once more. Gouging the water from his eyes, he peered about him.

He looked into the pistol muzzles of three men who had crept soundlessly from out the dusky undergrowth directly in front of him.

For a long second Hugh stood there, moveless and aghast. The three men were as motionless, as wordless, as he. He knew who and what they were. And he was unarmed—cut off, weaponless and helpless. This, then, was the end of his long trail.

A faint snarl—wolves do not bark—broke the spell of silence. Collie had come out of the doorway. At sight of the men he had dropped the towel from between his

teeth and stood at gaze. But his involuntary snarl had
carried a message to Glamis. Impulsively, wholly without
conscious volition, Hugh shouted:

"Collie!"

There was more than the mere calling of the name.
Hugh's cry fairly vibrated with fear and with stark des-
pair. And its message went straight to Collie's brain.
Even as a dog knows every inflection of his master's tone,
so, tenfold, did this creature of the wilderness recognize
the awful need behind Glamis's summons. He flew into
action.

These men were threatening his god! Collie forgot all
at once to be a dog and reverted back to the wolf. He did
not speed across the clearing a frontal charge, giving
tongue to mortal defiance as he went. Instead, his stomach tucked itself high under his loins; his tail whipped in
between his legs and plastered itself to the uptucked stomach; he dropped close to earth and made for the nearest
cover, like a gray wraith.

"One more squawk for help," decreed the nearest of the
three federal officers, breaking the trio's menacing silence,
"and we'll take you in, dead, instead of alive. Our orders
leave us full discretion which we're to do. Now suppose
you just put these wet hands of yours high above your
head—*high,* I told you. . . . That's better. Keep 'em
there. Dawson, go through him for artillery. He—"

The speaker's crisply efficient words ended in a strangled scream. Seventy pounds of noiseless gray demon
had launched itself from the undergrowth directly behind
him and had landed full on his back. A double set of teeth
had torn away the officer's whole left cheek in a single
rending slash; and those same ravening jaws were now

seeking the throat as the man plunged forward under the impact of Collie's leap.

By the time the victim had fairly touched ground the jaws had found a mark. Not in the throat, but in the left shoulder blade, which they cracked as readily as though it were a nut. And Collie, all caution now flung aside, was raging at the other two strangers.

A slash, aimed with the devilish craft of his breed, cut a tendon in one officer's leg and let him down to earth in a yelling heap; just as the third of the visitors found coolness and time to level his automatic at the ramping creature and to pull the trigger.

The high-powered bullet, at point-blank range, drilled Collie clean through, coming out at the far side. With a yelp which held more of wrath than pain, the giant wolf rolled over twice on the ground, then gathered his feet under him again and sprang foaming at his assailant's face. Once more the officer fired, point-blank, at the on-flying gray devil. This time his bullet shore a cleft along Collie's side, a mere flesh wound that had no power to stop his charge.

Down went the man, dropping his pistol and clawing frantically at the frightful creature which ravened above him.

The wolf's yelp, as the first pistol shot bowled him over, had brought Glamis out of his trance of amazed horror. The sight of his adored pet, wounded, yet fighting so gallantly for him, restored him to his wonted quickness of thought and action. One of his enemies was thrashing about, nursing a mangled cheek and a broken collar-bone. The second sprawled, hamstrung, on the ground. The third was reeling back under the frenzied weight of the wolf that had just smitten him in the chest. Taking advantage of all this, Glamis made a bolt for the near-by cover. Once in its shelter, he knew himself a good enough woodsman to elude these men of cities. As he ran he shouted:

"Collie!"

As ever, on the call, the mighty wolf responded. Leaping over his falling victim, Collie made after his master. The two reached the high bushes side by side, just as the third officer caught up his pistol and fired a futile shot after them.

There was a momentary crashing in the undergrowth. Then a dead silence. Man and beast were well skilled in the forest runner's art of traveling rapidly through the woods without making a sound.

And so, in mazy convolutions, at top speed, they fled through the familiar tangle of thickets. This until they reached a glade a mile beyond. There Hugh stopped for breath and to plan his course. Collie came very close to his side and pressed his head lovingly against the panting man's knee. Glamis let one hand drop gratefully on the wolf's broad head.

"If it hadn't been for you, old friend," he murmured, "I'd have been—"

He broke off, surprised, in his idle words of praise, for the great head was no longer under his hand. Quietly, without cry or other manifestation, Collie had sunk to the ground at his master's feet. Glamis looked down wonderingly. The wolf lifted his head in an effort to lick the hand that was just beyond his reach. He wagged his tail once, then shivered and lay over on his side, with a tired sigh as of one who has come to the end of a long journey. It is not every hero that can fight like a wild cat and then travel for a mile—with a bullet wound through his body. Now that the gripping need of battle and of escape seemed to be over, Collie allowed himself the luxury of dying.

Ten minutes later the third federal officer made his way to the glade, following easily the track of blood drops. There he found that he, too, had come to the end of his quest; for Hugh Glamis, arch-swindler and fugitive from federal law, was sitting on the ground, crying like a heart-broken baby. In his lap he held tenderly the head of a huge dead wolf. At sound of the officer's feet at the glade edge Hugh looked up, listlessly, into the muzzle of the menacing pistol.

"All right," he said, his voice as dead as the chum whose furry head he was clasping. "All right. I'll come along. There's nothing to stay here for—any more."

XIII. The Dogs of Sunnybank

I WAS just thirteen. I had saved nine dollars. Looking back, over a bumpy stretch of decades (wherein, so often, I saved money conscientiously until the last cent of it was gone), I fail to understand how nine whole dollars could have been amassed by me, at such an age. I realize that this is the weak link in my story. But it happened, never the less. Nine unsquandered dollars. Only one motive could have been mighty enough to hold me to that harsh course of saving. And that motive was a dog.

I took my nine dollars to the New York dog pound. There I bought the most wonderful animal I had ever seen. He was a collie.

If such a collie were to be led before me to-day in the judging ring at a show, I am afraid that a cruel sense of justice would make me "gate" him. But there would be a lump in my throat while I made this miserable sacrifice to show points.

For my first collie was beautiful. If his head was short and thick, if his dark eyes were big and round, if his dense coat had a strong suspicion of kink in it, he was none the less magnificent. His coloring was black and white, with a hint of tan—what now I know for "tricolor."

I had no way of guessing at his name, so I called him Argus. In less than an hour he was responding to that name as if it had been his from birth.

Argus was my first collie. He was my first dog. True, there had always been dogs at The Place, since many years before my birth. I had been brought up among them, but none of the lot was actually mine. That made the difference.

I devoted all my out-of-school hours to Argus's education. He learned with bewildering ease, but I learned ten times as much from him as he ever learned from me.

For example: from studying Argus I learned that the best type of thoroughbred may know the meaning of fear, but that he is able to rise above it for the sake of his master or of his own self-respect. I learned that he does not sulk when he can't have his own way, but shows a gay philosophy at such times that assuredly is more than human. I learned that he obeys the law, not through dread of consequences, but because that law is ordained by the master he worships. I learned that treachery and meanness have no place in his cosmos. I learned from him a new and exalted meaning of those outworn phrases, "loyalty," "forgiveness," "humor," and "devotion."

Here at The Place ("Sunnybank," at Pompton Lakes in the hill-and-lake region of northern New Jersey), we breed thoroughbred collies. We did not plan to do this, to any extent. We just happened to. Years ago, when Lad and Bruce were in their prime, it occurred to me that it would be more satisfactory to breed their successors than to buy them at a time when we might be heartsick over the deaths of The Place's two great collies.

One must look ahead in such matters. For, while many humans live too long, all dogs die too young. Your dog is not in his fullest prime of brain and strength and chumship until he has passed his third birthday. And in a pitifully short span of years thereafter the muzzle begins to whiten and the free gait to stiffen and the sight or the hearing to fail. After that there is nothing to do but to watch with increasing soreness of heart the steady breaking up of the once-perfect strength and spirit.

There are few sadder experiences, and none that is more mercilessly inevitable. Yes, and there are few better criterions of a man's kindness than his treatment of the dog that once was his guard and chum and that is now only his pensioner. Read over again Kipling's "Power of the Dog." He puts the thing better, in a handful of jingled words, than could I in a thousand pages.

So, in a small way, we began to breed collies. Our only purpose was to find two dogs that should develop into true successors of Lad and Bruce. And, by the way, out of the hundreds of pups bred since then, we have yet to find those successors.

Yet, we have found great dogs among them; splendidly human and stanch and clever and beautiful dogs—collies that have been dear to us and that no cash could buy. And, in the course of another ten years or so, we may chance upon the combination which shall produce a second Bruce or a second Lad. Or we may not. It costs nothing to hope.

In the meantime, unless The Place were to be overrun with generation after generation of thoroughbred collies, it became necessary to sell most of the members of each successive litter. And there trouble set in.

I shall not forget the gloom that hung over the first sale of a Sunnybank collie pup. He was a fine and loveable little chap, five months old. The Mistress spent an hour grooming him, for the arrival of the man who had bought the youngster.

And during that hour she and I decided that he was far too beautiful to part with; that we were going to keep him forever. The buyer could have another pup in his place. But when we looked over the remaining eight puppies the very same objection applied to the sale of any of them. So, by exercise of will power, we forced ourselves to stick to the original plan.

When the purchaser called for his new-bought collie he must have thought he had happened in on a pall-bearers' convention. The whole Place was holding a Lodge of Sorrow.

As in the miracle of the headless man who walked from Paris to St. Cloud, "it is the first step that counts." Afterward, it waxed decreasingly hard to let our cherished baby collies go to good homes and at good prices. But to this day there is always a bit of a twinge somewhere in my cardiac region when I lift a fluffy and loving Sunnybank collie pup into the car of a buyer.

As a rule, I try to be out of the way (the Mistress is *always* out of the way at such times) and to leave the matter to my superintendent,—Robert Friend,—who enjoys it little more than do we. At such rare times as a sale falls through, there is wholesale rejoicing.

All of which is ridiculous, past words. And I make no defence of it. Except—except—well, there's something tremendously appealing about a collie pup of one's own raising! It's rotten to have to sell him.

I hedge such sales around with the true statement that applicants can buy pups quite as good as ours, and at somewhat lower prices, from any of a dozen reliable breeders whose addresses I offer to furnish. Also, I refuse to sell a collie to any one living in a city. And I refuse to ship a collie by express. Buyers must come to Sunnybank in person for their dogs. One would think these restrictions were quite enough to keep purchasers away. Human nature, though, is far queerer than dog nature; rebuffs seem to act as incentives.

I could sell five times as many pups, if I bothered to breed five times as many. Buyers have come to Sunnybank for them from a score of states. Two have come from as far away as California.

No two collies are alike in characteristics—even in the supposed characteristics of their breeds. My big dog, Bobby, (old Bruce's son, Sunnybank Robert Bruce), for instance, had a sagacious patience that would have fitted better the body of an elderly St. Bernard. No ordinary event of life seemed to ruffle him. A motor car broke his leg in two places, when he was a puppy, and the anguish of bonesetting could not wring a whimper from him.

When I came to the door of my room in the morning, Bob was always lying across the threshold. And at first sight of me he sprang up, put his paws on my chest, and burst into a salvo of hysterical shrieks and howls and moans that would disgrace a moon-baying puppy. It was a dramatic reunion after eight hours of separation. Bob reveled in it.

For several minutes this rackety welcome lasted. Then

he quieted down and spent the rest of the day in silence—
always except when the sight or sound of a motor car woke
him to furious action. He limped no longer, but he never
forgot the cause of his broken leg, and an approaching car
sent him into paroxysms of rage.

Bobby is dead. Blithely would I spend a year's income
to bring him to life. In many ways he was the wisest
dog I have known. Tell him anything, once, and a year
later he would remember it. His understanding of human
speech was uncanny. Also he had a shrewd life-philosophy
that was all his own. He was my loved and adoring chum.
To this day I miss him, keenly.

Then there was Treve (Champion Sunnybank
Sigurd), a prize-winner of note and a thing of perfect
beauty. He was a flyaway, excitable mass of gold-and-
white. He was the only dog on the Place that did not
love to be petted. He drew impatiently away from the
touch of my outstretched hand. Yet whenever I chanced
to be absent from home for the day, Sigurd would go de-
jectedly to the hall table, take my cap between his teeth,
slouch into my study, and lay it on the floor beside my
desk. Then he would lie down, with one forepaw and his
nose on the cap, and remain thus all day, growling if
anyone ventured near. On my return in the evening he
showed no special interest in me.

His one rare form of demonstrativeness consisted in
coming up to me, putting his head on my knee, and growling ferociously for perhaps three minutes. I gather that
this was meant as a sign of affection.

Every now and then some one asks me if I don't find
collies treacherous. My invariable reply is, "If I did, I
wouldn't keep them."

Of all the long line of Sunnybank collies, I recall one—
and one only—to which that term "treacherous" might
perhaps be applied. He was a gentle, friendly dog, with
an elfin sense of humor. An elderly peddler used to stop
at the Place, once a month, with his wares. The peddler
had a wooden leg. The collie used to gallop out in wel-
coming fashion to greet him, on these visits, and, invari-
ably, as the man moved on toward the house, the collie
would drop back a step and bite him. Always in the
wooden leg.

Never by any chance did he bite any one else. And
never did he bite any part of the peddler except the wooden
leg. No growl went with the bite. It seemed merely
exploratory—or at most the exposing of a fake. Apparently, his powers of scent told him that the leg was not
real, and his uncanny sense of fun did the rest.

Wolf was the fiercest of our collies. It was not safe
for any stranger to take the slightest liberty with him.
Left alone, he was aloofly courteous to guests. But he
would not suffer familiarities, except from the Mistress or
myself. Very small children alone were exempt from this
rule. From them Wolf would endure any mauling.
Only once did I know him to protest at the familiarities
of a child. That was when a friend called, bringing along
her four-year-old son. Wolf sat down beside the baby,
and the two were having a jolly time together, when a
growl of utter disgust from the dog made us all look
around. The baby piped up, triumphantly:

"I bitted off one of Wolfie's whiskers; and it tasted just
like a worm!"

Do you wonder at the growl?

In June, 1923, every newspaper in America told at

much length of Wolf's hero-death. He died saving a worthless cur from destruction under the wheels of an express train.

Bunty was a roly-poly collie, of Sherlock Holmes tendencies. She found things nobody else could find.

It appears that most servants have *caches*—hiding places where are buried broken china and glass and such garments as are too badly torn or burned by the laundress to be sent upstairs with the clean clothes. Our own Sunnybank maids, of one vintage, had such a *cache*. None of the rest of us knew where it was. But Bunty knew.

Picking, by choice, a time when there were guests on the lawn, Bunty would canter up to them, bearing in her mouth some humble—not to say intimate—garment that she had resurrected from the *cache*. This she would display with chaste joy, to all beholders, in every detail of its ragged and grimy unloveliness, and would end the performance by depositing the horrible prize in the Mistress's lap. We were never able to track the collie to the *cache,* but to her it was an inexhaustible treasure house.

Then there was Lady, at one time the only dog, except Lad, allowed in the house. Lady had a favorite corner of the fireplace, where she was wont to drowse on cold evenings. Once in a while Lad, coming indoors earlier than she, would chance to pick out this nook. Lady had too much finesse to rout her mate out of the nest. Instead, with fur abristle, she would rush toward the front door, growling menace to some imaginary tramp. Lad, at the sound, would spring to his feet and dash doorward. As soon as he was well under way, Lady would slip back and take possession of the vacated hearth corner.

By the way, we humans make fools of ourselves **over**

our dogs, sometimes. A ten-line news dispatch in one of the papers a few years ago gave a notable instance of this. It told of a seventy-year-old countryman, in the Middle West, and of the collie that had been his sole comrade and housemate for eleven years.

Penniless and broken in health, the old man went to the poorhouse, his dog at his heels. He begged admittance; and was told he might find refuge there, but not his dog. The aged collie must shift for himself as best he could, in the wintry outer world.

The man listened to the decree. Then, without a word, he whistled to his dog and plodded back to the forest hovel which served them for a home. There, next day, a neighbor found the two. There was a bullet through the brain of each. Between them, where they lay side by side, was the rusted army rifle with which the old man had solved the problem of taking his collie chum along with him.

I cite this true anecdote only to show how absurdly far a sane human may sometimes carry his affection for a mere soulless dog. True, the collie would of course have chosen poverty and hunger and cold, sooner than leave his master for comforts that the latter could not share. But that is only because he was a dog and not a logical and soulful human.

Humans usually know better than to do such ridiculous things. Witness the numbers of men and women who move away from a neighborhood and leave behind them the family dog to shift for himself. Not being gifted with soul and intellect, your dog has not the brain to desert you for some better-off master, or to leave you in the lurch when your presence becomes inconvenient to him.

I have been talking in long-winded prosiness about col-

lies, because I am mildly daft on the theme. But there is
another kind of dog that I want to commend to your favor.
To be accurate, he is not really "another kind of dog."
He is "many other kinds of dog." I am talking about
the cross-breed—the so-called mongrel.

It is the custom to sneer at mongrels and to feel shame
in confessing the ownership of one of them. And there
could not be a worse mistake. The mongrel has more
cleverness, more stamina, and sometimes more beauty than
any thoroughbred. The best type of mongrel is often the
very best dog alive.

Instead of being ashamed of owning one, be ashamed
that you have not brought out his million fine traits
of smartness and stanchness and general worth-whileness.
Those traits are all there if you'll bother to look for them.

THE END.